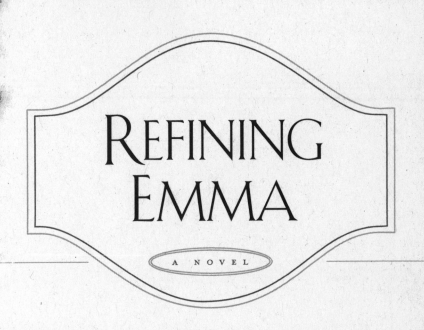

REFINING EMMA

A NOVEL

Delia Parr

BETHANY HOUSE PUBLISHERS

Minneapolis, Minnesota

Refining Emma
Copyright © 2007
Delia Parr

Cover illustration by Bill Graf
Cover design by Paul Higdon

Published by Bethany House Publishers
11400 Hampshire Avenue South
Bloomington, Minnesota 55438

Bethany House Publishers is a division of
Baker Publishing Group, Grand Rapids, Michigan.

Printed in the United States of America

Paperback: ISBN-13: 978-0-7642-0087-8 ISBN-10: 0-7642-0087-9
Large Print: ISBN-13: 978-0-7642-0395-4 ISBN-10: 0-7642-0395-9

The Library of Congress has cataloged the paperback edition as follows:

Parr, Delia.
    Refining Emma / Delia Parr.
        p.   cm. — (Candlewood trilogy ; 2)
    ISBN 978-0-7642-0087-8 (pbk.)
    1. Boardinghouses—New York (State)—Fiction. I. Title.
PS3566.A7527R44   2007
813'.54—dc22

                                                                    2007007105

WITHDRAWN

REFINING
EMMA

table, even as her mind struggled to make sense of what was happening. A thunderstorm in the depths of winter would be highly unusual, but this winter was odd. By this time of year, Candlewood was typically buried by one snowstorm after another, but they had yet to see more than a dusting of snow so far. This clap of thunder, however, felt different somehow and far stronger than anything she had ever experienced at any time of year.

She quickly glanced around the table again and saw her own surprise and confusion mirrored in the others' expressions only moments before an ear-shattering roar forced her to her feet. With her heart pounding, she pushed her chair away from the table, scrambled to her feet, and scurried from the kitchen. She raced through the dining room to the center hallway and charged past the two front parlors to get to the front door, her companions following on her heels.

Emma hurried outside to the wraparound porch, which offered a commanding view of the skyline and the town below, as well as the skies overhead. As the other women gathered beside her, leaving Reverend Glenn waiting just inside the front door, frigid wind whipped at her skirts. She wrapped her arms at her waist and stood close to the porch railing as she searched the night sky in vain for visible signs of what had to be a horrendous, mammoth storm system.

She furrowed her brow. The skies above Hill House were clear. Not a single cloud blocked the light of the full moon or the stars twinkling brightly on a bed of velvet that stretched across the full breadth of the horizon. Not a sliver of lightning sliced through the sky. Save for the sound of the swirling winds, the night was thick with silence.

Shivering, she lowered her gaze and studied the outline of the town below as the wind continued to whip at her body and chill her to the bone. As usual, only fireflies of light marked the homes and businesses there, including the factories and warehouses along the frozen canal, where workers had yet to finish their workday.

Confused that she could find no explanation for the rumbling sound that had sent them all rushing outside from the supper table, she nevertheless let out a sigh of relief to relax her tense muscles. She flinched the moment she heard a loud blast, accompanied by an amazing flash of light that illuminated the factories in the center of town. She watched, wide-eyed, as flames shot high into the sky. Once the heavy, gusting winds filled the air with the distinctive smell of phosphorous and burning wood, she knew the source: the match factory.

She clutched her heart. Horrified by the thought of workers who might have been killed or injured in the blast, she abandoned her own concerns and tucked her secret deeper inside her troubled heart. As Mother Garrett and her two young charges pressed closer to her at the railing, Emma pointed to the flames and what seemed to be a massive fire that was spreading quickly, even as she struggled to accept the undeniable thought that the rumble they had heard earlier had come from the same area. "Did you hear that? Do you see that? It—it must be the match factory. There must have been an explosion there. And now . . . now it's on fire," she groaned.

"My father! My brother!" Liesel wailed and ran from the porch.

Emma charged after her, running down the steps and across the front yard. She caught up with the young woman before they reached the front gate. Beneath the gentle light of the swaying lantern that hung over the gate in the wrought-iron fence, she tried to pull Liesel into her arms, but the sixteen-year-old kept struggling to get free. "Let me go! I have to go! My father and my brother work at the match factory. I . . . I have to go. . . ."

"It's not safe. With the canal frozen, there's little to be done to keep the fire from spreading, especially in this wind," Emma argued.

Liesel nearly pulled free, but Emma kept a firm grip on one of her arms. "I have to go! Please! I must go!" she pleaded.

"I know you're worried about your father and your brother, but you can't go alone," Emma said, realizing she could not expect to keep the young woman from going into town to check on her family. "Besides, you wouldn't get very far dressed as you are before you froze to death. Just . . . just calm down long enough to put on your cape and bonnet and a pair of gloves. I'll get mine and go with you."

Ditty joined them and put her arm around her distraught friend. "I'll go with you, Liesel. Don't worry. I'm sure your father and brother are fine. You'll see. Come inside. We'll both get dressed properly and then we'll go straight to your house." She paused and looked up at Emma. "Is it all right, Widow Garrett? May I leave with Liesel to take her home? We'll be careful."

With her cheeks stinging from the wind and the smell of smoke getting stronger and stronger, irritating her nose and throat, Emma hesitated. Now was not the time to remind the two young women they were still under punishment for their misadventure last fall and were not allowed to leave Hill House without an adult to accompany them. "Only if you promise not to go anywhere near the match factory. It's far too dangerous, and you'll only be in the way. Stay together and go directly to Liesel's house. I'll need to go into town to see how I can help, too, but you two can go ahead. I'll stop to see you both in a little while. If everyone is all right, then I'll bring you both back here," she said as she ushered the two young women back to the house.

Mother Garrett and Reverend Glenn, along with Butter, were waiting for them in the front hallway. While the two young women rushed to their room to get their winter outerwear, Emma tried to rub warmth back into her arms. "I told Liesel and Ditty they could go to Liesel's house to make sure her brother and father are all right. I think I should go into town to see how we can help."

Mother Garrett dabbed at her eyes. "There are bound to be some people who'll need a place to stay, at least for the night. I'll make up some beds while you're gone."

Reverend Glenn, his aged face wearied with concern, reached down to pat his dog on the head. "I think it would be best if I went down to the parsonage. Reverend Austin will need some help, but you go ahead. You'll make it faster without me and Butter here."

Emma locked her gaze with his and smiled. "Maybe I would, but I'd rather not go alone. We can go together," she suggested, then turned to take his coat from the oak coat rack and handed it to him. "We'll need to bundle up first before we can leave." She silently prayed that God would help them all to transform the horror of this night into a channel for His glory and to guide them to those who would need their help the most.

1

ALL OF CANDLEWOOD was in mourning.
Four days after the explosion and fire
at the match factory, which had quickly spread
to other businesses and homes, Emma Garrett
was almost ready to leave Hill House at midmorning, but she was already tired. She stole a
glance at the mirror above the small dresser in
her bedroom and quickly looked away. Although her pale blond hair had been neatly
braided and coiled at the nape of her neck and
her dark brown gown fit her slender frame well,
her blue eyes were dull with exhaustion and
faint circles under her eyes had darkened over-
night.

With little energy to waste worrying about
her appearance, she hurried down to the first
floor. For the past three days she had spent end-
less hours in town helping to care for those injured in the tragedy, only to return each night

to work side by side with her staff to accommodate the townspeople who had been left homeless and were temporarily living at Hill House.

After stopping only long enough to don her hooded cape and thick gloves, she opened the front door and stepped out onto the front porch, quickly closing the door behind her. One glance at the brick lane that led to the bottom of the hill made her sigh. Garnering enough energy to climb back up that hill at the end of this day would take far more energy than she had right now, and she dared not think about how difficult it would be later tonight.

She lifted her gaze and scanned the scarred town below. The tragedy that had befallen her beloved Candlewood had brought heartache and misery to many others, but Hill House was intact and her loved ones, as well as Liesel's father and brother, had been spared. She should scarcely be worrying about having enough energy to climb back up that hill tonight to get home—not when so many others were struggling to climb up from the ashes of their grief to rebuild their very lives.

Emma blinked back tears of frustration, fatigue, and sorrow as guilt tugged at her conscience. Given the scope of the tragedy, she felt selfish for worrying about her own troubles. In all truth, she had found neither the time nor the opportunity to share her secret with anyone at

Hill House. If she were really honest with herself, she would admit that she really did not want to tell them she had been caught in a legal quagmire that had nullified her purchase of Hill House, nor that she was living in a perpetual state of limbo while she waited for the legal owner of Hill House to arrive and decide whether or not to let her purchase the property again.

She carried her secret alone, except for her lawyer, and she had not heard a word from him for months.

Before she slipped into self-pity, Emma concentrated on the troubles facing the other townspeople. Even from this distant vantage point, she could see that the match factory had been reduced to rubble, along with several other businesses and nearby homes. The immediate area surrounding the core site of the initial explosion and fire was nothing more than a blackened crater of complete devastation. Other buildings in town, scattered about like dark pock marks, had sustained a wide variety of damage, ranging from minimal to severe.

Sadly, the timing of this tragedy in winter only compounded the destruction. Had the explosion and fires occurred between April and November, volunteers could have used the water in the canal to fight the fires. At this time of year, however, the canal was frozen solid, and volunteers had been forced to watch almost helplessly until the fires burned themselves out.

Unfortunately, they would not know until the spring thaw if the walls of the canal itself had sustained any damage from the explosion. The general consensus was that, at best, the canal would have leaks that would necessitate draining the canal to make the repairs in the spring. At worst, this entire section of the Candlewood Canal would have to be rebuilt, a prospect that threatened economic destruction far beyond the immediate losses within the town itself.

As she studied the town, she could see some of the roofs on the storefronts and homes along Main Street, including the General Store, which she had sold four years ago before buying Hill House. It appeared to be merely scorched or just blackened with soot. From here, she could not see the cracked and broken windows or the store signs that were covered with ashes or soot, but she knew they were there. She had seen them every day as she walked along Main Street.

Because of the direction of the wind the night of the fire, all of the workers' homes on the very southern edge of town had escaped any damage at all. Likewise, most of the homes and businesses at the far north end of Main Street had fared well, confining most of the devastation to the very center of town, although there seemed to be little rhyme or reason in terms of which buildings had been destroyed or damaged, while others escaped unscathed.

Emma drew in a deep breath and stiffened her back. Homes and businesses, even livelihoods, would be rebuilt eventually—but the loss of life and the serious injuries of those hurt in the explosion or fires, however, had left many hearts and dreams broken, and they would take much longer to heal.

Determined to help the healing process continue and to keep the uncertainties of her own life at bay, she tugged her hooded cape tight against her, descended from the porch, crossed the yard, and let herself out the front gate. The frigid air was still heavy with the acrid scent of charred wood and smoke that irritated her raw throat. The closer she got to the bottom of the hill, the more acrid the air became, and she snuggled her face deeper against the inside of her hood, grateful for the soothing aroma of lavender that scented the fabric.

She turned onto Main Street at the end of the lane and hurried into town past a number of intact homes. Like Hill House, they were also overflowing with families whose homes or businesses had been destroyed or damaged. Some of those families would stay in Candlewood to rebuild their lives; sadly, others would leave to seek shelter with friends or family elsewhere and never return.

When she reached the church, Emma

paused for a moment as the echoes of the church bell tolling incessantly only the day before yesterday rang once again in her mind. She glanced at the empty church and sighed. Nearly everyone in town had congregated here for a sad and solemn burial service, and many had been forced to stand outside in the biting cold for lack of room inside. They had all walked together in a sad procession to the cemetery behind the church where Emma's grandparents, parents, and beloved husband lay at rest.

There, below a bleak, gray sky, the workers killed in the tragedy—seven men and three boys—had been laid to rest.

Emma whispered another prayer for the families they had left behind before she continued on her way. As she passed the parsonage, she made a mental note to stop there later on her way home to see Reverend Glenn. He was staying there temporarily with Reverend and Mrs. Austin to be closer to the families who had suffered the loss of a loved one and to comfort those who had been injured. His presence at Hill House, however, was sorely missed, and she hoped he might come home soon.

Traffic on the roadway increased as she neared the heart of the business district, but few shoppers were strolling out and about on the planked sidewalk simply because most people were too busy working to help the town recover. The sounds of construction and deconstruction filled the air with both sadness and hope. While some men razed buildings too damaged to be salvaged, other men were busy repairing those that were not, and wagon after wagon hauled away charred debris, some of which was still smoldering.

She stopped for a moment in front of town hall, where people were hurrying in and out with an assortment of donations. Draped in black bunting, the new town clock had been stopped at 6:24, the precise time of the first explosion.

Inside the two-story brick building, however, town leaders like Mayor Calloway and Sheriff North were still organizing volunteers to help the victims touched most directly by the tragedy and making plans for the town's rebuilding and its economic recovery, as well. Women and their children were either accepting donated clothing and household utensils or sorting through them in the basement, while others on the first floor accepted donations of foodstuffs that were quickly delivered to those in need. Still other women were down the street at the Emerson Hotel, which had been turned into a makeshift hospital, where they cared for dozens of wounded workers.

Anxious to add her own efforts in that regard, Emma hurried her steps. When she finally arrived at the hotel, the lobby was crowded with other women volunteers who were standing in line, waiting to be directed to specific patients by Dr. Jeffers. Before she had a chance to take her own place in line, she spied a tall man with dark hair and soft gray eyes heading toward her.

She was so surprised to see her lawyer and financial advisor, Zachary Breckenwith, that she took a misstep. Somehow she managed to stay on her feet and waited for him to reach her, relieved he had to work his way across the entire room, if only to give her time to sort through the unexpected rush of emotion his presence created.

He was back.

He was really back.

Mr. Breckenwith had been summoned the better part of seven weeks ago to his aunt's sickbed in Bounty, the next town north along the canal. She had passed away within hours of his arrival, and he had honored her wishes and brought her back to Candlewood to be buried beside her husband.

Breckenwith had left almost immediately after the funeral to return to Bounty and subsequently to New York City to fulfill his obligations as executor of his aunt's estate, and Emma had not seen him or spoken to him since then.

She studied him as he drew closer. Taller than most men, he carried himself with an air of confidence just shy of arrogance. His stride was purposeful, his expression steady. When he locked his gaze with hers, her heart began to pound against the wall of her chest.

After sharing a professional relationship with this man for five years—in which he had challenged her business decisions more often than not—Emma had been more than shocked when he had stepped across the professional boundary separating them and expressed a more personal interest in her.

As it turned out, Breckenwith had been right to urge caution when she had first been approached by the executor of the estate that offered Hill House for sale. Instead, she had ignored her lawyer's advice and immediately bought the property, only to learn this past fall, some four years after the fact, that the executor had absconded with her money and failed to file the transaction with the courts, as well.

Emma was forced to wait now for the legal owner, indeed the actual heir to the estate, to arrive in Candlewood at some point in the near future to inspect Hill House and decide whether or not to allow her to buy it again. But she had also been waiting for Zachary Breckenwith to either take the first formal step toward courting her or to redraw the professional boundary between them. Perhaps now she would finally know his intentions.

She caught her breath for a moment, still unsure which would be a more daunting task— working with him as a lawyer or developing a more personal relationship with him as a suitor.

In point of fact, she had not followed his advice during his absence to begin looking at other properties, if only to be prepared should she be forced to move out of Hill House. In that regard she was not anxious to see him on a professional basis, simply because she did not want to face the possibility that she might indeed lose Hill House, a reality he would be quick to point out to her.

She couldn't face that yet. Not when she still hadn't decided what she might want to do instead of operating the boardinghouse. Not when she still had not decided how to tell Mother Garrett or Reverend Glenn that they would have to move again.

When Zachary Breckenwith finally reached her, he greeted her warmly. His hooded gaze, however, mirrored her own exhaustion. A widower of fifty-two, he was only a year older than she was, but the deep wrinkles across his forehead and the fatigue in his eyes dispelled his image of energy and optimism.

"You're back," she noted, dismayed she could only manage to state the obvious. "Have you finished your work on your aunt's affairs?"

"I rode in late yesterday afternoon," he replied and shook his head. "Although it's good to finally be finished and return home, I'm still trying to come to terms with what happened here."

She nodded. "As we all are."

"I was told you'd probably arrive about

now," he offered. "Since I met here earlier with another client, I decided to wait for you here instead of walking all the way up to Hill House to talk with you."

Her smile wavered a bit and her heart began to beat with both dread and hope. "You needed to talk to me?" she asked, wondering if perhaps he had news about the owner of Hill House coming to Candlewood.

He took her arm. "Let's take a walk outside, shall we? I'm told they have more than enough volunteers here already today, and I have a personal favor to ask of you."

Disappointed that his business with her today seemed not to fit any of her expectations, she let him escort her outside and across the street to walk along the planked sidewalk. Underfoot, more than a few scorch marks from flaming debris dappled the wooden walkway. As they walked past the storefronts, she tried to sort through her feelings for this man, but failed. Filled with self-doubt, she wondered if she had misread his intentions where she was concerned, at least on a personal level.

Yet here he was, this confusing man, about to ask her for a favor. A personal favor.

She slid her gloved hands into her cape pockets for warmth as they walked. "If you have something you'd like me to do for you, please consider it done. It's the least I can do, considering how supportive you were in helping us resolve Widow Leonard's problems with Mr. Langhorne last fall," she prompted, hoping to steer the conversation away from herself as well as her legal problems.

He chuckled. "That was easy work. All I had to do was stand by in case the plan you had all worked out ran into complications. I know Widow Leonard went home with her sons for the winter, but I trust your mother-in-law is well?"

Emma smiled. "She's very well, thank you. But I'm afraid Mother Garrett's been more than a little lonely without her friend and companion." Her smile drooped. "Now that the boardinghouse is full again, she's too busy in her kitchen to have time to be lonely, although I wish it were for a different reason. Entertaining guests on holiday is far easier than providing for people who have lost everything they owned, and I must admit we were all looking forward to a bit of rest until spring when we would normally be receiving guests again," she said. She dared not admit, however, that the strain of keeping her troubles from Mother Garrett was taking its toll on their relationship.

"You've been very generous to those who needed help," he noted.

"Others have done the same or more," she countered.

He drew in a long breath and shook his head. "I was worried that buying my aunt's house last fall, before she moved to Bounty, might be a bit extravagant, especially with young Jeremy deciding not to pursue his study of the law and returning home. Given all that's happened, I'm just pleased to have room to offer to so many others who need a place to stay, even temporarily. I moved myself into my office yesterday to free up another bedroom, but I'm afraid there isn't any more room for as much as a mouse at this point, which Mrs. Ellis has been quick to point out. To her credit, she's come around quite a bit since the tragedy," he added with just a hint of a smile on his lips.

Emma nodded but did not offer a comment. Rumors had painted a rather acidic picture of his housekeeper, Amanda Ellis. The sixty-something widow had been referred to him by a friend of his late aunt. Widow Ellis, reputed to be the most opinionated woman ever to put head to pillow in Candlewood, apparently did not confine her opinions to matters concerning house and home, which did not endear her to the men in town. Emma, however, had done little more than exchange pleasantries with the woman when they had been introduced last month, and she was not about to make any judgment about the housekeeper based on anything less than her own personal experience, although she had heard that the energetic widow had also alienated many of the women in town by openly criticizing a number of them.

He paused his walk, looked directly at her, and furrowed his brow. "Did you say Hill House is full?"

"Yes, it is," she said, stopped abruptly as he did, and clutched her cape tighter at her throat to keep out the cold air. "At least for now. Everyone there is trying to make more permanent arrangements until their homes can be repaired or rebuilt, but I'm not sure how soon any of them will be able to leave."

He frowned, and Emma cocked her head. "Why do you ask? I thought everyone who needed a place to stay had been given one."

"Until Sheriff North came to see me again this morning, I thought they had. Unfortunately, he has a couple who need a place to live, probably indefinitely, and he's just about out of other options. He's incredibly busy handling other problems, so I told him I'd speak to you about it. Since I don't have room for them, he was wondering if you might. Apparently not," he added thoughtfully.

"Tell them to come to Hill House," she suggested without hesitation.

His gaze lit with disbelief. "But you said you were full."

"And you said the sheriff had nowhere else for them to go. We'll make room somehow."

He cocked his head. "In all fairness, I probably should tell you who they are before you agree to take them in."

"Why? Should it matter?"

"It might," he admitted with a frown.

She returned his frown. "Well, it shouldn't matter at all. Hill House is open to anyone left in need by this tragedy. Tell this couple they're more than welcome to come as soon as they can. I have one stop to make, but I can be home within the hour. I'll try to see if we have anyone ready to leave. If not, I'll just have to close off one of the parlors for them, like we did for the Founders' Day celebrations last September. Actually, you can tell them Mother Garrett will be serving dinner at one o'clock, so they can join us. You're welcome to come, as well."

He rubbed his brow and started them walking again. "I'm afraid you'll need two rooms, not one."

"I thought you said this was a couple who needed a place to live."

Sighing, he slowed his pace. "I thought I said I had a couple of people who needed a place to live. If not, I should have. At this point, I'm afraid I'm so far past being tired, I can't even remember what I said exactly."

She shrugged. "Maybe you did. I probably just misunderstood and assumed this was a married couple."

"Either way, it's not, but I still think you should know who they are before you agree to take them in at Hill House."

"It doesn't matter. I'm not sure how, but I'm

sure we can manage two separate rooms. But now that you've pricked my curious side," she added, "you may as well tell me who they are."

He drew in a long breath. "It's Lester and Orralynne Burke."

Emma froze in place, forcing him to stop, as well. The favor he asked of her was too much to even consider, despite her earlier assurances to the contrary.

She stiffened her back. She had already taken in fifteen people who had been touched by this tragedy, and she would find room for another fifteen before she would even consider taking in that troublesome pair.

She simply would have to refuse.

Politely, of course.

Bracing her feet, she looked up at him. She was prepared to argue against anything and everything he might say to convince her to change her mind, but Emma felt she owed him at least the opportunity to try. "Give me one good reason that I should even consider taking in the Burkes, other than the fact that I'm indebted to you."

He shrugged and offered her the one reason she could not argue against. "Because I truly believe the sheriff when he tells me they have no other place to go."

2

EMMA MIGHT NOT BE ABLE to question the sheriff's concern or her lawyer's sincerity, but given the Burkes' reputations, she did question the notion that they actually needed a place to live.

She quickly challenged her lawyer's claim. "I haven't heard a word about them or their cottage being damaged. Their cottage is a good distance from all of the fires, after all. Has anyone bothered to check and see if there actually was any damage, or are you just taking the Burkes' word for it?"

He looked down at the planked sidewalk and stubbed a scorch mark with the toe of his boot. "I can't tell you why their home wound up being severely damaged by fire any more than I can tell you why some of the buildings closer to the match factory are still standing. All I know is that Sheriff North has had to find a different place for the Burkes to stay for the past three nights. Apparently no one who was kind enough to agree to take them in the first place can tolerate them for more than twenty-four hours. Since, one by one, they all refused to take them for another night, Lester and Orralynne have got no place to go tonight or any other night to come."

"I'm not surprised," Emma said. "Neither one of them bothered to attend services for the people killed in the explosion and fire. They're probably the only ones who live for miles around who didn't come."

With a snort, he shook his head. "Short of offering them a jail cell for lack of anything else, which might make more than a few people smile for the first time in days, the sheriff thought I could ask you first. As a favor to him. And to me," he added. "As soon as I have room in my house, they can move in there with me. I . . . I just can't promise how soon that would be."

Her reaction was both immediate and instinctive. She stiffened her back and clenched and unclenched her jaw. "That's one very big favor," she quipped.

He locked his gaze with hers. "I wouldn't ask you if I thought the sheriff had a real chance of finding any other place for them to stay. I may not have lived here all my life, as you have, but I've made Candlewood my home for five years now. That's long enough to know what

I'm asking on the sheriff's behalf. I know that taking even just one of the Burkes into your home would present a few problems for you, let alone both of them, but they refuse to be separated."

Emma huffed. "A few problems? I can think of several," she countered, her complaints tumbling out in a rush. "Everyone at Hill House will be affected. Mother Garrett will be beside herself. Liesel and Ditty, who are still on punishment for sneaking out to meet with their friends without permission, if you'll recall, will probably be reduced to tears by supper. I'll be lucky if they don't quit by this time tomorrow or at least ask to go home for a spell. And once he finds out, Reverend Glenn might just be tempted to stay at the parsonage indefinitely.

"As for the others who have come to Hill House because they've been forced out of their homes, I prefer not to imagine the looks on their faces when they see Lester and Orralynne Burke arrive. I don't want to think about what they might actually say when they realize the Burkes have come to stay indefinitely, either."

Emma paused for a moment, then addressed more personal concerns. "And what do you suggest I do if the owner of Hill House arrives in the meantime and witnesses the chaos bound to erupt? Any chance I might have had to convince him to sell the property to me again will be ruined. Unless you've heard from him and know he's arriving later, perhaps in the spring?"

"No, I'm afraid I haven't heard from him or his lawyer. I spent a lot of time last night sorting through the correspondence that arrived while I was gone, but no. I can't tell you when he'll be arriving," he admitted.

Breckenwith glanced down for a moment. When he looked up at her again, his gaze had softened. "You're right. You can't take in the Burkes. There are too many people at Hill House already, and I won't ask you to risk losing Hill House should the owner arrive. I'll tell Sheriff North that you don't have any room. Maybe I can think of somewhere else for them to stay. But I thank you for considering the idea. Apparently that's more than most people did when the sheriff approached them earlier today," he offered.

He hesitated for a moment, as if he wanted to discuss something else. Instead, he simply tipped his hat. "If you'll excuse me, I need to find Sheriff North to let him know that the Burkes still need a place to stay," he murmured before walking away.

Emma gritted her teeth and forced herself to stand perfectly still. Offering a temporary home to Lester and Orralynne Burke would be more than problematic. It would be pure disaster.

These two people had made enemies with

nearly everyone in Candlewood who had lived there for any length of time. She did not have the official town records at her fingertips, but Emma would venture to guess there were very few people who had not been taken to court to face some sort of complaint filed by one or both of the Burkes. By their very presence at Hill House, Orralynne and Lester would destroy whatever peace they all had been enjoying during the quiet season more than the other fifteen townspeople ever could.

In a matter of hours, the discord in the household would be intolerable. Emma did not want to consider what life would be like after a few weeks with the Burkes in residence, and she dared not entertain the notion that she might have her one and only chance to repurchase Hill House occur while the Burkes were in residence should the legal owner arrive.

As much as she tried, however, she could not quiet the echo of Reverend Glenn's admonition that the right way to handle a problem was not usually the easy way, especially since he had been proven right when she had turned to him for advice in the past. In response to the tragedy that had struck the town, the right thing to do, of course, was to recognize that everyone who suffered directly from the explosion or the fires needed to be helped.

The easy way out of the problem facing her now would simply be to consider that she had done her Christian duty by volunteering to nurse the wounded by day and by taking in so many others at Hill House. She could let the sheriff worry about finding a temporary home for the Burkes. The fact that so many others had refused to take in the Burkes would be his problem, not hers.

The harder way, of course, would be to bring the Burkes to Hill House.

Unfortunately, no matter how much she tried to justify taking the easy way out of helping this pair, she could not stop guilt from tugging at her conscience. How could she refuse to give shelter to anyone in need, when she believed that if God had truly led her to Hill House, He would help her to keep it for that very reason?

The answer was as plain as it was simple: She could not refuse to take in the Burkes.

Regardless of how difficult it would be, she simply could not turn them away. She had to trust in God's plan . . . for all concerned.

Before she lost her conviction and changed her mind, she gathered up her skirts. "No, wait," she cried and ran after her lawyer. When she finally caught up with him, she was winded and her throat was raw from the cold. "I . . . I know it'll be hard to take in the Burkes, but it's the right thing to do. Tell them to come to Hill House," she managed as she struggled to catch her breath. "Tell the sheriff to bring them by at one o'clock for dinner. He's welcome to stay for dinner, too," she added.

Half a smile lit his features. "Are you positive you want to take them? I don't want Sheriff North to drag them all the way up to Hill House, only to discover you've had a change of heart."

"Yes, I'm sure. I won't change my mind," she insisted, although she feared it would take a miracle to soften her heart against the two of them.

His smile broadened. "Thank you. I'm not sure if the sheriff will be able to stay for dinner, but I'll tell him to have the Burkes there by one. You're a good woman, Widow Garrett."

"Good?" She shook her head. "Not yet," she admitted and tugged her cape tighter around her shoulders. Traveling down this particular path to goodness would be troublesome indeed, and she was just as certain that Mother Garrett would be convinced Emma had lost her mind, adding yet another layer to the estrangement building between them.

"Perhaps in a few days, when everything is more settled, we might be able to meet to discuss other, more personal matters," Mr. Breckenwith suggested but left to find the sheriff before Emma could answer.

Intrigued by the prospect of seeing Zachary Breckenwith again soon, Emma headed straight for the parsonage, as she had originally planned, to see Reverend Glenn before returning to Hill House.

As she walked, she carried her concerns about the Burkes with her and tried comparing this new challenge with one she had faced just this past fall. A family feud between James and Andrew Leonard had inspired their mother, eighty-one-year-old Widow Frances Leonard, to run away from home. She had come directly to Hill House.

Widow Leonard, now affectionately called Aunt Frances by her adoptive Hill House family, had been a blessing to all of them. Keeping peace within Hill House had been relatively easy while she had been living there, in part because she was so easy to love. The fact that her sons both lived some miles from town also helped to keep dissension at bay. In the end, however, faith in God and the power of prayer, along with a little ingenuity, had helped to restore the broken bonds of brotherhood, and Aunt Frances had returned home with them for the winter. Come spring, however, she would come back to Hill House as a beloved member of Emma's family and staff for the tourist season.

Keeping peace at Hill House while the Burkes lived there would be a far greater challenge. Anxious to get out of the cold, she hastened her steps, but her mind kept pace, racing from one concern to another.

Neither Lester nor Orralynne Burke could

ever be considered anything but miserable. The antagonism between the two of them would quickly spread and envelop everyone else.

Emma's foremost responsibility would be to protect her staff and her guests. Contemplating the notion that by coming to Hill House, these two people could be reformed and transformed into lovable human beings was absurd. Only a miracle could do that, perhaps one far greater than turning water into wine.

"I don't want to do this. I don't like doing this. But I will," she grumbled. "I will."

She chanted the mantra under her breath, step by step. As the wind whipped at her back and pushed her down Main Street toward the parsonage, she hoped her faith would nudge her toward true acceptance, if not goodness.

Now, more than ever, she needed to speak with Reverend Glenn. He would know how to help her—he always did. He would give her the wherewithal to make sure that by the time she got back to Hill House, her heart would be filled with graciousness instead of resentment, and hope instead of fear. After all these months of praying the owner of Hill House would arrive soon, she found it completely disconcerting to now pray he would not come before spring.

With Reverend Glenn's help, however, her faith in God would hold firm. Then and only then would she be able to focus all of her efforts on ending the open rebellion she would face when everyone else learned Lester and Orra-lynne Burke were moving into Hill House.

As she approached the parsonage, the commandment to love thy neighbor as thyself suddenly came to mind. When the neighbors just happened to be the Burkes, however, the commandment took on even greater meaning and offered an impossible challenge.

Learning to love them as neighbors had already proven to be a stretch of faith for almost everyone in town, including Emma.

Learning to love them while at the same time living with them at Hill House was just too much to expect of anyone.

Indeed.

3

DESPITE HER HOPES otherwise, Emma did not have Reverend Glenn's counsel to buoy her spirits as she trudged back up the hill to the boardinghouse. When she had stopped at the parsonage on the way home, she discovered he had gone along with Reverend Austin to visit some of the families touched directly by the tragedy. Although he was not expected back until very late this afternoon, she had been pleased to learn he planned to return to Hill House tomorrow.

Since she was arriving home much earlier than anyone expected, she thought the element of surprise might provide the very opening she needed to announce her news about the Burkes. By the time she got to the top of the hill, however, she had to stop to catch her breath and paused to gather her thoughts at the same time.

With the Burkes in residence, the boarding-house was going to be very, very crowded.

Between the permanent residents and staff and the fifteen townspeople who were already living temporarily at Hill House, the total number was already twenty. Some of her guests, like Judith Massey, who was expecting her first child in a matter of months, and Anson Kirk, a seventy-three-year-old widower, stayed close to Hill House during the day. They provided what help they could to Emma's overburdened staff, although Mother Garrett still maintained tight rule over her kitchen, which she had proclaimed off limits to the townspeople in residence.

Other guests, namely Judith's husband, Solomon, the Ammond brothers, John and Micah, and both the Wiley family and the rest of the Kirk family, which included four adults and six children all told, only ate and slept at Hill House. They spent the better part of their day either salvaging their belongings or repairing their damaged homes so they could return there as quickly as possible.

In the scheme of things, adding two more guests should not make all that much difference, which is exactly how Emma intended to broach the subject with Mother Garrett first, before she informed anyone else. Hopefully the Burkes would not arrive early, so Emma would have the time to prepare her staff, as well as the other guests.

By the time she reached the front gate and let herself into the front yard, her hands and feet were numb and so were her cheeks. As much as she longed to get inside as quickly as possible, instead of using the front door and increasing the risk of encountering any of her guests, she skirted the wraparound porch, passed the outside entrance to her office, and proceeded around the back of the house to reach the kitchen.

She stopped along the way for a moment to peek inside the chicken coop built close to the house. Despite her frozen state, she was anxious to check on the flock of eight chickens that had adopted Hill House as a home after escaping from their crates in a bizarre accident on Main Street last fall. Inside the coop, Faith, the dominant chicken-turned-rooster, was roosting with several others on an old ladder that served as a perch while the rest nested together for warmth.

"If all else fails, I may have to recruit you and all of your friends to keep the Burkes under control," she teased, ever mindful of the role Faith had played in chasing away Mr. Langhorne, a wealthy investor from back East. He now lived some miles from town after both failing to convince Emma to marry him or to buy the Leonard properties.

Satisfied that the chickens were faring well in the cold, she let herself into the kitchen and walked straight into a wall of blessed heat coming from both the fireplace and the cookstove. The room was also heavy with the delicious aroma of beef stew, and her stomach growled.

Gratefully, she found Mother Garrett in the kitchen alone, standing at the sink scrubbing pots and pans. Six loaves of freshly baked bread, three bowls of custard, and two apple pies cooled on the kitchen table. Emma noted the droop of her mother-in-law's shoulders and frowned. The fact that Mother Garrett did not stop working to greet her indicated the older woman was in a bit of a mood, which was as rare for the seventy-six-year-old widow as it was out of character.

"If you've come home to tell me those people are going to move into Hill House, you're too late," Mother Garrett murmured without bothering to turn around.

Emma's heart sank. She had suspected that gossip about the Burkes would spread quickly in a town as small as Candlewood, but she never thought the news would precede her home. "I'm sorry," she murmured as she removed her bonnet and gloves and unbuttoned her cape. "I should have come home right after agreeing to have them move in with us. I stopped on the way home to see Reverend Glenn at the parsonage, but he wasn't there. I only stayed long enough to have a cup of tea with Mrs. Austin. She told me Reverend Glenn would be coming back to Hill House tomorrow. Who told you about the Burkes?"

Mother Garrett's ample body shook as she

scrubbed hard on a bread pan. "John Ammond told me, not that it matters much one way or the other. This isn't my boardinghouse. It's yours. You're free to invite anyone and everyone you like to stay here. But considering you decided to invite the Burkes, it might have been nicer if you had told me first, instead of letting me hear it from someone else."

Alarmed by the hurt tone to her mother-in-law's voice, Emma hung her outerwear on a peg by the back door, walked over to the sink, and stood beside the woman with whom she had shared the last thirty years of her life. When she saw the tears threatening to spill down Mother Garrett's cheeks, she placed one hand on top of hers and held it still. "You're right. I'm sorry. I should have come straight home to speak with you first. It's so cold outside, I didn't want to have to go all the way back to the parsonage to tell Reverend Glenn, and I didn't have the heart to say no when Mrs. Austin asked me to visit with her."

Mother Garrett sniffled, blinked back her tears, and tugged her hand free to resume her task. "What's done is done. The Burkes are coming. Like everything else that's happened in Candlewood for the past four or five days, there's little I can do about it."

Emma took a step back. "I knew you'd be concerned, but I never thought you'd be so upset with me."

Her mother-in-law set the pan down. When she turned around and looked at Emma, tears were flowing freely and silently down the older woman's cheeks. "I'm sorry. I'm not really upset with you. If anything, I suppose I should be proud of you for taking in those people, because I'm certain no one else will. But I'm just feeling so upset about anything and everything these days, I'm simply out of sorts, and I'm not sure what to do with myself. I even sent Liesel upstairs to help Ditty with the cleaning before I broke down and cried right in front of her."

She paused and swiped at her tears with the hem of her apron. "It's not just about the Burkes. It's everything. I miss Frances. I miss Reverend Glenn. I'm afraid to say it out loud, but I think I even miss that mongrel of his, too. And I miss sitting in front of the fire at night with you and watching Liesel and Ditty do their stitches on their samplers. Not that you joined us very often. You seemed happier spending more and more time alone this winter, and I've missed you. Very much."

She dropped her gaze and shook her head. "There are so many people staying here now, the only place for me to go at night is back to my room, all by myself. And on top of everything we're already doing, we have to contend with the likes of those Burkes. It isn't right and it isn't fair."

When Mother Garrett looked up, her eyes

were wide and filled with fresh tears. "When I think about the accident and all the people who died or got hurt or lost their homes, I'm just ashamed of myself for feeling the way I do. I never thought of myself as being selfish, but that's what I've become—a selfish old woman."

Emma hugged her tightly and patted her back, even as guilt tightened a wide band around her heart. Avoiding Mother Garrett because of her legal problems with Hill House had been wrong and unfair. "You're not selfish at all," she insisted. "I'm sorry I haven't spent as much time with you as I usually do, but I promise I will, as soon as there's room," she teased. "You're just overworked and overtired. Ever since the explosion, you've been working in this kitchen day and night preparing food for up to twenty people at each meal. Even with Liesel helping, it's too much for you, which is partly your fault and partly mine. Instead of leaving you here alone all day, every day, to volunteer in town, I should have spent more time at home helping you. Not that you didn't contribute to being overworked in your own way."

"Me?" Mother Garrett pulled back and locked her gaze with Emma's. "It's not my fault there are so many mouths to feed. Not that I'm complaining, mind you. It's not their fault that they've lost more than I can even imagine, but I'll be the first to admit I'm looking forward to everyone going home so we can have our quiet times together again, like we used to." She paused and shook her head. "See what I mean? I'm just pure selfish."

Emma chuckled. "No, you're not. You're just disappointed, and so am I. But you're the one who keeps insisting you don't need more help in the kitchen, even when the guests offer to lend a hand. That doesn't make you selfish. It makes you stubborn."

Her mother-in-law shrugged. "I suppose that's better than being selfish, but that doesn't change the fact that I like to keep my kitchen in a certain order. I'm not letting just anyone in here to help."

Emma cocked a brow. "I don't suppose Anson Kirk would be the specific 'anyone' you had in mind, would he?"

Mother Garrett's cheeks turned pink. "You'd think he'd have more on his mind than paying attention to me. A man his age! And with his wife not yet in her grave half a year! The day you let that man set a foot in my kitchen to help me is the day I pack my bags. And that's a promise."

"I think he's just lonely," Emma countered.

"Lonely? Living with his son and daughter-in-law and four grandchildren? Ha! If I weren't a churchgoing woman, I'd tell you what he's lonely for is someone to warm his bed. But I am, so I'll just say he's lonely for something he won't find in this kitchen!"

"Mother Garrett!" Emma clamped her hand to her mouth.

"Oh, don't bother pretending to be shocked. Between us, we've fought off enough would-be suitors before getting married, and then fought them off again after becoming widowed. To my way of thinking, there are four kinds of suitors, one for each season, and he's definitely a winter suitor. That's the worst of them all."

Emma chuckled. In truth, she only remembered one suitor who had shown an interest in Mother Garrett, but that was years ago, right after her mother-in-law had come to live in Candlewood. She did not remember much, only that Mother Garrett had sent him packing after a spat. "I don't believe I've ever heard suitors described quite that way, as if a man's intentions are linked to the time of year he decides to call on a woman."

"That's because it's just something Frances and I talked about. She could tell you some tales, too," she murmured, then turned back to the sink and started scrubbing again.

Emma grinned and picked up a drying cloth. "I don't suppose you would care to share your collective wisdom with me and explain the differences between these seasonal suitors, would you?"

After rinsing a pot, Mother Garrett handed it to her. "It's simple, really. A summer suitor is a man who has little or nothing to his name but wants you to marry him so he can harvest everything you've worked hard to earn or to keep. That Mr. Langhorne? He was a summer suitor. He came calling in June, if I recall."

"But he had his own fortune," Emma argued.

"But he wanted yours, too. Except he didn't know you were smart enough to see him for what he was—a conniving, sneaky treasure hunter. Dumb, dumb man. Even that chicken you call Faith saw him for what he was." She chuckled. "I sure wish I could have seen that creature send the man running. Scared the hat right off his head, didn't it!"

Laughing, Emma dried the pot and set it aside as her mother-in-law continued her explanation. "Now, an autumn suitor, he's pretty crafty, and I personally think he's the craftiest of them all. He's thinking he should settle down, but he's a fickle one. He's got one eye on an unsuspecting woman in one town and the other eye on some poor woman in a different town. He's having trouble making up his mind, so he just travels back and forth until winter gets close. By then, he's either been found out or he's forced to make a choice because he can't travel in winter with all the snow we usually have."

She paused and worked at a piece of crust burnt into one of the corners of the pan. "Silas Knell was an autumn suitor."

Emma's eyes widened. "Was he the one who—"

"He's the only one I ever gave a serious thought about after moving here. It was right after you gave birth to Mark. I was helping Jonas in the store. Lo and behold, one day there's a letter for Silas. A pretty-smelling letter, too. Pity. Back in those days, as I recall, it was real hard to get decent wax to seal up a letter."

Emma gasped. "You opened it?"

"Read it, too. I didn't bother to seal it back up again, either, but I did send the poor lady a letter of my own to let her know she was welcome to marry that scoundrel because I sure didn't want him." She turned and handed the pan to Emma. "Here. I think that one's as clean as I'm gonna get it."

Emma took the pan and dried it. "At the time, I remember wondering what happened. Why didn't you tell me?"

"With three little ones plus the store, you had enough to worry about," Mother Garrett countered and wiped her hands.

"Aren't you going to finish? There's still one kind of suitor left. The spring suitor."

Mother Garrett put her arm around Emma and hugged her. "You know all about spring suitors. We both do. A spring suitor courts you because he loves you deeply enough to see a whole new life ahead, one full of promise and hope. That was my Joseph."

"And that was my Jonas," Emma whispered. She did not have a hand free, but she did not really need to reach into her pocket to take hold of her keepsakes, a simple treasure made of simple bits of cloth that celebrated special memories in her life and the lives of her children and grandchildren. Her memories of her beloved husband, now eight years at Home, were precious and tucked close to her heart.

Before she let fond thoughts of the past distract them both from the challenges of the present, Emma smiled. "Thank you for reminding me how blessed I was to be married to your son." She cleared her throat. "Speaking of blessings, what about Judith Massey? Didn't she offer to help you in the kitchen just this morning?"

Mother Garrett let go of Emma and tidied the sink. "She did, but she's teeming. She should be resting."

"She's not sick. She's going to have a baby. Besides, sitting around only gives her more time to worry about her home and whether or not it's going to be repaired before she has her baby. She'd be better off keeping busy with you. Or don't you like her?"

"Despite my opinion of Anson Kirk, there's not a soul on this earth I truly don't like, with two exceptions I'm not going to name because I'm trying hard to be kind."

"Then let Judith help you."

Her mother-in-law sighed and shook her head. "If it makes you happy, I'll talk to her at dinner."

"It makes me happy."

Mother Garrett sniffed.

Emma grinned. "I probably should have talked you into doing this days ago. Did you say Liesel and Ditty were upstairs? I should tell them the Burkes are coming, too."

"John Ammond saved you that bother. When he came back to tell his brother the news, he didn't just tell me, you know. He told everyone here, which means you only have to bother yourself with two things, since the folks coming back here for dinner will no doubt have heard about it in town."

"Only two? What are they?" Emma asked as she donned an apron and grabbed another drying cloth.

"First, you have to worry about finding enough room for the Burkes, which is going to be nigh impossible, if you ask me, unless you intend to hang their sleeping cots from the ceiling. You might want to consider asking the chickens to move over and make room in the coop, but I have a feeling those critters will refuse and stop laying the few eggs we're getting this winter for spite, just because you asked them."

Mother Garrett dried her hands one last time on her apron. "Second, between Liesel and having Judith helping out in the kitchen, you don't have to worry about me. I can take care of Anson Kirk, too. But I wouldn't plan on volunteering in town anytime soon. You're going to be far too busy playing peace-keeper here at home."

Mother Garrett was right. As much as she wanted to continue volunteering in town, Emma had no choice but to stay home at Hill House and meet her obligations to everyone staying there. She looked at her mother-in-law, shook her head, and groaned.

It was definitely not easy living with a woman who was usually right.

4

EMMA WAS RUNNING out of time.

Making room for twenty people, even at Hill House, required more than an organized mind. Adding the Burkes, without asking anyone to move from one room to another, also required more mental patience and stamina than Emma possessed at the moment.

With less than an hour before dinner and with the Burkes expected momentarily, she sat behind her desk in her office and pulled a scrap of paper from the clutter she stored in one of the drawers. She used a pencil to draw a quick sketch of the bedrooms on the second floor, made a list of all the people staying at Hill House, and labeled each room with the names of the occupants.

The six primary guest rooms on the second floor were filled. Solomon and Judith Massey had one of the two rooms at the front of the house, while the Ammond brothers shared the other. Mr. and Mrs. Kirk and their four children shared the two rooms across from one another in the hall behind the Masseys. Mr. and Mrs. Wiley and their three children shared two similar rooms in the hall behind the Ammonds.

Four smaller rooms that stretched across the back of the house were also occupied. Anson Kirk, unfortunately, was staying in Aunt Frances's old room next to Mother Garrett, and Liesel and Ditty were sharing the room next to Emma's. Her original plan to close off one of the parlors for a married couple would not work. Not for the Burkes.

To accommodate the brother and sister, Emma would have to close off both parlors, which she could ill afford to do, since the guests used them both at night. If the Burkes could manage two flights of stairs, she could put them in the garret where there were two small bedrooms separated by a sitting room, but not in this cold weather. There was only one small warming stove in the sitting room, and they would no doubt file a complaint against her for trying to freeze them to death.

She let out a sigh and doodled on the paper. She hesitated to ask Liesel and Ditty to go back up to the garret to share the sitting room. Not that the two young women would argue with her. But Emma had moved them down to the second floor from the garret to keep a closer watch on them, and she was reluctant to change that now.

She probably could move Anson Kirk out of the room next to Mother Garrett and put him in the garret. That way she could move Orralynne Burke into his old room, but that might be a bit like trading a little problem for a bigger one. Instead, Emma could offer her own bedroom to Orralynne and sleep in her office. She had done that for Aunt Frances willingly for a few nights at the end of the Founders' Day celebrations, and she would probably have to do that now, though not quite as willingly.

That left only Lester Burke without a room. Like it or not, she might have to close off the library for him, but that meant she would not be able to cut through the library to access her office, since the only other entry was from her private bedroom upstairs, where Orralynne would be staying, or from outside.

She tossed the pencil to the desk and scrunched up her paper. Maybe someone would come back for dinner, announce they were leaving this afternoon for home, and solve her problem for her. As long as she was dreaming, she may as well hope the Burkes would decide not to come to Hill House after all because they had been offered better accommodations.

The sound of a wagon going past the side of the house drew her attention to the window. But by the time she dragged herself out of her chair to take a look, the wagon had already turned into the backyard and all but disappeared from view.

She let the curtain fall back into place. "It's probably Steven bringing the supplies from the General Store. And not a day too soon, either. Not with twenty mouths to feed," she murmured, then hurried to the kitchen to help Mother Garrett put everything away.

By the time she reached the kitchen, Mother Garrett was already opening the back door. Along with a blast of cold air, Andrew Leonard and two of his nephews, Harry and Thomas, walked into the kitchen carrying baskets of foodstuffs.

Andrew set his down on the floor. "If you tell these two rascals here where you want everything, they'll store it away for you. I'll just get the rest and be right back," he promised and disappeared back outside.

Wide-eyed, Emma approached Harry. "What's all this?"

He grinned. "When we heard about the fires, my father and Uncle Andrew wanted to do something to help."

Thomas nodded. "Father is at town hall with our brothers unloading a wagon there, but since we thought you'd probably be taking in some folks, too, we wanted to bring you some extra supplies."

Harry held up the burlap bag he was carrying. "We even brought some feed for the chickens."

"You're all so good to us. Thank you," Emma said.

"Come with me, boys," Mother Garrett suggested. "I'll be right back, Emma. I'm taking them down to the root cellar to make sure they store everything in the right place. Thomas, you can come with me now. Harry, put that feed by the back door and bring that basket of turnips down for me, will you?" she asked, leading Thomas down the cellar steps.

"How's your grandmother?" Emma asked Harry.

He winked and nodded toward the door. "You should ask her yourself," he whispered.

As if on cue, Andrew poked his head into the kitchen and glanced around before leading his mother inside.

Emma stifled a yelp of surprise when Aunt Frances put a finger to her lips. "Not a sound, Emma dear. I thought I'd surprise Mercy," she whispered.

Emma rushed to her and hugged her tight. "You're half frozen! Let's get you over to the fire and warm you up. What were you thinking coming all this way in the cold just for a little visit?"

Andrew cleared his throat and held up one hand. "Don't blame me. I tried to warn her not to come." He hoisted up a basket of sweet potatoes, motioned for Harry to do the same, and they promptly disappeared down the cellar steps.

Aunt Frances smiled and spoke in a whisper. "As soon as we heard about the tragedy and how many people lost their homes, I had a notion you'd be taking in a lot of them. How many do you have staying here?"

Emma helped the elderly woman remove her outerwear. "Fifteen, with two more arriving sometime today."

"That many? Oh dear. Poor Mercy must be plumb tuckered to the bone. My joints are pretty stiff, so I don't think I could do much sewing, but I'd surely love to stay and help her in the kitchen. I'd enjoy visiting with Reverend Glenn, too, but with that many people here, I don't suppose you'd have room for one more, would you?"

After storing the woman's garments on a peg, Emma pulled a chair close to the fireplace and helped Aunt Frances to sit down. "For you? Always. Unfortunately, I'm afraid I have someone staying in your old room, but you can take my room. I was planning to move downstairs and stay in my office anyway," she insisted and immediately cancelled her plans to put Orralynne Burke in her room. Instead, Emma would have to put the woman in Liesel and Ditty's room and have the two young women move back up to the garret.

When they heard Mother Garrett talking her way back up the cellar stairs, Emma helped Aunt Frances to her feet and stepped out of the way. The moment her mother-in-law reentered the kitchen and saw Aunt Frances, the look of pure astonishment on her face quickly turned to joy that put a sparkle back into her weary eyes and a bounce to her step.

Emma watched the reunion of the two friends and offered prayers of gratitude for having Aunt Frances back here at Hill House, if only for a short visit. For the first time in a long while, Emma wondered what it might be like to have a friend her own age, perhaps someone who might stay at Hill House from time to time, or even better, someone who lived nearby so they could visit each other more often. Although she did not have the burden of operating the General Store day and night any longer, she still had little time or opportunity at Hill House to enjoy the same type of friendship and companionship with a friend her own age that Mother Garrett shared with Aunt Frances.

In all truth, however, she longed even more for the friendship and companionship she had found in her marriage to Jonas.

Unfortunately, the only female guest close to her own age who was staying at Hill House at the moment was Orralynne Burke. The likelihood that Emma could become friends with that woman was even less than the prospect that Emma would find a suitor at her door in the spring ... which was twice again as likely to happen as having the legal owner arrive and simply hand her the title to Hill House.

5

T HE BURKES WERE late for dinner.

In all fairness, there were only four rules at Hill House, and they were simple enough for anyone to follow. Attend services every Sunday you were in residence. Show respect for other guests, as well as the staff. Conduct yourself with proper decorum at all times. And finally, be on time for meals.

Without even crossing the threshold, however, Orralynne and Lester Burke had already broken one rule, and Emma suspected it was probably only a matter of hours before they broke the others.

When Sheriff North finally arrived with Emma's newest guests, everyone else staying at Hill House was already at the dining room table, halfway through dinner. Because of the cold, Emma had been waiting just inside the front door, ready to open it as soon as the couple reached the porch. She held the curtain back on one of the glass panels on either side of the door and watched the brother and sister as the sheriff helped them to disembark from a buggy parked just outside the front gate.

Over the years, Emma had seen the Burkes from time to time, though not recently. But Orralynne and Lester had not changed much. Like a pair of well-worn, mismatched shoes, the brother and sister did not look like they belonged together at all. Orralynne was the same age as Emma but younger than Lester by three years. Where she was slender, with fair skin and hair, Lester was bulkier, with olive skin and dark, curly hair.

Their disparate appearances lent visual evidence to the rumor that they had been sired by different men. Their mother, Beatrice Burke, who had been widowed shortly after Orralynne's birth, had gone to her grave two years later, however, insisting they had only one father, Charles Burke.

With no other living relatives, Orralynne and Lester had been raised together, moving from one household to another each year, depending on which family submitted the lowest bid to the town for their care. In time, Lester had been apprenticed to a tailor, which gave him a trade and allowed him to support both himself and his sister to this day.

When they came through the gate and crossed the yard to reach the porch, they each wore a perpetual scowl that testified to their miserable dispositions, perhaps the inevitable scars of their desperate childhoods. Sadly, Orralynne was also troubled with a number of minor physical frailties, while Lester had been born with a deformed foot and now leaned heavily on a cane for support.

The moment the guests reached the porch, Emma dropped the curtain back into place. Bracing herself, she opened the door and stepped out into the bitter cold to greet them. "Welcome to Hill House. I hope you'll be comfortable here," she said as she looked from one to the other and smiled.

Lester's dark eyes snapped with irritation. "I'd be comfortable in my own house, but I suppose I'll just have to make do staying here. Frankly, this is the last place I'd choose. Not that I have any say in the matter." He looked around the porch and frowned. "In all truth, I'm surprised anyone would pay honest money to stay here at all, given the history of the place."

Orralynne nudged him with her elbow. "Move over. Stop crowding me," she snapped. She cast a dark glance at Emma but waited until the sheriff passed them and carried some of their bags inside before addressing her. "I don't fancy staying here, either, but I trust you won't think about putting us out come morning like the others did. We're tired of being shoved around like pieces of old furniture no one wants anymore."

She lifted her chin in defiance and locked her gaze with Emma's. "Until we can have our home repaired, we've both decided that we're not being forced out again. Regardless of what you might like to do, we want to remind you that it's your Christian duty to help us."

Emma clenched her jaw. Being reminded of her duty as a Christian by a woman who had not been to services for years soured the taste in her mouth. She swallowed hard, turned the other cheek, and stepped aside. "You're welcome to stay as long as you like. Please come in out of the cold."

Lester struggled his way inside first, and Emma followed Orralynne back into the house, where they gathered in front of the massive oak coat rack.

Sheriff North was waiting for them just down the hall at the bottom of the staircase with the several bags he had carried inside. "I'm not sure where to put these bags."

Emma pointed straight ahead to the room just behind him. "You can put Mr. Burke's in the library and the rest in my office." When he turned and walked down the hall to deliver the bags, she explained the arrangements she had made for them. "I'm afraid we don't have any guest rooms available upstairs, and there are none at all on the first floor. Instead, we'll set up some sleeping cots for you in the library and my office, which are adjoining rooms. My office isn't very big, but it should do nicely as a bedroom for you, Orralynne, and there's an outer door there so you can come and go as you please without having to use the center hall. The library is large enough to allow for a sitting area for both of you, and you'll be close to the dining room, too."

Lester snorted. "We prefer eating alone, so we'll take our meals in the library. I'm certain you must have a small table you can put there. As a matter of fact, I believe we were expected for dinner."

Emma could make a stand here and now and insist that they both take their meals in the dining room—although the opportunity to have the two of them virtually sequestered in a make-shift suite of rooms in the back of the house, at their own request, might be better all around, despite the inconvenience of giving up her office. Her only concern was that travelers and guests who arrived typically used the outer door to her office to register for their stay, but since no guests were scheduled until spring, she easily set aside her concern. "Why don't you hang up your outerwear on the rack before I show you to your rooms?"

When Lester eyed the garments already hanging there, his gaze filled with disdain, as if the coats and bonnets did not measure up to his standards as a master tailor.

Orralynne, on the other hand, simply shook her head and shrugged. "Thieves are everywhere these days. I'll keep mine in my room," she insisted and turned to her brother. "If you're wise, you'll do the same, but do what you will, as long as you don't complain to me when your coat or hat disappears."

Stunned, Emma barely had the wherewithal to hold her tongue to defend her household and her guests. No one at Hill House had ever been labeled a thief or had lost a single item to thievery. Instead of arguing the point, however, she led them down the hall and into the library, where the sheriff was waiting for them.

"Unless there's something else you'd like me do, Widow Garrett, I need to get the rest of the bags so I can take the buggy back to the livery."

"No, thank you. You've done more than enough already." Her words sounded cool, even to her own ears, and she smiled to soften them. "Please give Joy my regards, and Pamela and Patricia, too," she added.

Struck by the memory of seeing Mother Garrett and Aunt Frances sitting at the Norths' kitchen table, each holding one of his little girls while his wife, Joy, prepared supper, her smile grew. "Aunt Frances is back for a visit. I'm sure she and Mother Garrett would love to stop in to see them."

He grinned. "Anytime. Joy would love the

company," he replied and said good-bye to the Burkes.

Once he took his leave, Emma turned her attention back to her guests. "While you make yourselves comfortable, I'll check on dinner for you and see if we can't find a table we can set up for you in the library, as well." She pointed to the door in the far wall. "My office is right through there, if you care to unpack. We'll move some sleeping cots into these rooms later today."

With high spirits, she left quickly before either one of them could argue with her. If the rest of the Burkes' stay followed the same pattern as their arrival, and if they remained isolated in the back of the house, which is what they seemed to want, keeping peace at Hill House might be just a bit easier than she could have hoped.

6

PEACE LASTED ALL of thirty minutes.
While Mother Garrett and Aunt
Frances served dessert in the dining room,
Emma finished making up two dinner trays.
She handed one to Liesel and the other to Ditty.
Although she felt slightly uneasy about sending
the two young women to deliver the trays to the
Burkes, there was no sense delaying the inevi-
table. Sooner or later, Liesel and Ditty would
have to contend with them, and Emma pre-
ferred to be close at hand the first time they did.

As long as they followed Emma's advice,
however, they should be fine. She eyed the two
young women and cocked her head. "Before
you leave, tell me again what you need to remember."

Liesel did not let much in this world intimi-
date her, with the exception of losing her position here, and she grinned. "Deliver the tray.
Smile a lot. And turn the other cheek. Don't get

upset if they say anything that's nasty or un-kind."

"And don't trip," Ditty added. "I know you didn't say so, but that's because you wouldn't want to hurt my feelings. But I think I've been doing much better, and I promise to be very careful so I don't trip and drop the tray."

Emma chuckled. Ditty was a hardworking young woman, uncommonly tall but incredibly clumsy. She really had improved over the past few months, apparently "growing into her own feet," as Mother Garrett liked to say. "I know you will. Just remember: If you encounter any trouble at all, leave the trays on the small table we just carried down from the garret and come get me. I'll be right here waiting for you."

Once the girls left the kitchen, Emma filled a plate with beef stew for herself, buttered a thick piece of bread, and nibbled off the crust. The moment she heard a large crash coming from the same direction as the library, she gulped down a last bit of bread. With visions of disaster nipping at her heels, she charged out of the kitchen and ran through the dining room, past her startled family and guests, who made no effort to go anywhere near the library.

She got to the center hall just as Liesel and Ditty came scurrying out of the library. Slam-ming the door behind them, they turned about and leaned back against the door to catch their breath.

Tears coated Liesel's cheeks.

Ditty's face was flushed dark pink, and her chest heaved as she drew in deep gulps of air. Like Liesel, her apron and the bottom of her skirts carried several telltale stains from the food on the dinner tray she had been carrying.

Emma swallowed hard. Despite all Ditty's good intentions, she must have either tripped or dropped the tray she had been carrying, and Emma faulted herself for sending the young woman to the library in the first place. She went directly to the two of them, realized she was still holding her buttered bread, and shoved it into her apron pocket before taking each of the trembling young women by an arm. "Take a deep breath. Both of you. Don't worry, Ditty. I'm sure it was an accident."

Ditty's eyes widened and filled with fresh tears. "I didn't have an accident. I didn't trip at all. I didn't!"

"*She* did it," Liesel argued as she pointed behind her. "She did it. That Miss Burke did it, not Ditty."

Emma let go of them and wrinkled her nose. "Miss Burke dropped the tray?"

"No," Ditty cried. "She didn't drop it. She threw it at me."

Emma gasped. "She . . . she what?"

"It's true. Well, almost true. She didn't throw it at Ditty as much as she just put her hand under that tray and shoved it right back at

Ditty. I saw her," Liesel argued.

"No!"

"That's just what she did," Ditty protested. When she looked down at her apron and skirts, she managed a bit of a smile. "I didn't get hit too badly with the food, though. I was pretty quick. After helping to feed all my brothers and sisters when they were babies, I've gotten used to dodging food."

"But the library is a mess," Liesel countered. "The dinner is spilled all over the floor and I think it hit some of the chairs, too. Mr. Burke said we had to clean it up before he could eat, so he wants us to fix another tray for him, too, because the food on the tray we already gave him will be cold by then."

"Widow Garrett! Come here at once! Widow Garrett!"

Emma ignored Lester's booming command and kept her focus on unraveling the details of the girls' encounter with the Burkes. "Did she . . . did she say why she flipped the tray at you?"

Ditty shrugged. "I'm not sure. One minute I was setting the tray down and the next that tray was heading straight for me."

"I remember what she said," Liesel offered. "She said if they were going to be living here at Hill House, the least you could do was to treat them as well as the other guests and serve their meals on china instead of crockery."

"Widow Garrett! Come here! Now!"

Emma's head started pounding and irritation pulsed through her veins, but she ignored Orralynne's command exactly as she had done with Lester's. "I'm sorry this happened," she managed. "I'll see to it that this doesn't happen again. Liesel, go with Ditty and see if you can't help each other to get those stains out of your skirts while I speak to the Burkes."

Liesel nodded and urged Ditty toward the kitchen.

As the two young women crossed the hall, Emma called after them, "Fetch me a pail of water, some soap, and a few cleaning rags, will you?"

Liesel looked back over her shoulder and rolled her eyes. "Could you maybe see if the Burkes could leave the room while we clean it up?"

"You're not cleaning up the mess. Just bring everything I asked for and leave it outside the library door," Emma said. She turned and reached for the handle on the library door, then hesitated for a moment to clear her head.

On the one hand, she wanted to charge inside the library and give both of the Burkes a good tongue-lashing. On the other hand, after raising three sons, she knew better than to react to any tale without at least attempting to get the other side of the story first.

The Burkes were a troublesome pair, which

made both Liesel's and Ditty's account of their encounter more likely than not. But the Burkes still deserved the same benefit of the doubt Emma would have given to anyone else, especially if she had any hope of learning to love them as her neighbors.

At the moment, however, tolerating them seemed a bit too much to ask, even for a woman trying desperately to be good.

7

EMMA CLOSED HER EYES long enough to whisper a prayer for patience and understanding before she knocked on the library door and opened it. She stepped inside, took one look around the library, and choked back her disgust.

Just as Liesel had described, the gleaming wood floor, which Emma and Ditty had cleaned and polished only last week, was splattered with chunks of beef, turnips, carrots, and potatoes. It appeared gravy had sloshed on one of the new leather chairs. A bowl of custard, along with a generous slice of apple pie, had landed on the floor, as well, right next to a pool of hot tea still dripping from a teapot lying on its side next to the upended dinner tray.

As she approached the Burkes, she drew in a deep breath and squared her shoulders. She looked directly at Orralynne but deliberately kept her voice soft. "Tell me what happened."

Orralynne sniffed. "You can see that for yourself. There's a mess that needs to be cleaned up."

Lester waved his hand toward the floor to get Emma's attention. "It's about time you got here. You need to tell one of those servant girls to hurry back here to clean this up."

Emma swallowed hard. While she held tight to her determination to hear both sides of the story, she was sorely inclined to lay blame directly with the Burkes. "Before I do anything, I need to know exactly how your dinner wound up on the floor."

"That's where it landed," Orralynne explained. "Not that I threw it there deliberately, although I was tempted. I merely gave it a shove and it slid right off the table. That wouldn't have happened if anyone had bothered to cover the table with a tablecloth," Orralynne said without a smidgeon of apology in her voice.

"You shoved your dinner tray? Why?" Emma asked.

Orralynne huffed. "It's difficult enough to know you've given the other guests proper bedrooms, while we're forced to make do in these rooms." She pointed to the tray in front of her brother. "You shouldn't treat us like nobodies and serve us our dinner on ordinary crockery. Not when I've heard all about the fancy china you use to serve your hoity-toity guests. What's good for one guest should be good for all."

With the girls' account essentially confirmed, Emma tried to keep hold of her temper and remain patient. Unfortunately, after turning both cheeks earlier, she did not have another one left. She reacted immediately and instinctively, stared directly at Orralynne, and held up her hand to count off her complaints on her fingers as she made them.

As she did, her voice rose with each complaint. "First, Liesel and Ditty are not servants. They're both valued members of my staff, and I'll remind you to treat them, as well as everyone else here, with respect. Second, you may never, ever throw anything at anyone for any reason, for as long as you're living here. Third, if you intend to eat anything between now and when you leave, you'll clean up this mess you've made or go hungry."

"B-but—"

"Let me explain something," Emma continued, astounded that this woman would be so brazen as to mutter a protest of any kind. "If you insist on dining on china plates, you'll go hungry more often than not. With twenty-three people staying here now, I don't have enough china for everyone, which you would have known if you had dined with everyone else, instead of insisting on having special private accommodations. Of course, that would mean you'd have to be on time for your meals. You were both over half an hour late for dinner today."

She paused to catch her breath and looked from Orralynne to her brother and back again to make sure she still had their full attention. "In the future, I'll expect you to take your meals in the dining room, on time, just like everyone else, so there won't be any more misunderstandings. We have breakfast at eight, dinner at one, and supper at six. We don't accommodate anyone who is late and misses a meal. Ever."

Lester struggled to his feet, knocked his chair to the floor, and waved his cane at her. "I cannot and will not allow you to speak to my sister or to me in that tone of voice."

Orralynne remained seated, but her cheeks flushed scarlet. "You can't tell us what to do, Emma. We're adults. We're not children anymore."

Emma's tenuous hold on her temper snapped. "No, you're not, which means you should have learned by now that you can't use being an orphan or being sickly as an excuse to be demanding or obnoxious or rude or mean. As proprietress of Hill House, I certainly can and will ask you to follow the same rules as everyone else as long as you're living under my roof, which means I'll also expect you to attend services every Sunday."

Horrified that she had lost all semblance of control and courtesy, she clamped her mouth shut as a warm blush stole up her neck to her cheeks. Trembling, she blinked back tears of embarrassment and frustration and struggled to find her voice. "If you can't or won't comply, I'm sorry, but you'll simply have to leave. It's entirely up to you," she whispered, turned, and walked out of the room.

The moment she shut the door behind her, she leaned back against it, closed her eyes, and concentrated on taking one long, slow breath at a time to keep from dissolving into tears. As a businesswoman, whether she was operating the General Store or Hill House, she had developed a number of strategies. Depending on the situation at hand, she had either been conciliatory or forceful. Occasionally, she had even been coy.

But she had never, ever allowed herself to lose her temper or to speak so forcefully to anyone, most especially a guest at Hill House.

When she heard footsteps approaching, she opened her eyes, found Ditty and Liesel arriving with the cleaning supplies, and pushed herself away from the door.

She managed half a smile. "Just put everything right here on the floor. When you get back to the kitchen, tell Mother Garrett I'll be upstairs for a bit."

While the two young women did as she requested, Emma started for the staircase rather than let them see how upset she was.

"Widow Garrett?"

Emma looked back over her shoulder. "Yes, Ditty?"

"You never had time to eat your dinner. Would you like me to bring you something to eat?"

Emma pressed her lips together and swallowed hard. "I'm not very hungry anymore, but thank you."

Liesel glanced down at the cleaning supplies. "What about the mess in the library? Are you sure you don't want us to clean it up?"

"Very sure," Emma whispered and walked slowly but steadily to the staircase, seeking the privacy she would find in the solitude of her bedroom. She was halfway up the stairs before she remembered that Aunt Frances had moved into that room. She could not even escape to her office because Orralynne had already settled herself there. The only place in the entire boardinghouse that offered any retreat at all was the garret.

She climbed up the stairs, turned down the hall, and walked up the last flight of steps to the third floor. Feeling like an exile in her own home, she was ashamed of herself and completely certain she did not fit anyone's description of a good woman at the moment, especially not Zachary Breckenwith's.

Not after the way she had behaved in the library.

She paused just a few steps from the top and reached for the pocket in her gown for her keepsakes. Instead, she realized she had reached into the wrong pocket the instant she grabbed hold of the buttery bread she had slipped into her apron earlier.

"I give up. There isn't a thing I can do right today," she grumbled, plopping herself down on the step to wipe the butter from her hand with the hem of her apron. When she finished, she pressed her hands together and wrapped her fingers tight to make a single fist.

With a sigh that came from deep within her spirit, she closed her eyes, bowed her head, and rested her chin on her fingers. She realized that her troubles did not start and end with the Burkes.

The uncertainty of not knowing when the legal owner of Hill House would arrive and whether or not he would agree to sell the boardinghouse to her was growing harder and harder to bear. Continuing to keep the whole matter a secret from Mother Garrett, as well as the others, was growing more and more difficult, even as she weighed the fairness or unfairness of her decision. She blinked hard to hold back tears of frustration and fear. She had worked so hard and so long to make a home here for all of them, and she could barely consider the prospect of losing this very special place for much longer. Not alone. Not without someone who would listen to her deepest fears and soothe her troubled spirit with patience and understanding and love. With humbled heart, she turned to the One whose presence and love had always been constant in her life.

"Please help me, Father," she prayed. "I want to be a good woman. I want to accept your will for my life, and I want to follow your teachings and help the Burkes. But they haven't even been here a day, and I've already lost my way. Please, I need your help."

She drew in a long breath. "I'm frustrated, and I'm angry. I know life for Lester and Orra-lynne has always been difficult, but without knowing you and loving you, their burdens are many and their words and actions are as bitter as their hearts. Forgive me, Father, but I wouldn't mind a bit if either one of them simply vanished from the face of this earth. I know they're my neighbors, but . . . but they're just so difficult to love."

She pressed her cheek against her hands. "Please guide me. Help me to return their un-kind words with understanding and their de-mands with patience. Help me to protect my family and the others who have come here seek-ing shelter from the discord these two people have already brought into my home. If you'll just show me how to begin, I'll do my best to follow and allow your plan for me to unfold in your time. Amen."

With every breath she took, with every beat of her heart, she entrusted Him with her worries and her guilt. In return, in the quiet of the moment and with the surrender of her will, she received the gift of acceptance that only His love and His presence could bring. When her heart filled with peace, she received the answer to her prayer and knew exactly how to begin.

She rose, retraced her steps all the way back to the first floor, and walked down the center hall to the library.

Determination gave her the strength to gather up the cleaning supplies Liesel and Ditty had left on the floor and knock at the door.

Faith and faith alone gave her the courage to open the door and step inside.

8

THE LIBRARY FLOOR was still littered with the contents of Orralynne's dinner tray, but the Burkes had vanished.

Emma's heart skipped a beat. Fearful she had forced them out with her impatience, she was halfway to panic when she spied Lester's travel bags sitting on the floor in front of the glass-enclosed bookcases on the far side of the fireplace. The door to her adjoining office, which had been open earlier, was now closed.

She cocked her head, heard the sound of muffled voices coming from her office, and assumed the Burkes had both gone there to discuss what to do, rather than stay in the library to clean up the mess.

Feeling grateful she did not have to explain herself or apologize immediately, she sidestepped her way to the table. The plates on Lester's dinner tray were empty. Apparently, he had not been too upset to eat his meal; she hoped he had had the decency to share it with his sister.

She set down her cleaning supplies, retrieved the tray and tableware from the floor, and set them back on the table. Working on her hands and knees, she wiped up the food from the floor and put the soiled cloths on the tray before washing the floor clean and rubbing it dry.

Next, she tackled the leather chair and washed it down. When she was done, she stored her cleaning supplies and both dinner trays out in the center hallway. After taking a final glance around the room to make sure she had not missed anything, she approached the door to her office in hopes of establishing peace between herself and the Burkes. She also had to remove her guest register and other important papers from her desk, as well as the personal items she had stored there when Aunt Frances moved into her bedroom.

Emma knocked on the office door and opened it. She took one step inside but immediately braced to a halt. Orralynne was sitting behind Emma's desk, which riled her immensely, while Lester occupied one of the two chairs facing the desk. A man Emma had never seen before sat in the other.

Even though he was sitting down, the middle-aged stranger appeared to be very tall, if the length of his legs were any indication. He had a very narrow face and pinched features that made him look as if his face had been pressed in a vise, much like the one Reverend Glenn used when he whittled crosses out of candlewood for their guests.

Although she was surprised to find a total stranger sitting in her office, she was utterly stunned by the smiles on the Burkes' faces and the amiable atmosphere in the room. "Excuse me. I . . . I didn't realize you were entertaining a guest," she managed.

"He's not our guest," Orralynne crooned. "He's yours."

The stranger shot to his feet, towering over everyone else in the room. "Widow Garrett? Allow me to introduce myself. My name is Malcolm Lewis. I'm an artist. I recently finished some work in Bounty. I was just explaining to your guests that I was hoping to secure some work here in Candlewood, but once I arrived this morning and learned of the recent tragedy, I realized that's probably not going to be possible. In point of fact, I haven't even been able to find a place to stay for the night. I have a small wagon filled with my supplies that I use for my travels. I'm not loathe to admit that I've slept more than a few nights in that old wagon, but never in weather as cold as this," he admitted.

Orralynne smiled coyly at him, shocking Emma yet again. "I assured Mr. Lewis you would be able to make room for one more, especially for a man of artistic talent. He's also been kind enough to agree to paint our portraits, which would help to pass the time until some of the others can leave and return to their own homes and we can move into more proper accommodations. Perhaps you might have need for some of his services, as well. In addition to portraits, he also paints landscapes and does stenciling."

Lester nodded. "Fortunately, I was able to salvage most of my tools and a good supply of fabric, which Sheriff North has been kind enough to store in his office. I've agreed to make Mr. Lewis a new suit of clothes in exchange for his services. I'll be using the library for my work room, so even when a proper bedroom becomes available, I'll require that additional accommodation. In the meantime, I assume you'll have those sleeping cots you promised us set up shortly."

He eased from his chair and grabbed hold of his cane. "Come along, sister. You can help me unpack. I'm sure Widow Garrett would like to discuss her own wants and needs with Mr. Lewis," he suggested before looking at the artist. "Mr. Lewis, please join us when you're finished here."

Emma was shocked speechless. She hardly had room for another guest, and she certainly did not need the Burkes to encourage this man to stay here to paint their portraits. Before Emma could organize her objections or even think to apologize to the Burkes for her behavior earlier in the library, Orralynne got up and followed her brother to the door. She turned to face Emma and smiled. "I told Mr. Lewis about our little accident at dinner. Are the cleaning supplies still available? I'd like to take care of that little spill before he joins us."

Emma's eyes widened. "I've taken care of that for you," she managed. "I'd also like to apologize for—"

"There's no need for apologies," Orralynne insisted before walking into the library and shutting the door behind her.

Emma stared at the closed door for several long moments and tried to reconcile her experience with the Burkes now with what had occurred earlier in the library. If she had stepped into a dream, she did not want to wake up. She had never seen such a turnabout in attitude. Not in all her years tending the General Store or in the two years she had been welcoming guests to Hill House.

At the same time, however, she did not want to allow a guest to dictate whether or not there was room to accommodate another guest or determine whether or not Emma would allow her library to be turned into a tailor shop.

"Widow Garrett?"

At the sound of her name, Emma turned,

smiled at Mr. Lewis, and reclaimed her rightful place behind her desk. "I feel very badly that you've arrived under such difficult circumstances," she offered. "At the moment, unfortunately, I believe your assessment of finding it hard to get work in Candlewood is probably correct. Most folks are still reeling from our recent tragedy, and they probably won't be inclined to think about using their funds for themselves when so many others have such need."

He shrugged. "After spending most of my life moving from one town to another every few months to secure work, I've learned to be grateful for the blessings I have today. I try not to worry about the ones I'll receive tomorrow. Fortunately, I'm as happy painting landscapes or portraits as I am doing stencil work or creating silhouettes, so I manage to find enough work for myself one way or the other."

She cocked her head. "I believe you might be rather unusual in that regard. Most artists have one or two specialties, or so I've been told."

"Perhaps that's true," he replied. He leaned down, pulled a sketchbook from a satchel on the floor, and handed her the book. "If you like, you can look over some samples of stenciling and other work I've completed in the past. I've put some letters of introduction inside the book, as well, along with a list of the prices I charge for my work. Of course, that's only if you're agreeable to my staying here at all so I can paint the Burkes' portraits. I'd need to spend a few weeks on them, at least. Like Mr. Burke suggested, I'd be spending most of my time in the library with them so I would try not to be in the way. After that, unless I'm fortunate enough to find additional work, I'll be on my way."

Emma laid the sketchbook on top of her desk. Though sorely tempted, she held back from looking inside. Once she did, she would be certain to find a design for the center hallway she found pleasing—and she felt she could not incur such an expense when her ownership was in question.

She was, however, reluctant to send this man away since he had managed to tame the Burkes' negative attitudes so easily and so quickly, even though she had no room to offer him.

When she suddenly remembered that Reverend Glenn would not be returning to Hill House until tomorrow, she sighed with relief. "I do have one room open just for tonight," she admitted and quickly explained that the room actually belonged to the retired minister. Because of his difficulty walking or managing stairs, she had converted a storage room off the kitchen into a bedroom for him. "Beyond that, since Reverend Glenn is expected home tomorrow, whether or not you can stay will depend on the other guests and how quickly they'll be leaving."

He smiled, softening the hard planes to his features, and rose from his seat. "The room will be fine for the night. Like I said earlier, I'm grateful for today's blessings. Tomorrow will take care of itself. In the meantime, if you'll excuse me, I left my other bags outside in the wagon. I'd like to bring them inside before I spend some time with the Burkes so we can discuss plans for the portraits."

While he made several trips in and out of the house to retrieve his bags, Emma laid his sketchbook on top of her guest register. The only thing she left on top of the desk, other than the oil lamp, was a small decorative sampler. She scooped up the personal items she had moved into her office and moved everything to the back staircase that led upstairs to her bedroom. On impulse, she removed her apron, spread it out on top of her desk, and dumped the clutter she had stored in both desk drawers on top. After putting the drawers back, she wrapped up her apron and carried it with her.

By the time she made two trips up to the garret on the third floor and returned one last time to her office, she was flushed and winded. Mr. Lewis, apparently, was sequestered behind closed doors in the library with the Burkes, and his bags were lined up in her office.

In order to get to the kitchen to tell Mother

Garrett they had yet another guest, at least for the night, Emma had three choices. She could go back upstairs to her bedroom, take the hallway to Mother Garrett's room, and use the back staircase that led to the kitchen, but she did not think she could face climbing all those stairs yet again. She could cut through the library like she usually did, but that meant she would interrupt the Burkes.

Instead, she decided to take a faster, simpler way. If she slipped out the door to the porch, she could go around the house and get to the kitchen door in less than a minute. "I can tolerate the cold that long without my cape," she muttered.

After crossing the porch and descending the steps, Emma rounded the house but immediately braced to a halt. The wind whipped at her skirts and nipped at her face and carried away what little scream escaped from her throat. Her heart slammed against the wall of her chest.

Straight ahead only yards away, a panther was crouched low, inching closer and closer to the pen housing the chicken coop. Fortunately the animal was upwind, facing the other direction, which gave her a few seconds to react and escape. Instead of racing back to safety, however, she was frozen immobile, too stunned to see an animal only rumored to roam this area several decades ago to do anything other than to watch with horrid fascination.

Until the chickens in the coop started squawking.

Startled back to reality, she stared at the wire pen. While it was strong enough to keep the chickens close to the coop, it would be too weak to hold up against the strength of this predator. She looked around frantically and picked up a rock the size of a loaf of bread.

Using both hands, she hurled it as best she could in the panther's direction, hoping to startle it rather than hit it and hurt it. Almost immediately, Faith fluttered out of the coop, squawking her heart out.

The panther straightened up but hesitated, as if momentarily shocked or confused by the commotion. Emma could now see that the poor creature was very thin and obviously hungry. Still, her protective instincts overruled her common sense, and her need to protect her chickens was greater than her desire to see the panther assuage its hunger on them.

She grabbed a smaller rock and tossed it toward the panther. This time the animal turned and looked directly at her. Acting on pure impulse, she imitated Faith and then some. She grabbed her skirts and started flapping them like wings while screaming at the top of her lungs. "Go away! Scoot! Go! Go! Go!"

To her utter amazement, the panther quickly turned and leaped over the stone wall along the perimeter of the backyard. With her body shaking as much from fright as from cold, she offered a silent prayer of gratitude while she tried to catch her breath.

Faith, on the other hand, patrolled the inside of the pen, still agitated and still squawking.

"You're all right for now," Emma murmured before she hurried to the kitchen door. The moment she got inside, she slammed the door shut and collapsed against it.

Mother Garrett, who was sitting with Aunt Frances sharing a cup of tea while they peeled apples, looked up and frowned. "In case you've forgotten, it's the middle of winter. Next time you decide to go outside without your cape, I hope you have the sense to wait until spring. Your lips are almost as blue as your eyes."

Emma tightened her jaw to keep her teeth from chattering. "I'm sorry. I was only trying to take a shortcut to the kitchen so you'd be the first to know we have another guest. Mr. Lewis is here. He's an artist. He'll be staying in Reverend Glenn's room for the night. And the Burkes will be taking their meals with us in the dining room. And in case you're interested, on my way to the kitchen I encountered a panther that was headed straight for the chicken coop. But don't worry. I chased it off."

Her mother-in-law dropped the apple she was peeling. "A panther? Here? In the backyard?"

"And you chased it off? All by yourself?" Aunt Frances asked.

"Yes, yes. But Faith helped," Emma quipped and plopped into the chair next to Mother Garrett. Now that the crisis was over, she started shaking. Hard. She wrapped her arms at her waist and pressed her elbows to her body, rocking in rhythm to the tremors rippling through her body from head to toe.

Mother Garrett took the knitted blanket she kept in the kitchen to keep the drafts off her legs and wrapped it around Emma's shoulders.

Aunt Frances went to the cupboard for another cup, fixed some hot tea for Emma, and handed it to her. "Drink this. You'll feel better."

Now settled, Emma took the cup and curled her hands around it. "The panther will be back for the chickens, and the next time, it might get to them. The wire pen just isn't strong enough to hold it back. That animal is starving. I could almost make out its ribs," she whispered. "It's not safe to go outside now. Not for anyone. What are we going to do?"

Mother Garrett patted Emma's back. "We'll send for the sheriff. He'll know what to do. At the very least, he'll have to alert everyone in town to be on the lookout for the panther."

Emma closed her eyes and sighed. "He's already got enough to do. He doesn't have the time to go from household to household to warn everyone. We'd probably be better off if we could get someone to go to the General Store and the hotel and tell the tale. Gossip will spread the news faster."

Mother Garrett grinned at Aunt Frances and stood up. "We can do that much."

"You can't go into town! What about the panther?" Emma argued.

Aunt Frances waved away Emma's question. "I doubt the animal will venture out of the woods again for a while, but I'll grab an umbrella for each of us. That way, if we do spot the panther, we'll have something to use to protect ourselves."

Emma snorted. "An umbrella?"

Aunt Frances narrowed her gaze. "Did you ever get poked with one?"

"No, but—"

"Enough said," Mother Garrett argued. "We're going to town. While we're there, we'll stop at the General Store and ask that nice Mr. Atkins to send Steven up here with supplies to strengthen up that pen for the chickens, too. And don't argue with us. We're your elders," she added.

Mother Garrett untied her apron and laid it across the back of her chair. "Come along, Frances. If we hurry, we can be back well before supper. Emma, you rest up and don't worry about finishing up these pies. Liesel just went upstairs to fetch Judith Massey. She wanted to help after she took a bit of a nap."

Emma set down her tea. "Please. You really can't venture into town alone. It isn't safe," she countered, also anxious that Mother Garrett and Aunt Frances might be so busy matchmaking again for poor Mr. Atkins, they would forget the real purpose for their trip into town.

Aunt Frances got up, stored her own apron away, and grinned. "We'll take Anson Kirk with us. He's just sitting in the front parlor waiting for us to finish up in the kitchen so he can try sweetening up to one of us anyway. A good walk in the cold might settle him down a bit."

Grinning, Mother Garrett hooked her arm with Aunt Frances's. "Maybe we can lose him in town."

Before Emma could choose another argument to make to convince the two women not to leave, they had already left the kitchen. "Oh, I'll rest easy now," she grumbled and took a sip of tea. "Why shouldn't I? I only have two elderly women venturing outside, using one old man and two umbrellas to protect themselves from a starving panther that's roaming about the area looking for a meal. I've got an artist in residence now, sixteen other townspeople, and the Burkes, not to mention a flock of chickens who probably are so agitated they won't lay a single egg for weeks, assuming Steven can get here with stronger wire anytime soon."

She shook her head. If she had any sense at all, she would find that old pair of skates of hers, strap them on, and skate away up the frozen canal to escape this lunacy.

Then again, the last time she strapped on those skates, she had fallen, twisted her ankle, and spent two weeks in bed.

"At least I had a bed then," she griped and settled for another sip of strong, hot tea.

9

THE BOARDINGHOUSE WAS so quiet two hours before supper, Emma could almost pretend the day was normal.

While Liesel and Ditty were busy straightening and cleaning both parlors, Emma sat at the kitchen table and helped Judith Massey crimp the top crust on the last of the apple pies while the others finished baking. The kitchen was warm and heavy with the sweet scent of apples and cinnamon, but the companionship was just as heartwarming.

Unlike Emma, who was getting closer to old age every day, Judith was in the prime of her life. Just months from delivering her first child, she had a mop of unruly dark curls that framed her full, round face.

Since Emma had sold the General Store to purchase Hill House before Judith and her husband moved to Candlewood from Connecticut a few years ago, she only knew them in passing and hoped to get to know this young woman better. "You're probably close in age to my three sons," she prompted as she twisted the edge of the crust on one of the pies between her fingers.

"I'm twenty-four," Judith replied, working in tandem with Emma on a separate pie.

"My youngest, Mark, is twenty-four."

"He doesn't live nearby, does he?"

Emma shook her head. "No. In fact, all my boys moved away when they got married," she replied and paused to turn the pie to reach the dough on the other side. "Mark is living in Albany. Benjamin is my middle child. He moved west to Ohio. Warren is living in New York City."

Judith frowned. "You don't see them often, then."

"They come back home from time to time for a visit, but they write. In fact, they're all planning to bring their families home in April to celebrate my birthday, and I'm looking forward to seeing all of my grandchildren together at the same time. I have seven," Emma said proudly.

"Solomon's parents are both deceased, but this will be my mother's first grandchild. I don't have any brothers or sisters. I was hoping she would be able to be here when the baby was born, but she and my stepfather won't be able to visit until summer."

Emma shook her head. "Life gets very complicated when our children grow up and move away," she said, wondering what it would be like to be able to share in the ordinary moments of day-to-day living with her sons and their families.

Judith used a knife to trim the last bit of excess crust from one pie, then handed the knife to Emma. "Your life here at Hill House has certainly gotten more complicated with all of us suddenly appearing on your doorstep. I can scarcely believe how many pies we need just for supper."

Emma chuckled. "We've got over twenty people to feed, but that's only a few more than we have now and then during the tourist season. You're used to baking for two, but that will change soon enough, won't it?"

"By mid-March, I believe, but the midwife tells me babies don't always arrive on time. You know Mrs. Sherman, don't you?"

"Very well. She helped all three of my boys into the world."

Judith caressed her swollen abdomen. "I . . . I almost wish it were a bit longer. I just love the feeling of having the baby inside, where it's safe and warm." She blushed. "I suppose that sounds silly."

"Not at all," Emma countered as she trimmed another pie crust. "I had the same feelings carrying my boys. Until my time got close and they got bigger. Have you chosen any names yet?"

Judith snatched a piece of raw crust and nibbled on it. "I think Solomon really wants a boy so he can teach him to help in the cobbler shop. In that case, we'll call our son Isaac. If it's a girl?" She shrugged. "We can't decide. I think I'd like to call her Susan, for my sister. She died when she was very young."

"How old was she?"

"She'd just turned thirteen the week before she got the measles," Judith murmured. "Solomon thinks it would be better if we named the baby something else, so I wouldn't be sad every time I called her Susan."

"What do you think?"

Judith let out a sigh. "Maybe he's right. But I think I'm going to have a boy, so I won't have to worry about it. At least, not this time." She sniffed the air. "Do you think it's time to check the pies in the oven?"

Emma rose from her seat. "I'll do it. You finish up that last crust." She opened the oven, saw the crust on the two pies was golden brown, and reached for a pair of heavy cloths. "You're right. The pies are done."

After setting both pies on trivets Mother Garrett had put out at the far end of the wooden table, she slid two more into the oven to bake. Instead of returning to her seat, Emma picked up the remnants of raw crust for a moment. On a whim, she retrieved a whole apple from the larder and peeled it.

She coated the outside of the apple with butter and dusted it with cinnamon before she sat down next to Judith again. She rolled out some dough and pressed it around the buttered apple. "Has anyone ever made one of these for you yet?"

Judith furrowed her brow. "For me? No, why?"

"I always thought it was an old wives' tale, but maybe it was just something my mother made up herself. Each time I was carrying a babe, my mother would bake a whole apple for me, just like this."

She retrieved a small baking tin, placed the pastry apple inside, and popped it into the oven before taking her seat again. "When it's done, we'll let it cool until we have dessert after supper. Then you can scoop a spoonful of apple from the center and count the seeds on your spoon. If there are an odd number, you're supposedly having a boy. If there are an even number, it's a girl." Emma chuckled. "I'm not sure how reliable it is, but I always got an odd number of seeds, and I had all boys."

Judith cocked her head. "What if I don't get any seeds at all? Do I try again?"

Emma laughed. "Fortunately, that never happened to me, but my mother said it meant you'd be having twins."

Judith glanced down at her abdomen. "Really?"

"No, I'm teasing. You just try again."

"Oh, good. I'm not sure I know what to do with one baby, let alone two."

Emma took the younger woman's hand. "You'll do just fine. Mrs. Sherman is very good about helping new mothers. I'm sure there'll be neighbor women who will stay with you for the first week or two. And I'm here, too, if you need help. Just send for me."

"Thank you. I will."

"What about your home? How are the repairs coming along?"

Judith's dark eyes welled with tears. "Thankfully, Solomon's cobbler shop on the first floor was spared or we wouldn't have any hope of repairing anything. Since the fire started on the roof, our living quarters upstairs were pretty badly burned. We lost everything we couldn't carry out in a hurry. I shouldn't complain, though. Other folks lost everything they owned. Solomon thinks it'll be the better part of a month or two before we can move back home."

"Then you'll be there in plenty of time to have your babe."

Judith sniffled. "I hope so. We can't stay at Hill House for that long."

"Why not?" Emma asked, anxious to know if Judith was aware of the sad history of the house she had converted into a boardinghouse.

The younger woman dropped her gaze to

her lap. "Solomon said I was being foolish to worry about it, but I . . . I would be lying if I said it didn't bother me. I know what happened to the people who lived here when the house was first built."

Emma swallowed hard. "And you're afraid that because Mrs. Foxleigh died in childbirth, along with her babe, that the same thing might happen to you," she said gently.

Judith lifted a teary gaze and nodded. "I know it's foolish, and I don't mean to appear ungrateful but—"

"It's not foolish at all," Emma argued. "It's perfectly natural for you to feel especially vulnerable to what happened here. I hadn't brought the matter up before because, frankly, I wasn't sure if you knew about the original owners."

Emma paused and put her hand atop Judith's. "If it makes you feel better, I can promise you that as your time draws near, if you're not back at home by then, I'll see about making arrangements for you to stay elsewhere. Unless you'd like to move now," Emma offered. "I'm not sure if it's possible, but I can certainly try to find another place for you and your husband."

Judith sniffled again. "You're very kind, but I'd like to stay here for a while to see if I can go home first before I put you to all that bother. That might be difficult, though, now that the Burkes are here."

Emma put her arm around the younger woman. "I wouldn't worry about them. They're far too busy with Mr. Lewis to be bothered with much else." She quickly explained the Burkes' plans to have their portraits painted. "That's why they'll be in the library most of the time."

"They filed a complaint against Solomon, you know," Judith murmured. "Or Mr. Burke did. He said Solomon didn't repair a shoe right. The one for his deformed foot."

Emma drew in a long breath. "No, I didn't know, but I can't say I'm surprised. How did the complaint get resolved?"

"Solomon won in court, but he repaired Mr. Burke's shoe again anyway, for free. Not that it made any difference. Every time Mr. Burke brings in another pair of shoes, he barks at Solomon and threatens to file another complaint if he doesn't do it right."

Emma hugged her. "Mr. Burke won't be barking at anyone while he's here." She rose and started cleaning up their work area. "If it makes you feel any better, I'll make sure to sit next to you and Solomon at supper. That way, I'll be right there to remind the man how cold it is outside, which is where he'll be if he forgets his manners."

Judith chuckled. "Don't forget to tell him about the panther."

"That too," Emma replied and whispered a silent prayer for the trio who had gone to town to warn the others about the panther. On second thought, she added a prayer for the poor panther that had no idea how dangerous it would be to run into those three.

Supper was a boisterous affair, filled with the joyful noise of laughter, lively conversation, and enthusiastic celebrations that easily eclipsed the presence of the Burkes.

Naturally the panther sighting and the town-wide alert were the centerpiece of the hoopla, and everyone was intrigued to have an artist in their midst. The announcement by the Wiley family that all five of them would be leaving after supper to return to their home was only supplanted by other hopeful news. All five members of the Kirk family, except for the elderly winter suitor, would be leaving the following day, on Saturday.

While Liesel and Ditty carried in slices of warm apple pie for dessert for everyone, Emma placed the baked apple and a plate in front of Judith and sat down next to her.

Before she attempted to take a spoonful, Judith quickly explained the ritual to everyone. For his part, Solomon merely smiled in that characteristic way a man smiles at his very-pregnant wife, as if he would agree the sky was green and the grass was blue, if it pleased her.

Beaming, Judith scooped a spoonful of

apple from the center and let it slide onto the plate. Under the watchful eyes of everyone present, she used the tip of her spoon to separate the seeds from the pulp and counted them out loud. "One. Two. Three. Four." She smiled. "It's a girl. Oops. No, look! There's one more. Five. It's a boy!"

Solomon grinned from ear to ear.

Everyone else clapped, especially the children, where the boys outnumbered the girls five to two.

Emma's heart swelled. The spirit of goodness that prevailed, with friends and neighbors and guests gathered together around this table, was the epitome of everything she had hoped and dreamed would be the essence of Hill House. As she slipped her hand into her pocket and caressed her keepsakes, she whispered a prayer to thank Him for the many blessings she had received, along with a prayer that the owner of Hill House would arrive soon so she could convince him to sell the boardinghouse to her.

"I wouldn't start calling the babe Isaac until he's actually here," Mother Garrett teased. "Just in case the seeds are wrong."

Judith blushed. "It's just in fun. I know that. All we really want is a healthy babe."

"With God's grace, I'm sure you and your babe will be fine," the older woman replied. "You've had no problems so far."

Orralynne shook her head. "I don't think it

matters much if you've had problems or not," she quipped. "Lucy Smith had a babe a few months back that was stillborn, and some years back, Elsie Taylor's baby only lived a day or two. I didn't hear they had any problems before their babes were born. In any event, I suppose you'll still need a name for the babe. There's no telling what could happen when the babe is born, especially if you're still here. You must know what happened to the last woman who gave birth at Hill House."

The stunned hush at the table was immediate and heavy; even the children grew silent.

Judith's bottom lip quivered, and her eyes filled with tears. Solomon's face flushed scarlet. When his wife bolted from the table and ran from the room, he followed her, but not before he cast a dark look in Orralynne's direction.

Orralynne looked around the table, as if struggling to understand what she had done wrong. Apparently frustrated by the stony faces glaring back at her, she stormed from the room.

The happy mood was irrevocably broken, destroying the camaraderie that had filled the room throughout the meal.

One by one, everyone left the table until Emma was sitting there alone, left only with the bittersweet memory of a wonderful evening that had ended far too soon and on far too bad a note.

This time, when she thought about escaping, she made a mental note to find those ice skates of hers. She wanted to take them with her when she went to speak with Orralynne. That way, Emma could give the woman a choice: Either Orralynne apologize to Judith, or Orralynne could strap on those skates and start skating north and keep skating—until she decided she would.

10

EMMA WAS A WOMAN on a mission, poised to engage in a battle of wills with Orralynne, and she chose her weapons carefully. One pair of skates, a bit rusty and dull, but serviceable. Two gifts usually given to guests when they left: a wooden cross made of candlewood, whittled by Reverend Glenn, and an embroidered handkerchief, handmade by Aunt Frances. And three very heartfelt prayers for guidance, wisdom, and patience.

Fully armed and equally determined to win, Emma planned her approach carefully. Given Orralynne's flustered state, she suspected the woman had holed herself up in her room, Emma's converted office, rather than the library, where Lester would likely be with Mr. Lewis. She ruled out using the outer door to reach her office to avoid the risk of encountering the panther again. She also dismissed going to her office indirectly via the library for fear

Lester might block her way.

Instead, she slipped into her second-floor bedroom, where Aunt Frances would be sleeping later, and cautiously descended down the familiar staircase that connected her bedroom to her office. Although it was now dark, she carried no candle to light her way and let the dim light coming from the oil lamp on her desk in the room downstairs guide her steps.

She did not want to frighten Orralynne, only to have her run from the office. When she was halfway down the steps, just after the grandfather clock chimed the hour of eight o'clock, she announced her presence. "Orralynne? It's only me, Emma. We need to talk," she said, keeping her voice as gentle and non-threatening as she could.

No response.

When she got to the bottom of the steps and looked about the room, she gasped and dropped the skates she held in one hand and the cross and handkerchief she held in the other. Pale and wan, Orralynne was sitting in front of Emma's desk. With her skirts twisted and bunched at her thighs, she had braced her elbows on the top of the desk and scrunched the bottom of her skirts together to create a bowl of sort to catch the blood still dripping from her nostrils.

Although Emma knew that Orralynne had suffered from serious nosebleeds as a child, she had no idea they continued to plague her or that the nosebleeds would be so severe. Blood was everywhere, on the fabric in Orralynne's hands, the top of her desk and the oil lamp, and even the small, framed sampler Emma had left on her desk.

Both alarmed and horrified, Emma rushed to Orralynne's side and bent her knees to lower herself to get face-to-face with her.

Orralynne's complexion was ashen, and her features were splashed with blood. When her pale blue eyes filled with embarrassment, even mortification, Emma's heart constricted. "Are you all right? How can I help? Do you want me to send for Dr. Jeffers? Or your brother?"

Trembling, Orralynne tightened her blood-stained hands holding her skirts, sighed, and ever so slightly shook her head. "Go away, Emma. I'll . . . I'll be fine. The blood's nearly stopped flowing," she managed in a shaky voice.

"I'm not leaving you alone. Not like this."

A single tear escaped and trickled down Orralynne's cheek. "It's ugly and disgusting and messy," she snapped.

In that angry, bitter response, Emma could almost hear the echo of those very same words shouted by caretakers who had no love or pity to share with the young, sickly orphan girl Orralynne had once been.

"Go away. Just go away. I don't want you

here. Once the blood stops, I'll need to rest awhile before I can clean up everything, but I will. I will," Orralynne insisted.

Once again, Orralynne's words opened the window to her spirit and unwittingly let Emma see the hurt inside and hear the voice of a young girl, scared and alone and forced to handle the consequences of her physical maladies.

Emma tugged the other chair closer to Orralynne and sat down. "Don't worry about cleaning up anything. Are you sure there isn't something I can do? Maybe I should get you some cold cloths for your forehead. That would make you feel better, wouldn't it?"

"No. Go away. And you don't have to be nice to me," Orralynne whispered. "I can manage on my own."

"I'm sure you can, but there's no need to face this all by yourself. Not this time," Emma replied. She massaged the woman's shoulder for a moment with her fingertips. "I'm going to get you those cold cloths. I'll be right back."

Orralynne's eyes widened. "You can't tell Lester. You can't tell anyone!"

"I won't," Emma promised, although surprised that Orralynne would keep something like this from her brother. With little time to waste, she chose the quickest and easiest way to the kitchen, let herself outside into the cold, and prayed the panther was far, far away. Guided by the lights coming from the windows, she raced to the back of the house, where it was pitch-dark. When she passed by the chicken coop, she could not see anything, but all was quiet. Still, she hoped Steven would be able to strengthen the pen Monday morning, as Mr. Atkins had promised.

When she charged into the kitchen, she found Liesel and Ditty sitting together in front of the fire. They were working on their samplers. Ditty looked up and frowned. "What were you doing outside in the dark? Aren't you afraid of the panther?"

Liesel kept on stitching. "Don't be silly. Widow Garrett isn't afraid of anything. Besides, she chased that panther off earlier today all by herself."

"Well, I'm afraid of lots of things, and that panther is on the top of my list at the moment," Ditty countered.

"I just need to gather up a few things," Emma explained as she rubbed warmth back into her arms. "Where are Mother Garrett and Aunt Frances?"

Liesel put down her sampler. "They're in the parlor with the Ammond brothers, trying to work out a new tavern puzzle. Would you like us to do something for you?"

Emma hesitated, but then decided she could get back to Orralynne quicker if she enlisted the two young women to help. "As long as I can trust you not to ask any questions and to keep this to yourselves, I'd be very grateful for a little help."

When both Liesel and Ditty got up, Emma set each of them to separate tasks before tackling one of her own. Ten minutes later, she was headed back out the kitchen door. Loaded down with most of what she needed, she had to walk more slowly this time, which only heightened her worry that the panther might be lurking nearby. When she finally got back to her office, her teeth were chattering and her hands were numb, but she was safely inside again.

Orralynne had moved from the desk to her sleeping cot, where she sat upright with her feet on the floor. She was still wearing her blood-stained gown. The moment Emma looked at her, the woman turned away and stared at the wall. "I told you I could manage alone."

Emma set down her load and rubbed her hands together to get them warm again. "You'll feel better if you can manage to get out of your gown. Did you bring a dressing gown, or would you like to borrow one of mine? We're about the same size."

"No. I don't need to borrow anything. I was just about to change."

"Good. Then while you do that, I'll wash up the desk," Emma suggested. After she handed Orralynne the cold cloths she had brought for her, Emma turned her back to the woman. Working quickly, she wiped down the top of the desk and the oil lamp, as well as some drops of blood on the wood floor that miraculously had missed the carpet.

When she picked up the sampler to wipe it clean, she read the simple message to herself: *God is love*. With the tip of her finger, she traced each of the letters stitched in dark green thread. Ironically, several pinpricks of blood had splashed onto the sampler and dried dark crimson, a poignant reminder of the precious blood spilled by His Son in the ultimate act of pure love. She set the framed sampler back down on her desk without trying the remove the tiny blood stains.

When she finally turned around, Orralynne was sitting on the sleeping cot with her feet flat on the floor. She had wiped her face clean, and she was wearing a dark blue dressing gown that was belted tight at her waist. With her shoulders drooped and her gaze downcast, she looked totally bereft and as limp as a soggy piece of bread. Her gown lay in a crumpled heap on the floor at her feet, but the poor woman looked like she had neither the strength nor the desire to pick it up.

Emma swallowed the lump in her throat. "What do you usually do now? Do you lie down for a spell?"

A long, long breath. "I can't lie flat. Not for a while. Sometimes the bleeding starts up again, and I'd choke. I'll . . . I'll just sit here. There's nothing more for you to do. You can leave now."

Emma glanced at the sleeping cot and the single pillow resting at the head. "I have an idea. I'll be right back." She scooted back up the stairs all the way to the garret, grabbed four extra bed pillows stored there, and stopped on her way back downstairs on the second floor to put pillowcases on them.

When she got back to her office, she propped all of the pillows at the head of the sleeping cot. "Try lying back now. You may have to adjust the pillows a bit, but you should be able to rest better if you lie back against all five pillows. There's enough of an incline that if the bleeding starts up again, you won't start to choke."

To Emma's surprise, Orralynne simply turned, pulled her feet up to the cot, and leaned back against the pillows. Emma did not know if the woman was too exhausted from the loss of blood to argue or if she had finally decided that having someone care for her was somehow now acceptable.

In either case, Emma let the woman rest and busied herself tidying up the room. She wrapped up Orralynne's gown and stored it near the door alongside the other cleaning rags and a pail of bloodied water. She picked up the skates she had dropped and stored one in each of the empty desk drawers, along with the cross and the handkerchief. After she pulled a chair next to the sleeping cot, she dimmed the light and sat down.

Orralynne's eyes were closed. Her breathing was slow and even. She may have actually fallen asleep.

In the quiet of the moment, with only the sound of their breathing in the room, Emma let her mind wander away from the adult woman lying in the sleeping cot. She looked back to the past, searching for memories of the little girl Orralynne had once been.

Since she and Orralynne were nearly the same age, Emma's memories were from a child's perspective; even so, she recognized how painful it must have been to arrive at the town hall, along with other impoverished children and adults, to wait and see who would bid, if anyone, to be paid by the town to care for them for the coming year.

Not everyone who took in the orphaned or the elderly or the poor did so with charitable hearts and good intentions. Even fewer would step forward to care for children as sickly as Orralynne had been, or as deformed as her brother was. Some, however, were kind and good.

Emma closed her eyes. With a little struggle, she recalled at least four, no, five families who had taken in Orralynne and her brother. For several years, they had been separated, then reunited for several more, and finally separated again when Lester had been sent away to apprentice with a tailor in Hampton, Pennsylvania.

To his credit, Lester had brought Orralynne to live with him in the very same cottage they occupied before the fire after his apprenticeship ended and he returned to Candlewood to open his own tailor shop.

Emma bowed her head. While she had grown up knowing nothing but love and tender affection, both Orralynne and her brother had known only loss, as well as rejection, loneliness, and shame. The irony of their situation now, as adults, dependent again on townspeople willing to take them in, was almost too much to fathom. Was it any wonder they were still bitter? Or unkind? Or peevish or ill-natured?

She pressed her hand to her heart. Her spirit wept for the past, filled with hope and determination to be the instrument of His healing love. Quietly, she got up from her chair and retrieved the handkerchief and cross from the desk drawer. She placed them on top of Orralynne's travel bag, turned out the light, and sat down to resume her vigil, just as the grandfather clock struck the hour of ten.

"You're still here."

Orralynne's voice roused Emma just before

she dozed off again. "Yes, I'm still here. How are you feeling?" she asked, disconcerted by having a conversation in the dark.

"What time is it?"

"The last time I remember hearing the grandfather clock, it was four-thirty, so it's—"

Orralynne sat up. "Four-thirty? In the morning?"

Emma yawned. "Thereabouts, yes."

"But you're still here."

"Yes, I'm still here," Emma repeated.

"Why?"

"Because I wanted to make sure you—"

"Never mind." Orralynne sighed. "I know why you're really still here. It's about Judith Massey. You can say what you've come to say, but in truth, I need a drink of water first. My mouth tastes wickedly sour."

Emma stood up. "I'm sorry. I couldn't carry any more than I did. I'll have to go to the kitchen to get you a drink, but it won't take long. Unless you're feeling up to it and would like to go with me. There's plenty in the larder we can snack on, if you're hungry."

Orralynne sighed again. "I'm not going outside. Not with that panther lurking about."

"If you're strong enough, we could use the stairs to my room, but . . . No, we can't. Aunt Frances is asleep by now in my room. She'd be frightened if we woke her up."

"Can't we just go through the library?"

Emma cleared her throat. "Not with your brother in there. We'd wake him up. Anyway, it wouldn't be proper for either one of us to be in his bedroom, especially while he's sleeping."

She heard Orralynne slowly swing her feet to the floor and get to her feet. "Lester wouldn't wake up if a pair of mules pulled a freight boat loaded with squealing pigs past his cot. I'll go first. As long as it's dark in the library, too, you won't see a thing you shouldn't see. Just follow me," she whispered.

So Emma did, praying with every step that Orralynne was right and Lester would not wake up.

11

FOR BOTH EMMA and Orralynne, the moment of truth had finally arrived.

Emma sat on one side of the kitchen table facing the fireplace. Orralynne sat on the other side, still pale but somewhat revived by the warm apple cider and buttered molasses bread they had shared in virtual silence.

Like the first rays of the morning sun, a low fire burning in the fireplace chased away the chill in the kitchen and bathed the room with the gentleness of first light. The hurt and disappointment created by Orralynne's thoughtless words at dinner, however, hung heavy in the shadows, like a curtain of awkwardness.

Emma, however, was unable to remain silent anymore—not if she hoped to restore peace within Hill House. "We need to talk about what happened earlier tonight," she prompted, hoping Orralynne had had time to consider what she had done to Judith.

The woman flinched and lowered her gaze. "I had a nosebleed. I'm sorry for the mess I made, but you shouldn't have cleaned it up. I told you I would do that. If . . . if there's anything stained to ruin, I'll see that it's replaced."

Although Emma had been referring to the earlier incident at dinner with Judith Massey, she was reluctant to correct Orralynne, if only to learn more about the woman's affliction in order to be able to help her. "Nothing was ruined," she offered, dismissing the tiny spots of blood on the sampler she kept on her desk. "How often do you have a nosebleed?"

Orralynne did not lift her gaze. "When I was a child, I would have one five or six times a year. These days, I don't have one very often at all, so you needn't worry that you'll be bothered helping me or cleaning up again. Even if I do have another one while I'm here, which I doubt, I won't cause you any more trouble in that regard. I can take care of myself."

"I'm not concerned about cleaning up. I'm more troubled by the fact that you have the nosebleeds in the first place. When you were little, did you ever see the midwife, Mrs. Sherman? She usually takes care of the women and children in town when they're ill. Or what about Dr. Jeffers?"

Orralynne sighed. When she lifted her gaze, her eyes appeared even darker than usual. "Orphaned children who are wards of the town don't usually merit much attention or concern. Even so, most of the time I knew when to expect a nosebleed, so I just tried to live through it as best I could."

Curious, Emma cocked her head. "How did you know to expect a nosebleed?"

Orralynne looked past Emma's shoulder, as if looking back into the past, and her eyes shimmered with misery. "Usually I got one in the weeks right before I would find out if I would be passed on to another family. More likely than not, I'd be moved, and the nosebleeds would start again, but just for a while."

Just imagining the fear and confusion that must have triggered the nosebleeds, Emma's heart grew heavy. "I'm sorry. That must have been a scary time for you."

Orralynne tilted up her chin. "I was scared because I was young. I was only five when my mother died. But I'm not scared anymore. I've learned to accept my affliction. In point of fact, I did see both Mrs. Sherman and Dr. Jeffers after Lester came back to Candlewood and took me to live with him. She tried to help, but there was little she could do to stop the nosebleeds from starting in the first place. Dr. Jeffers suggested I should take Riley's Bilious Pills."

She snorted. "Those pills made me so sick! I felt like my head was stuck in the middle of a cloud. I couldn't get out of bed most days, and I still had a nosebleed occasionally, so I dumped those pills into the trash pit."

Emma nodded. "We used to sell them at the General Store. I've heard more than one woman say the same thing," she admitted. Encouraged by Orralynne's willingness to talk openly with the usual rancor, she tried to learn more. "Why do you think you had the nosebleed tonight?"

Orralynne's cheeks suffused with pink, and her eyes flashed, as if Emma had struck a match and reignited her old self. "You want to know why? I'll tell you why. Because I don't want to be here. Because I want to be home, where I belong. Because I know no one here at Hill House wants me or my brother here, not even you. Not really. If you did, you would have taken us in the night of the fire instead of letting us be humiliated not once, but three times when we were put out by those other families."

Stung by the truth of the woman's accusation and bewildered by how to reply without antagonizing Orralynne any further, Emma moistened her lips. "Well, I . . . I—"

"Don't deny it. I know it's true, so don't bother to lie or to try to defend yourself," Orralynne demanded. "You're supposed to be a woman who follows the Word. Or do you just follow your own rules at Hill House and attend services every Sunday but leave your faith in the pew when you leave, like most everyone else in this hypocritical town?"

Emma dropped her gaze and drew in a deep breath. She folded her hands on her lap before she looked up at Orralynne again. "You're right. It's true. I did hesitate to bring you and Lester here to Hill House. But in the same vein of truth, you should know that I didn't have any idea your brother's cottage had been damaged by the fire or that you needed a place to live until Zachary Breckenwith told me this morning."

Orralynne's eyes widened. "Even so, I'm sure you had to be persuaded to take us in."

"Not by him and not by the sheriff," Emma countered. "I had to persuade myself."

Orralynne huffed. "Guided by your faith, no doubt."

"Yes," Emma said, keeping her voice low and nonthreatening. "And since you're so insistent on being truthful, perhaps you'll admit that from the moment you both arrived, you've done your best to make it as difficult as possible for me to be happy that I had invited you here."

When Orralynne's blush deepened, Emma shook her head. "It's almost as if you want people to . . . to dislike you or to turn on you."

"Why should I expect anything else?"

"Because you can't let the past dictate the present or control your future, that's why. You had a difficult childhood. No one denies that, and if they do, they're too foolish to consider. But you're not a child any longer. You're an adult. If your stay here today is any indication, you spend so much time being embittered you don't even realize how you hurt people by what you say or what you do."

Orralynne stiffened. "I suppose now we're really getting to the heart of the matter. You didn't really want to help me tonight when I had the nosebleed, any more than you wanted to sit and have something to eat with me now. You just wanted the opportunity to . . . to reprimand me, to make me feel badly for telling Judith Massey the truth."

"That's not true," Emma argued. "I just wanted to talk with you about what you said to her, but I didn't want you to feel badly. I wanted you to understand why what you said upset her, so you wouldn't do it again."

Orralynne shrugged. "I don't see why it's my fault she got so upset. Just because no one else told her the truth doesn't mean I have to go along with them. Every word I said was true. She can have a stillborn babe, like Lucy Smith or her babe could only live a few days, like Elsie Taylor's. Or the woman who died right here at Hill House giving birth to a stillborn babe."

Emma pressed her hands tighter together. "That may be, but don't you think Judith knows all that? As her time gets closer, don't you think that she's frightened and worried by all that could go wrong?"

"I wouldn't know. I've never been married.

I've never had a child, and I never will."

"Perhaps not," Emma whispered. "But you know what it's like to be afraid." She let her words rest for a few moments in the silence that marked Orralynne's only response. "What Judith needs now, more than anything else, is to know that she has people around her, good neighbors and friends, who care about her and who will support her now and after her babe is born. Wouldn't you like to be a good neighbor for her, if not a good friend? Wouldn't you have wanted that for yourself when you were a child? Or even now?"

Without meeting Emma's gaze, Orralynne traced the rim of her empty plate with her fingertip. "I suppose you're going to force me to apologize to her, regardless of what I think."

"Only when you're ready, but I wouldn't wait too long. The longer a hurt brews and festers, the deeper it gets, and the harder it is to forgive," Emma replied and decided she should follow her own advice. "Although you insisted otherwise earlier, I really need to apologize to you. I shouldn't have spoken to you or your brother so harshly after the supper tray ended up on the floor."

She paused to let out a long breath. "It's up to you, Orralynne. If you and your brother prefer dining alone for the remainder of your stay here, then of course you may. But I hope you'll

continue to take your meals with us in the dining room."

Emma rose and started to clear the table.
"Except for the elderly Mr. Kirk, the rest of the
Kirk family left after supper and the Wileys are
leaving after breakfast in a few hours. We'll be
spending the better part of the day today cleaning their rooms. Judith and Solomon will be
staying, of course, and so will the Ammond
brothers. That means the two rooms at the
front of the house will still be occupied, but
you're welcome to come upstairs with your
brother later this afternoon and decide which of
the other four rooms you'd like to have. I'll tell
Mr. Lewis to do the same after you've made
your choice, and you can tell Lester that he can
still keep the library for his own use, as well."

As she set the mugs and plates into the sink,
she pulled the winter curtains aside to look out
the window and saw the first light of day, a
hopeful omen that she and Orralynne might
also be beginning anew. She heard footsteps
overhead and smiled. "Mother Garrett will be
coming downstairs soon to start breakfast, and
I expect Liesel, Ditty, and Aunt Frances won't
be far behind her," she said and turned around.

Emma caught but a glimpse of Orralynne's
dressing gown as the woman slipped from the
kitchen. Sighing, she had no idea whether or
not Orralynne would apologize to Judith or if
her conversation with Orralynne would reach

into the hurts buried deep within the woman's heart.

She did know, however, that she had tried her best. She closed her eyes and placed the matter in His hands with a simple but earnest prayer. "Please shower us with your goodness and your healing grace, Father. Amen," she whispered.

When she opened her eyes, she glanced around the kitchen and yawned. As much as she would like to collapse into a real bed and get a few hours of sleep, she had too much work ahead to give the idea more than a wishful thought. Instead, she washed and dried the dishes, stored them away again, and wiped the table clean so the kitchen would be in proper order when Mother Garrett came downstairs.

Since neither Liesel nor Ditty would be very happy about going outside to collect eggs for breakfast, despite Emma's assurances the panther had been chased off, she donned her cape, grabbed the egg basket, and slipped out the kitchen door.

The moment she turned toward the chicken coop and saw the wire fencing sagging low to the ground, her heart filled with horror. She dropped the basket and ran to the coop, only to have her worst fears confirmed.

The panther had returned after all.

Every chicken was gone, save for one who lay frozen motionless on the ground, its neck apparently broken. The straw and bedding were a mess. And feathers—so many feathers! They were everywhere. Inside the coop. Outside on the ground, like colorful autumn leaves scattered by a savage wind. And trails of blood.

Blinking back tears, she dropped to her knees. "Poor Faith," she whispered. "You must have fought so hard to protect your little flock of friends. Why didn't I hear the hubbub? Why didn't anyone hear it?"

She groaned. The panther must have struck during supper while everyone inside was talking and laughing and celebrating the good news that repairs on the Wiley and Kent homes had been completed. Burdened by guilt for not having had a stronger pen built sooner and by sadness at the loss of her little friends, she shook her head. "You were out here all alone, without a good strong fence to protect you. I'm sorry. I'm so sorry," she whispered.

She got back to her feet and scanned the backyard. Although there were more feathers lying scattered about on the ground, she held tight to a slim spark of hope. Maybe one of the chickens managed to escape. Perhaps more than one, since it was difficult to imagine that the panther had gotten to all of them. If there were any survivors, Faith would be among them, just as she had been among the chickens who had escaped after the accident on Main Street last fall. Faith had found her way safely to Hill House then, and Emma firmly believed Faith could do it again—if she had survived.

Hoping against hope, Emma picked up the basket she had tossed to the ground and hurried back into the house, praying she would find that ornery chicken waiting for her in exactly the same place where she had found it the first time.

12

Emma charged through the kitchen past Mother Garrett, who was slicing bread at the kitchen table. "The panther got to the chickens," she explained and dropped the basket onto the end of the table.

Without losing a step, Emma hurried through the kitchen to the dining room. She opened one of the double doors and stepped out onto the patio and quickly glanced around. The summer furniture, which had been covered with canvas for the winter, hosted only a scattering of dead leaves. Autumn debris also gathered in the corners of the patio at the base of the stone wall surrounding it and in the fireplace, but there was no sign of any of the chickens.

Acting on a hunch, she crossed the patio to get to the gate. She let her gaze travel down the terraced steps to the gazebo sitting at the bottom of the hill and the summer pen near the mulberry trees.

Again, there was no sign of the chickens.

The woods behind the gazebo were mostly barren now, and she could see clear through to the frozen canal in the far distance. The few pines in the woods, including candlewood trees, were still green with life but would offer little shelter for the chickens, especially now that the panther was roaming about.

She pulled her cape tight against the wind and shivered. Without protection, any of the chickens who might have escaped would not last long in this cold, assuming they could continue to hide from the panther. Disappointed and disheartened, she turned away from the gate and gasped.

Faith was just ahead, nesting alongside one of the other chickens, on top of one of the canvas-covered chairs that had been empty only moments ago.

Emma took measured steps to reach the two chickens that looked more than a bit bedraggled, since they had both lost a good number of feathers. She blinked back tears and stooped down. "You poor dears," she whispered and got a few weak squawks in reply.

In a quandary as to how to help them, she looked around the patio. There wasn't enough shelter from the cold here, and there was nothing she could do to prevent that panther from leaping right over the wall to get at them. Until the pen could be rebuilt and the fence strengthened, she could not move them back to the chicken coop behind the house, either.

With no other recourse, she slipped off her cape and laid it on the stone floor. "I guess you'll just have to come inside," she murmured. With the little chicken experience she had acquired over the past few months, she placed first one chicken and then the other on top of her cape.

Fortunately, the chickens were too frozen or too scared to offer much of a protest when she wrapped the cape around them, scooped them up, and carried them back to the house.

Unfortunately, Mother Garrett was waiting just inside the dining room, with her arms folded at her waist, her feet planted firmly on the floor, and a frown on her face.

With her teeth chattering, Emma nodded over her mother-in-law's shoulder. "W-would you p-please sh-shut the door for me? I'll drop one of them if I even try."

Mother Garrett took a step back. "Tell me you're not bringing those chickens inside the house," she quipped as she stepped around Emma to shut the door.

"I can't leave them outside! If they don't freeze to death, the panther will get them for sure."

Mother Garrett sighed but kept her gaze on

the chickens when she returned to block Emma's way. "And just where do you think you're going to put them? You've seen what they do to their coop!"

Emma shifted her load and shivered from head to toe. "I'm not sure."

"Frances should be downstairs soon. We could get her to help. Chicken soup sounds like a good idea for dinner to me, in which case you may as well leave them on the patio."

Emma's eyes widened. "I can't eat Faith! She's . . . she's my friend!"

"Well, you can't keep that friend in the house," Mother Garrett argued. "In case you've forgotten, Reverend Glenn is coming back today with Butter, and that old dog will tear up this house in no time to get to those two chickens."

"The root cellar! I'll fix up a pen down there. It'll only be for a few days, until Steven gets here Monday to redo the pen outside," Emma countered.

When she started for the kitchen, Mother Garrett stepped aside but followed on Emma's heels. "The root cellar? They'll eat half our stores, and what they don't eat they'll ruin with their droppings!"

"I'll fix it so they won't," Emma insisted. When she got to the kitchen, she stood at the door to the root cellar with the chickens squirming to get free. She could not open the door without putting them down, a sure invitation to disaster. She looked over her shoulder at Mother Garrett. "Would you open this door for me? Please?"

Mother Garrett tapped her foot. "I will, even though it's against my better judgment, but only with two conditions."

Emma gritted her teeth and struggled to keep the chickens in her grasp. "Go ahead. Name them."

"First, I get to say, 'I told you so,' as many times as I like when this idea of yours turns into a nightmare."

"Agreed," Emma quipped as first Liesel, then Ditty, descended the back steps into the kitchen.

"Good. Second, I don't want you—"

Suddenly Ditty slipped and knocked into Liesel, who fell into Emma. The chickens broke free and chaos erupted, forcing Mother Garrett to swallow her second condition. Emma dropped her cape and chased after the squawking chickens while Mother Garrett removed her apron, draped it over her head like a scarf, got down on hands and knees, crawled under the kitchen table to get out of harm's way, and crouched there.

Liesel grabbed a broom as Ditty, grinning, opened the door to the root cellar. "Shoo them over here!"

Emma flapped her skirts and chased one

chicken around and around the table while Faith perched on the hand pump at the sink. "Help me, Liesel," she urged. "Don't try to hit the chicken. Just block its way so it heads toward the cellar door."

After the third go-around, the plan worked and Ditty shut the cellar door to keep the chicken from coming back into the kitchen.

Panting, Emma stopped to catch her breath.

"Can I come out now?" Mother Garrett cried.

"Not yet. Faith is still free."

"She's sitting on the pump," Liesel added.

"What do you want to do now, Widow Garrett?" Ditty asked, joining both Emma and Liesel.

"We can't wait until dusk until the chicken falls asleep like we did last fall when she showed up on the patio," Emma admitted and looked toward the table. "Did you say Aunt Frances was coming down soon?"

Mother Garrett groaned. "Apparently not soon enough. Like I've tried to tell you before, I like chickens good and dead so I can cook them. I don't like them alive, and I especially don't like them flapping and squawking in my kitchen! And let me just say, 'I told you so,' before my heart gives out for good."

"I could try swatting it just a little with my broom to scare her," Liesel suggested.

"Then what? We play tag again?" Emma

argued. "I'm not sure I'll last through it a second go-around. Besides, we can't open the door to the cellar because the other chicken might run back into the kitchen."

Ditty shrugged. "I'll go down to the root cellar to make sure the chicken stays there."

"How?" Emma asked, half tempted to put both chickens back outside, panther or not.

Ditty picked up Emma's cape from the floor. "I'll use this to block its way while you and Liesel try to make the other one go downstairs."

Emma sighed. "All right. I suppose that's a good plan."

"No," Mother Garrett protested, "a good plan would be to open the back door and chase both of those critters outside where they belong."

Ignoring her mother-in-law, Emma walked over to the door to the root cellar. "I'll watch the door. Ditty, you go ahead downstairs, but be careful. It's dark down there. Try to find those candles Mother Garrett keeps down there and light them. Liesel, hold off with that broom until I tell you we're ready."

Emma opened the cellar door for Ditty and quickly closed it behind the young woman. "Ready!"

With the broom in her hand like a shotgun, Liesel approached Faith. "Be a nice chicken. A nice, nice chicken," she crooned. "Don't you want to join your friend?"

Faith squawked, ruffled up her feathers, and scooted from the pump to the sink to the kitchen table, knocking all three loaves of bread to the floor in the process. When Liesel chased after the chicken with the broom, it ducked away and scooted under the table.

Emma gasped, ran to the table, and dropped to her knees to look beneath it. Trembling, the chicken was nesting on Mother Garrett's lap, with its head resting on one of the elderly woman's knees.

Emma sat back on her haunches, locked her gaze with her mother-in-law's, and tried not to laugh at the apron sitting askew on her mother-in-law's head. "Don't move. Just hold very still. I'll think of something to get that chicken off of you."

To her surprise, Mother Garrett slowly reached out and gently, very gently, began stroking the chicken's back. "Poor thing. You're shaking all over. You're just as scared as I am, aren't you?" she crooned as she tugged her apron from her head and laid it over the chicken. "Well, you needn't worry. You're not headed for the soup pot. Not just yet, but if you keep flapping around my kitchen and ruining my bread, you're going to get there right quick."

She looked up at Emma and nodded. "Go ahead. See if you can pick her up now. She's not trembling so much anymore."

Emma leaned forward, scooped up the chicken with both hands, and caught Mother Garrett's gaze. "Are you sure you're all right?"

"I'm fine. I come from strong stock, just like that chicken of yours. Now get it downstairs and fix up some sort of pen for the two of them. No, wait. You haven't agreed to my second condition yet."

"I agree. Whatever it is, I agree," Emma insisted as she struggled to get to her feet without tripping over her skirts or dropping the chicken.

Mother Garrett crawled out from under the table. With her face flushed, she pushed the hair back out of her face and rearranged her skirts. "You can't tell one soul, living or dead, that I agreed to keep a pair of chickens in my root cellar. And that goes for you, as well, Liesel."

"We won't tell anyone," Liesel promised as she opened the cellar door for Emma.

"No, we won't," Emma agreed and started down the stairs with Faith in her hands and faith in her heart that this day would get better—because it simply could not get any worse.

13

AT MIDMORNING ON Saturday, when Reverend Austin pulled up at the front gate bringing Reverend Glenn and Butter back home, Emma was certain the day's turnabout was continuing.

With Aunt Frances's help and a little ingenuity, she had eventually set up a temporary pen for the chickens in one corner of the root cellar. All of the Kirks, except for Anson, had left to return to their home. Although he was upstairs helping Liesel and Ditty store away the extra sleeping cots and bedding, he had primarily remained behind to help Steven rebuild the chicken pen on Monday. Emma also suspected he had stayed to be close to Mother Garrett and Aunt Frances, much to their mutual dissatisfaction.

In the meantime, Solomon Massey and the Ammond brothers were in town organizing a group of men to go hunting for the panther.

Mr. Lewis was in the library, where Lester Burke was either sitting for his portrait or busy measuring the artist for his new suit of clothes. Emma assumed Orralynne was still in bed recovering from last night's nosebleed, since she had not appeared for breakfast.

The moment Reverend Austin's buggy came to a complete halt, Emma pulled a heavy shawl around her shoulders and hurried out the front door to help the retired minister into the house. When Reverend Glenn approached the fence with Reverend Austin on one side and Butter on the other, she already had the gate open. "Welcome home, Reverend Glenn. We've missed you," she greeted.

After suffering a stroke that had weakened his left side, Reverend Glenn relied heavily on Butter to help him keep his balance—which was the only reason Mother Garrett tolerated the mangy mongrel. The hat he wore covered the few strands of white hair left on his head but made his overly large ears appear even larger.

He looked up at Hill House before meeting her gaze and smiling. "I've missed all of you, too. It's good to be home."

"Thank you for bringing him back to us, Reverend Austin. Do you have time to come inside for a visit?"

"I wish I did, but I have several more stops to make in town and tomorrow's sermon to write," he said, stepping aside to let Emma take his place at the older man's side. He returned to the buggy, retrieved Reverend Glenn's travel bag, and carried it up to the porch while Emma walked alongside Reverend Glenn and guided him toward the front steps.

When the minister returned, he shook Reverend Glenn's hand. "Thank you, friend. I'll see you both at services tomorrow," he promised, then patted Butter's head before leaving and climbing back into his buggy.

Before he could pull away, Mother Garrett rushed out of the house with Aunt Frances close behind her. To Emma's dismay, the two women were both carrying an umbrella. "Wait just a moment, Reverend Austin," Mother Garrett cried.

The two elderly women stopped for a moment in the yard. They both welcomed Reverend Glenn home, with Aunt Frances explaining that she had come back to Hill House for a few weeks to help out, before Mother Garrett led the twosome out the gate to speak to Reverend Austin. "Frances and I wanted to go into town and thought we might ride back with you."

He climbed down from his seat and glanced at their umbrellas. "Expecting rain, ladies?" he teased.

"No. A panther," Aunt Frances replied as he helped her into the buggy first, then Mother Garrett. "We'll tell you all about it on the way."

The minister waved to Emma. "Don't

worry about them. I'll see that they have a ride home," he promised before driving away.

As Emma helped Reverend Glenn mount the steps, he started to chuckle. "I probably shouldn't ask, but since both of those women had quite a twinkle in their eyes, I was wondering if you could tell me what they were up to now."

She shook her head. "I'm not certain. On one hand, I have a feeling they might be busy matchmaking again. Mother Garrett is still convinced Mr. Atkins at the General Store needs a wife, and now that Aunt Frances is back, I'm afraid there's no stopping her. On the other hand, they might have decided to do some errands just to avoid being stuck at home with Anson Kirk. He's been paying both of them a fair bit of attention while he's been here."

Reverend Glenn paused for a moment at the bottom of the porch steps and took her arm. As he mounted the steps one at a time, Butter shadowed his master's progress. "Since Melinda died, Anson's been just plain lonely, but that won't be for long. He'll be married again by spring," he explained.

"I doubt he'll be able to convince either Mother Garrett or Aunt Frances to marry him. Mother Garrett already told me she thinks he's just a winter suitor," she blurted.

Trying to explain to the retired minister that a winter suitor merely wanted a woman to warm his bed seemed almost blasphemous, and her cheeks burned hot, a particularly odd sensation since the rest of her body was nearly numb with cold.

He paused on the second step before attempting the next. "I don't believe I've ever heard that term before. What exactly is a winter suitor?"

Her blush grew more intense. "It's nothing, really. Just something Mother Garrett and Aunt Frances made up about men who go courting during the winter and how they're very serious about getting married," she managed, mentally tripping over her words to avoid the impropriety of being totally honest and the indecency of a lie. "Did you ever think of remarrying?" she asked to change the direction of their conversation.

"It was a good while after Mrs. Glenn passed away, but by the time I decided to give the matter any serious thought, I had the stroke and that ended that. I couldn't support myself, let alone a wife," he admitted as he mounted the next two steps to reach the porch. "I don't think Anson will have much choice about remarrying, though."

"Why? Was he courting someone before the explosion and the fires?"

"No. But based on what I heard in town, there are several widows who have set their caps for him, including Widow Cates and Widow

Franklin. He may want to stay at Hill House for as long as he can instead of going home, just to avoid those two."

"Maybe you should tell Mother Garrett and Aunt Frances that bit of news," she said. She ushered him across the porch and into the house before turning back to retrieve his travel bag. She set the bag just inside the door and closed it tight against the bitter cold outside. After hanging up her shawl on the coat rack, she helped him remove his outerwear and stored it on the rack, as well.

He looked from one parlor to the other and smiled. "After living at Hill House for the past several years, I'd forgotten what a blessing it is to be rather isolated here. Troubles are few and gossip is little. I don't think I'd been back in town for more than a day when I'd already heard enough gossip to fill a couple of those freight barges on the canal."

"I suppose that's natural after a tragedy," she offered.

He shook his head. "There's been too much hurt and heartbreak already to add more with idle gossip and rumors, and it's far too easy to fall into the trap the gossipmongers set to create more." He paused for a moment, then sighed. "I'd given up thinking I'd even be able to help folks again like I used to do, and I have to admit to a certain amount of guilt about what I'm going to tell you now, but . . . being back in town and working with so many of the congregation these past few days felt awfully good. I'm afraid it's just been a reminder of all I've lost since the stroke," he admitted.

Emma swallowed hard. "I know," she whispered, all too aware of how important it was for her to feel needed, if only to her guests. "Would you like to sit awhile in the parlor? I'd like to tell you about who is staying at Hill House with us now," she suggested, hoping he would not mind when she told him she had let the artist stay in the retired minister's room last night. "I'll leave your bag here for now. Mr. Kirk can carry it to your room for you later. He's upstairs helping Liesel and Ditty store some things away at the moment."

He rubbed his left hand as if trying to warm it. "If you wouldn't be too troubled, I think I'd rather sit in front of the fireplace in the kitchen and talk with you while we share a pot of tea. I don't suppose Mother Garrett has any apple crisp in the larder, does she?"

She grinned. "I saved a piece from last night's supper just for you, and I even have a ham bone for Butter."

He grinned back and patted Butter on the head. "Being home is even better than I thought it would be."

———

". . . so perhaps it isn't quite as isolated from

troubles or gossip as you thought," Emma suggested as she concluded bringing Reverend Glenn up-to-date on the happenings at Hill House.

Like the companionable friends they had become, Emma and Reverend Glenn sat together in front of a good fire in the kitchen, warmed by both friendship and an entire pot of tea. Butter, as always, was asleep on the floor alongside his master's feet.

Although he was already weakened by several good bouts of laughter, the retired minister laughed again. "I'm not sure I can keep all this straight. In the five days I've been gone, you've had a run-in with a panther?"

"Yes, but I fared better than most of the chickens. Solomon Massey and the Ammond brothers are organizing some men to go after the panther, even as we speak."

"In the meantime, both your mother-in-law and Frances are gadding about town with umbrellas to fend off the beast."

She smiled. "Yes, I'm afraid they are."

"And two of the surviving chickens are penned up in the root cellar?"

"Yes, but only until Monday, when Steven is going to build a stronger pen outside. And don't forget: You can't tell anyone else there are chickens in the cellar. Mother Garrett made me promise you wouldn't."

He chuckled. "I won't tell anyone. Did you

say you had an artist in residence here, and that he's staying in my room?"

"Yes, but he's moving upstairs this afternoon."

He sighed, deflating the humorous atmosphere, and massaged his left arm. "And the Burkes are living here. Indefinitely. Mrs. Austin told me you had stopped by to tell me that, but I wondered if they were still here."

"Yes, they are, but . . ."

"But it's very difficult to have them here," he murmured. He gazed at the fire, as if mesmerized by the searing memory of his own encounters with the siblings. After several long moments, he blinked hard before turning to face her. "Orralynne was very, very cruel to my Letty once, you know."

Emma nodded. Letty Glenn had been a model of what a godly minister's wife should be. With no children of their own, both Reverend and Mrs. Glenn had devoted themselves to their congregation, which had made Orralynne's very public, very vocal assault on Letty Glenn during services one Sunday all the crueler.

"I know having her here with her brother will be hard for you. It's been hard for everyone, especially Judith Massey," she said, quickly relating the events surrounding the Burkes since their arrival, including the incident at supper last night involving Judith. She also explained that she had talked with Orralynne about the matter but did not break the woman's confidence to reveal that she had had a severe nosebleed.

"Poor Judith still looked upset at breakfast, and she retired straight to her room afterward," Emma continued. "I can only assume Orralynne hasn't apologized. In all truth, I've been looking forward to having you home so I could get your advice. I'm trying to do what's right, but I'm constantly frustrated because doing what's right for one guest seems to be so wrong for another. Just because Orralynne needs a place to stay at Hill House doesn't mean Judith should be upset by remarks Orralynne makes, whether she said them deliberately or not. Not with so many other worries already, and not with her time so close."

Reverend Glenn reached down to pat Butter's head. "In the end, what's right for one—or in this case, two guests—is always right for everyone concerned," he suggested. "It's the way we all get to that end that marks us as people of faith."

"I agree, or at least I think I do," she replied. "I tried following the Word and turning the other cheek, but I got slapped so hard on both cheeks that I just snapped and lashed out, which only made matters worse, I'm afraid."

She sighed. "Whenever Orralynne and Lester do or say something mean, I lose my footing. I . . . I feel like I've fallen over the edge of a cliff and I'm hanging from a ledge just below, holding tight to a rope of faith that grows thinner and thinner every time I struggle to climb back up to solid ground."

She looked down at her lap and toyed with the hem of her apron. "I've never, ever lived with such discord, especially not here at Hill House, and I can't understand why it's happening now," she admitted. "Can you help me to understand why?"

He leaned back in his chair. "I can tell you that you're not alone, Emma. I've spent the better part of the past week with grieving widows and fatherless children, men and boys suffering horribly from burns or other injuries, and families who've lost some or all of what they owned. All of them are asking the same question. They all want to know why. Why are they suffering such loss when they've tried to follow His Word? Why? Just . . . *why*? That's all."

She moistened her lips. "What did you tell them?" she asked.

"I told them many things, but also that they were asking the wrong question."

Disappointed, even confused by his answer, she cocked her head.

He smiled. "Asking why something bad has happened will only lead to the very struggle of faith you're experiencing. And I know that's true because I've done the same thing. Why did Letty have to die? Why did I have a stroke and lose not just my health but my pulpit, as well? Why must I be so dependent on others, especially you?"

He shrugged and shook his head sadly. "I know we've talked about this before, so you know how hard I struggled to find the answers to my questions. Just recently, in the aftermath of this terrible tragedy, I've come to believe that my answers never came, in part, because I had been asking the wrong question all those years. Instead of worrying about why these troubles had landed on my doorstep, the true question I should have been asking myself as a man of faith is very clear: Not why, but how? How can I be stronger in my faith, not weaker? Instead of wallowing in self-pity or fixing blame or seeking vengeance, how can I take what's happened to me and use it for His glory?"

"Not why, but how?" she repeated as she mulled the concept over and over in her mind.

"Perhaps without even realizing it, you've done just that in the past," he prompted.

"I have?"

"Many times, which helped me with my own struggles."

Her eyes widened with disbelief. "Me? I helped you with them? When?"

"The night Jonas died. I came to see you. Do you remember?"

She nodded, slipped her hand into her pocket, and felt through her keepsakes until she found the piece of cloth cut from the work apron her late husband had worn every day while tending the General Store until his death some eight years ago. "I remember you came to see me, but I'm afraid I don't remember much more than that," she whispered, consumed by the memory of holding her beloved husband in her arms while he drew his last breath on this earth before his heart stopped and his spirit passed through the gates of heaven to eternal life.

"Letty died some years later, but I clearly remember being humbled by the conversation I had with you the night Jonas died."

"I . . . I wasn't myself. I was distraught. I . . . I hope I didn't say anything to offend you," she gushed.

"On the contrary," he argued. "Understandably, you were distraught. Jonas's passing was very sudden and unexpected, but you were . . . you were absolutely yourself. Instead of pleading to know why your gentle, loving husband, the father of your three young boys, had died in the prime of his life, do you know what you asked me to do?"

She held tight to her keepsakes and shook her head.

"You asked me to pray with you, that with the death of your husband, you might be strengthened in faith and open to His will for you during your widowhood so that you might bring honor to your husband's name and glory to God in the difficult days ahead."

She bowed her head.

"Even then, at that most difficult of times, you asked how, not why, Emma. And as hard as it might be, that's what we all should do now. Instead of asking why the Burkes must be here at Hill House or why we must be surrounded by such discord, we should ask how we can accept His will that they're here and how we can be His instruments and serve His purpose."

He stretched out his hand. "Will you pray with me?"

She let go of her keepsakes, took his hand, and bowed her head.

"Father, we come to you with troubled hearts. Ease our troubles with your grace, and give us the strength to be joyous in our faith, to be faithful to your will, and to be gracious and loving to all. Amen."

"Amen," she whispered. "Amen."

14

B Y LATE SATURDAY afternoon, all of the vacant guest rooms at Hill House had been restored to order and thoroughly cleaned. Emma was bone tired. She wanted nothing better than to sit in the west parlor with Reverend Glenn and Aunt Frances, who were spending as much time together now as they had last fall. Unfortunately, Emma would not be able to rest or reclaim her own bedroom, as well as her office, until she had the Burkes and Mr. Lewis settled upstairs in proper bedrooms.

As promised, she gave Orralynne and Lester first choice of the bedrooms and led them down one of the upstairs hallways to the available rooms on the west side of the house. She opened all the doors so they could look inside. "As you can see, there are actually two adjoining rooms on this side that include a small sitting room and a bedroom that is half the size of the one across the hall. There are identical rooms available on the east hall, as well, so if you'd both prefer to have one large bedroom, there's one for each of you."

Orralynne edged ahead of her brother, whose limp was a bit more pronounced today, and poked her head into the large bedroom. She sniffed. "You might prefer this room, Lester. The beige tones in this room are a bit bland for my taste. What color is the large bedroom in the other hall painted?"

"Deep purple, with a touch of lavender. It's decidedly more feminine than this one."

Orralynne pointed down the hall to the room at the front of the house. "What about that one?"

"That's where John and Micah Ammond have been staying. The Masseys are in the front room in the other hall," Emma offered, hoping to dissuade the woman from taking a bedroom in that hall to avoid any further confrontations, since Orralynne had yet to apologize to Judith.

Leaning heavily on his cane, Lester went into the beige room. He immediately sat down on the edge of the double bed and waved his cane at them as if it were a royal scepter and he was sitting on a throne. "This room will do for me, but I'd remind you that I still need full use of the library," he insisted before turning his attention to his sister. "Go on. You may as well take the larger room in the other hall. There's no need to crowd yourself by taking the smaller bedroom across the hall from me and you have no need for a sitting room, even a smaller one."

Emma had one option left to convince Orralynne to remain in the west hall. "The other two rooms across the hall are small, but they do create a suite of sorts and offer a place where you could enjoy your privacy."

Before Orralynne could reply, her brother rejected Emma's suggestion outright. "I hardly think it would be proper to have my sister in this hall. Not with the Ammond brothers so close," he barked. "And what about Mr. Lewis? He'll be moving upstairs this afternoon, as well, and I should think he'd be better suited to this hall and have more need for a sitting room. He does have considerable supplies he needs to store."

Unfortunately, Emma could not find fault with Lester's suggestion. Although she was sorely tempted to take him to task for speaking to her so abruptly, she smiled at Orralynne instead. "Let me show you the purple room."

Lester waved his cane at them one last time. "I'll wait here until my bags are brought up."

Emma retraced her steps, then continued along the back hall. "My room is here at the end. The other three rooms are also for the staff," she explained before turning down the east hallway.

"If I owned Hill House, I'd have a bigger room for myself, not one that looks as small as a storage closet," Orralynne noted with disdain.

"I find my room comfortable. Since it's just above my office and there's a separate staircase, it's more convenient, too," Emma countered. After opening the door to the purple room, she stepped aside to let Orralynne enter first. "Well, what do you think?"

For the first time since she had arrived at Hill House, Orralynne was actually speechless. With her eyes wide with awe and wonder, she walked about the room. Emma had had the same reaction the first time she had walked into the room after refurbishing it. Though the room was too frilly to suit her personal taste, it was still her favorite guest room.

The walls had been repainted the same deep purple color the original owner had selected. Emma had replaced the heavy brocade drapes that had covered the single window with frothy lace panels trimmed with deep ruffles that matched the white coverlet and canopy on the four-poster bed. In addition to two rosewood bureaus and washstand, a chaise lounge upholstered in purple velvet, which held an assortment of pillows in lavender and white, sat in the far corner near a small warming stove.

Orralynne stopped at the window and pulled one of the lace panels aside. She held silent for several long heartbeats before letting the panel drop back into place. When she turned around, her eyes were glistening. "I don't believe this room will do. I'd like to see the other one."

Emma narrowed her gaze. If this room did not please the woman, none of them would. "Don't you like this room?"

Orralynne's back stiffened. "You know very well why I can't stay here in this room and sleep on that bed. Or do I have to remind you how quickly I could destroy it with a single nosebleed?"

Emma cringed. "I'm sorry. I didn't think about that."

"I wish I could say the same, but unfortunately, my ailment doesn't afford me that opportunity."

"No, I suppose it doesn't," Emma admitted. "Even so, you told me you don't have nosebleeds all that often. Since you suffered from one just last night, you shouldn't have another one soon. Maybe you should stay here after all," she said and shrugged her shoulders. "And if worse comes to worse, and you do have another nosebleed, then we'll just wash the bed linens. We do it often enough for other guests if they become ill. Which reminds me . . . I left the cleaning bucket and rags and your soiled gown in my office. I need to launder them before the stain really sets."

Orralynne narrowed her gaze. "You'd let me stay here? In this room?"

"Yes, of course."

"Why?"

Emma held tight to Reverend Glenn's advice and smiled. "Because, since you're apparently going to be here for an extended visit, you may as well be in the prettiest room we have. And because I think you really fancy this room as much as I do."

"I've learned not to fancy much of anything," Orralynne whispered and glanced over at the chaise lounge.

"Then we need to change that," Emma insisted. "You're looking a bit peaked. Why don't you rest awhile on the chaise lounge and think things over while I go back downstairs to get Liesel and Ditty to bring up your bags and your brother's. When I get back, if you change your mind, I'll show you the other room across the hall," she suggested and started to leave before Orralynne could proffer an argument.

"Emma?"

She paused in the doorway and turned around.

Orralynne had not budged a single step. "If you're so willing to let me stay in this room, why did you seem so set on having me take the room across from my brother?"

Emma drew in a long breath. "Since you've shared a home for so many years, I thought perhaps you might want to be closer to your brother."

"That's not the entire reason, is it?"

"No," Emma admitted. "In all truth, I didn't want either you or Judith to be uncomfortable. Living here at the same time will be awkward enough, given what happened at supper last night. If you stay here, you'll be sharing the same hall. I suppose I just thought it might be easier all the way around if you didn't have to worry about encountering each other going to and from your rooms."

Orralynne looked past Emma into the hallway. "I'm still not certain it's all that necessary to apologize. Even if I were, I'm not sure I know how to do that, or if she'll even be willing to hear me out."

"No, you won't—not until you try. I believe Judith is resting in her room while Solomon is in town," Emma murmured and continued on her way.

When she descended the steps to the center hallway, Mr. Lewis was waiting for her at the bottom. "Mr. Burke has chosen his room, but I'm afraid his sister isn't quite certain yet about the guest room she prefers."

"That's fine. I'm in no rush. I was wondering if I could trouble you for a moment of your time to speak to you privately."

She sighed. "If it's about doing any work here for me, I'm afraid I haven't had a moment to think about it."

"No. It's something far more important. It's

about Mr. Burke," he whispered, his dark eyes troubled.

"They're both upstairs, so why don't we use the library?" Emma suggested, since she did not want him anywhere near her office until she had an opportunity to remove Orralynne's soiled gown and the cleaning supplies.

Once they were in the library, where all four of the Burkes' bags were packed and ready to be taken upstairs, she closed the door to assure their privacy. He waited until she had sat down in one of the leather chairs near the fireplace before taking his own seat in a matching chair. "I hope you won't think I'm speaking out of turn, but I'm concerned enough to want to speak out anyway."

Emma braced herself to hear yet more evidence having the Burkes here at Hill House was indeed a heavy cross to bear for all concerned. "If something happened and you've changed your mind about wanting to paint the portraits—"

He waved her silent. "Not at all. As I said, this is about something very important."

She raised one brow. "I'm sorry. Please go ahead."

He pulled on his chin, accenting the narrowness of his face. "As you might expect, since I've spent the past twenty-five years sketching or painting for a living, I've got an eye for detail. I realize I only met Mr. Burke yesterday, but we've spent a considerable number of hours to-gether. I'm not at all privy to the precise nature of the man's deformity, but I'm certain some-thing is very, very wrong."

"From all I've been told over the years, he was born with a deformed foot. I did notice his limp was a bit more pronounced today than yesterday," she offered.

"Quite a bit more. In point of fact, he's barely putting any weight on that foot. When he does, he pales and begins to sweat. When I sug-gested perhaps he'd been injured in the fire at his cottage and that he might want to send for the doctor, he got so angry I was half afraid he might hit me with that cane of his. At the very least, I thought I should tell you about my con-cerns."

"Thank you. I appreciate that you came to me. I suppose it's possible that he's injured his foot," she admitted. "Unfortunately, I don't know him well enough to be able to tell if this is normal, if he has times when his foot is un-usually sore, or if indeed it's something that warrants the doctor's attention."

"Be careful how you proceed," he warned. "I doubt he'll take your concern with any more grace than he took mine."

"Probably not. I think I'll speak to his sister instead. She should know what to do." Emma got to her feet. "I came downstairs to ask Liesel and Ditty to carry the Burkes' bags upstairs for them. Hopefully, by the time we get back upstairs, Miss Burke will have made her choice and I can show you which of the rooms are available for you."

He smiled with relief and rose from his seat. "Thank you. I'll gather up my things and meet you back here."

Within ten minutes, Emma was leading both young women back upstairs. When they reached the second floor, she sent Liesel ahead with one of Mr. Burke's bags and had Ditty, who was carrying one of Orralynne's bags, follow her down the east hall to the purple room.

Emma stepped into the room, then stopped so abruptly when she realized the room was empty that Ditty ran right into her. The bag she was carrying hit the back of Emma's legs and knocked her off balance. She fell hard against one of the bureaus and cracked her hip on the corner.

Wincing with pain, she blinked back tears.

Ditty dropped the bag and ran to her. "I'm sorry, Widow Garrett. Are you all right? I didn't expect you to stop like you did."

Emma clenched her jaw for a moment until the pain subsided. "I'm fine. I'll be fine," she managed. "Don't be upset. It wasn't your fault. I was just so surprised to see Miss Burke wasn't here that I forgot you were right behind me. I thought for certain she would want this room for herself."

Gently, she massaged her hip and took a few tentative steps to make sure the only damage was a bruise she would no doubt wear for a spell.

"Where do you think she went?" Ditty asked.

"If she's not in one of the rooms across the hall, then she's either visiting with her brother, who's in the beige room, or waiting for us in the room directly across the hall from him."

"I'll check the room across the hall first," Ditty insisted but set her bag down before she hurried from the room. A single heartbeat later, she was back. "She's not there."

"I think we should just leave this bag here for now. There's no sense carrying it all the way to the other hall until we know for sure where she's going to stay. Why don't you go downstairs and help Liesel with the other two bags? I'll go and find Miss Burke," Emma suggested.

After Ditty went downstairs, Emma continued walking about the purple room. Once she could take a step without pain, she went out into the hallway. Intrigued by a spot glistening on the floorboards only a few feet away, she went to investigate, only to discover not one but a series of spots leading straight down the hall toward the Masseys' bedroom, where Judith was resting.

The door was slightly ajar.

With her heart pounding, Emma bent

down, touched one of the spots, and looked at the red stain on her fingertip with horror. "Blood . . . it's blood," she whispered.

With the debacle at dinner the other night when Orralynne raised concerns about the health of Judith's unborn babe, Orralynne's severe nosebleed, and Mr. Lewis's concerns about Lester's foot still fresh in her mind, Emma followed the trail of bloodstains down the hall, wondering if they would stop at Judith's room or continue on.

15

B LESSEDLY, EMMA'S CONCERN for Judith Massey and her unborn babe was short-lived and quickly proven unfounded.

When she was halfway down the hallway, Emma heard soft humming coming from Judith's room and smiled with relief.

Unexpectedly, the young mother-to-be opened the bedroom door, slipped out into the hallway, and shut the door behind her. When she turned about, she looked well-rested and happy, with her dark eyes sparkling and a quick smile on her lips the moment she saw Emma.

"You're up from your nap," Emma noted, returning Judith's smile with one of her own as they approached each other and paused to chat.

Judith laid one hand on the side of her extended abdomen and giggled. "Once this little one starts doing somersaults, I don't have much choice in the matter. Now that Aunt Frances is here to help Mother Garrett, and most of the other guests have gone back to their own homes, there's not much for me to do in the kitchen. I thought maybe I could visit with Reverend Glenn for a spell while I'm waiting for Solomon to come back," she said, her smile drooping into a worried frown.

"I wouldn't worry about your husband overmuch," Emma urged. "I'm sure he'll be back by supper, long before it gets dark. None of the men will be doing much more than organizing the search for the panther today, and since tomorrow is Sunday, they won't really start until Monday."

Judith brightened. "By then the panther could be long gone."

"Perhaps," Emma admitted. Anxious to ease the young woman's concern for her husband's well-being, she was just as anxious about sharing the news of Orralynne's move upstairs into a room very close to the young couple. "I was just going to speak to Miss Burke about room arrangements for herself. Her brother is going to be staying in the other hall. She'll either be staying in one of the rooms across from his, to be closer to her brother, or she might choose to stay in the purple room in this hall. I'm not certain yet."

Judith's eyes grew darker, and she glanced over Emma's shoulder toward the violet room. "I . . . I expected they'd be moving upstairs this afternoon. I was hoping they might both choose the other hall." She dropped her gaze. "That's selfish of me, I know."

"On the contrary," Emma insisted. "I understand your concerns, given how she upset you and your husband at dinner. I've spoken to her about that, and I don't believe she realized what she was doing at the time. I don't think she'll do anything like that again," she said reassuringly.

When Judith looked up, her eyes were glistening. "I hope not, but that's why I thought I might visit with Reverend Glenn. He always knows how to set a person's mind and heart at ease."

Emma nodded and smiled. "That he does. He's in the west parlor with Aunt Frances," she offered. When Judith started on her way, Emma continued down the hallway toward Lester Burke's room, where the trail of blood spots ended.

Before knocking, she quickly checked the room across the hall. Empty. She approached the door to Lester's room and stopped. Troubled by what she might discover once she talked with both Lester and Orralynne Burke, she took a deep breath.

Before she had a chance to knock, however, the door swung open. Orralynne locked her gaze with Emma's and proceeded to walk out of the room, forcing Emma to quickly step out of the way.

With a single yank, Orralynne shut the door behind her and cast Emma a hard glance. "Whatever you want with my brother will have to wait, although I daresay it's improper of you to visit a man in his private room, even if you are the owner of the boardinghouse."

"I wasn't here to visit him," Emma argued and stiffened her back. "I came here—"

"Regardless of why you need to speak to my brother, you'll simply have to wait. He's . . . he's feeling a bit indisposed at the moment."

"I know," Emma whispered, relieved that Orralynne appeared to be fine yet concerned about her brother. When Orralynne's eyes widened, Emma pointed to a smudge of blood on the floorboards. "I followed smudges of blood from the other hallway to here. I was worried. I thought perhaps you had—"

"Another nosebleed? No. I'm perfectly fine."

"Then I can only assume that the blood belongs to your brother and that he had come to the other hallway looking for you," she ventured, uncertain if the blood in the hallway was the result of Lester having a nosebleed, like his sister, or perhaps from his deformed foot.

Glancing down at the floorboards where there was a telltale smudge of blood, Orralynne shook her head. "That looks more like dirt to me. I can't believe you could confuse dirt or mud with blood."

"It's blood, Orralynne," Emma said gently. "Should I send for Dr. Jeffers?" she asked, anxious to secure whatever help Lester might need.

Orralynne paled and drew in a long breath. "No. No doctor. Please, I . . . I just need to get a few things from my brother's other bag for him. Liesel went to fetch it, but of course she's taking her good sweet time about it, so I thought I'd get it myself."

Before Emma could respond, Liesel and Ditty appeared at the end of the hallway, carrying a large travel bag between them. Liesel nodded toward Orralynne. "I . . . I'm sorry I took so long. I couldn't manage this bag by myself, so I waited for Ditty to come downstairs to help me," she managed as the two women huffed their way down the hallway.

"You should have asked Mr. Kirk or Mr. Lewis to carry this for you," Emma countered as she helped the two young women set the bag down on the floor in front of Lester's bedroom door.

Ditty's eyes sparkled with amusement. "They're both down in the root cellar handling a . . . a bit of a problem. Or two," she added.

Imagining all sorts of trouble those two chickens might have gotten into, Emma rolled her eyes but held back a groan. "Why don't the two of you see if you can help the others?"

Liesel cocked her head. "What about Miss Burke's other bag? It's still downstairs where you left it in the library."

"I'll bring the bag up," Emma offered and waited until the young women had left before turning her attention back to Orralynne and the trouble facing her on the second floor. "Would you like me to help you get this bag inside your brother's room?"

Orralynne stiffened. "No. I'll manage."

Still curious about the precise nature and extent of Lester's indisposition, Emma kept Mr. Lewis's concerns about Lester's limp in mind and pressed for more information. "I can have Liesel or Ditty bring up some fresh water if that would help your brother, or have some water heated up, perhaps?"

Orralynne looked at the door to her brother's room and then down at the floor again before looking back at Emma. "Some hot water would be best. My brother often needs . . . He uses warm compresses every day to ease the trouble with his foot."

Emma swallowed hard. Orralynne's explanation presented the very real possibility that the blood on the floor had seeped through Lester's boot, opening up the troubling possibility of an infection, which would pose a very real threat to the man's well-being.

Orralynne sniffed, as if reading Emma's mind. "It's nothing that can't be treated," she insisted, "although I daresay it could have been avoided. Unfortunately, because we've been forced to move four times in almost as many days, my brother hasn't had either the opportunity or the time to tend to his physical needs the way he should."

Although Emma still remained skeptical, she had little desire to antagonize Orralynne or question her judgment about her brother's condition or his needs. "Then I'm glad he finally has a room of his own, for as long as he likes," Emma murmured. "I'll bring some hot water up as soon as it's heated. Would you like me to put your bags across the hall so you can be close-by to help your brother?"

Orralynne tilted up her chin. "My brother prefers to tend to his own needs. As you recommended, I'll be staying in the purple room, but I'll wait here with him to make sure he has everything he needs before I leave. It might be best if we each had supper in our own rooms tonight, as well."

Emma nodded and hurried downstairs to set some water on the stove before carrying Orralynne's other bag upstairs. She quite forgot all about the trouble in the root cellar until she got to the kitchen.

Mother Garrett looked up from her place at the kitchen table, where she was frosting a cake, and greeted her with a smile. "I get to say 'I told you so,' but that's all I'm going to say. For now."

Emma let out a sigh, filled a pot with water, and set it on the stove alongside a pot of simmering chicken soup. "Mr. Burke needs some hot water," she explained. "Can I assume that's not one of my chickens in the soup pot?"

"Not this time."

Emma looked around the kitchen and furrowed her brow. "Where's Aunt Frances?"

"Downstairs in the root cellar helping Anson and that artist fellow with the chickens."

Emma shook her head. "Do I want to know what happened down there?"

Before she could answer, Liesel appeared in the doorway leading to the dining room. "I've got Miss Burke's bag. Should I take it upstairs?"

"I thought you were going to help Ditty and the others in the root cellar."

"There wasn't much room for me, not with everyone else there."

"Oh, then I suppose you can take Miss Burke's bag up for me. Put it in the purple room, will you? When Mr. Lewis is finished in the root cellar, you can show him the room across from Mr. Burke." She turned her attention back to Mother Garrett, who seemed overly preoccupied with frosting that cake. "Do I want to know what happened in the root cellar?" Emma prompted.

"That depends."

Emma shut her eyes for a moment and prayed for patience, as well as the grace to accept another lesson in humility now that Mother Garrett had apparently been proven right. Again. "That depends on what?"

"On whether or not you want a full accounting now or if you're willing to simply wait for the bill."

"What bill?" Emma asked as she gathered up some cloths and a pail with fresh water so she could wipe up the blood spots in the upstairs hallway before anyone else noticed.

"The bill from the General Store you're gonna have when I go down to see that nice Mr. Atkins and have him replace all the stores you lost to those critters."

"All the stores? All of them?"

Mother Garrett licked a bit of frosting from her finger. "No, not all. Just most of them. What those chickens didn't peck away, they ruined with their droppings," her mother-in-law quipped. "Fortunately, I had the good sense to have Ditty bring up some stores to fill the larder the other day, or we'd be having one skimpy soup for supper tonight and not much to eat tomorrow."

She paused and smiled. "I'm sure Mr. Atkins can get what's ruined hauled away for you. Some farmer's pigs will be mighty well fed. In the meantime, you might as well tell those poor folks in the root cellar not to bother trying to fix up another pen that won't hold. Supper will be ready soon, and they need time to clean themselves up."

Distracted by the sound of the bell at the

front door, Emma glanced at her mother-in-law. "Now, who could that be? Surely Solomon and the Ammond brothers wouldn't bother ringing the bell."

Mother Garrett cocked her head, then smiled. "I believe that might be our supper guest, but don't bother yourself. Judith will probably answer the bell. She's in the parlor with Reverend Glenn."

"Supper guest?" Emma shook her head. "I didn't invite anyone to supper."

"Oh, I did."

"You did?"

"I did, but I guess I just forgot about it until now, what with all the commotion of people moving out and that business in the root cellar. I'd better get Liesel to set another place at the table as soon as she gets back downstairs."

Emma hauled the pail of water to the doorway, set it down, and checked the water on the stove, which had yet to warm sufficiently. "When did you invite someone to supper?"

"When Frances and I were in town this morning."

Emma sighed. Between cleaning all day and getting the Burkes settled into their new rooms, she had not had a moment to herself to even think about freshening up for supper, let alone entertaining yet another guest. "I hope you didn't invite Mr. Atkins," she countered. "I'm sure he was pestered enough this morning when you and Aunt Frances went into town."

Mother Garrett stopped frosting the cake and held her frosting knife in midair. "Pestered? Did you say we pestered the man?"

"About getting married," Emma replied as she heard the front door open. "In between errands and spreading news about the panther, I imagine the two of you made some time to stop at the General Store. You were matchmaking again, weren't you?"

"Perhaps," Mother Garrett admitted as she spread another bit of frosting on the cake. "But we're not ready yet to make a match for him. Frances and I still can't agree on which young lady might suit him best. We're still working on that. So no, it's not Mr. Atkins we've got in mind. Not today."

Emma picked up the pail of water and grabbed the cleaning cloths with her other hand. "Then who's coming to supper? Who's the poor soul you're matchmaking for this time?"

"I never said—"

"Who?"

"Mr. Breckenwith."

Emma nearly dropped the pail of water. "M-my lawyer? Your . . . your matchmaking involves my . . . my lawyer? You actually went to his home and invited him to supper?"

Mother Garrett looked up, locked her gaze with Emma's, and grinned. "Frances and I didn't go to his home. We met him at the General Store, where he was ordering some supplies. He mentioned seeing you in town yesterday and said he'd probably be meeting with you soon. I merely told him that I was sure you'd want me to invite him to supper so you could meet with him afterward."

"I never said any such thing!"

"You never mentioned he wanted to meet with you when you said you'd seen him in town, either," Mother Garrett countered, "but I'll set that matter aside for now. That poor man has taken in so many folks, he's scarcely got any room for himself in that house of his, and word in town has it that the housekeeper he hired can't keep her thoughts to herself for more than a minute. He deserves a good meal he can eat in peace for a change. Besides, that man is taking so long to get serious about courting you, Frances and I decided he needed a good old-fashioned nudge in the right direction. We figured if we started now, the man would be ready to court you seriously by spring. And a spring suitor is the finest of them all, if you'll recall what I told you just the other day."

"You . . . you can't be serious. You—"

"Don't bother arguing with me or sputtering some nonsense about you not being interested in the man, either," Mother Garrett argued with a wave of her frosting knife. "I'm old but I'm not blind, and neither is Frances.

We watched that man and the way he looked at you for months, starting when Frances came to stay with us last fall. And we saw you looking back at him the same way. Then right after Frances left to spend the winter with her sons, he had to go to his aunt, bless her soul, and then handle her affairs after she passed. And you started moping about and daydreaming. I think you're lovesick, Emma. Just plain lovesick. You've just forgotten what that feels like."

Mother Garrett shook her head. "And it's getting worse, even with the fire and all the upset here at home. Seems to us you two need-ed someone to step in with a bit of match-making to help things along. Now, if we're wrong," she added, "just say so."

Emma blinked hard, unable to decide whether to laugh or to cry. Though she was ad-mittedly frustrated by her own growing interest in Zachary Breckenwith as a suitor, Mother Garrett was wrong. Emma had not been mop-ing about or daydreaming because she was lovesick. She had simply been scared that every-thing she had worked so hard to achieve here at Hill House had been for naught, and there was nothing she could do except wait for the owner of Hill House to arrive and resolve her situation, one way or the other.

Keeping the matter secret from Mother Garrett and everyone else who called Hill House their home had worried her, and now it had come back to haunt her in a way she could have scarcely imagined. Out of the corner of her eye, she saw the pot of water on the stove had begun to boil, an odd reminder of the state of her own affairs.

"You know me very well," she began, "but—"

"I should," Mother Garrett murmured as she set her frosting knife down and wiped her hands on her apron. "We've lived together for thirty years or so." She sighed. "We used to sit and talk all the time, just the two of us, but these days there never seems to be any time to do that, and I'm not just talking about the past week or so since the fire."

Emma swallowed hard. "I know. I'm sorry. It's just that . . . Maybe . . . maybe we could sit down together later tonight. Just the two of us," she offered, certain that keeping this secret from her mother-in-law had been a mistake.

"I'd like that," Mother Garrett whispered with a smile. "Now go on. Go back upstairs, clean up whatever it is that needs it. I'll send Liesel up with Mr. Burke's water. You just fix yourself up real pretty. But don't take too much time. It's not polite to keep a gentleman caller waiting too long."

Emma nodded and marched herself upstairs to the east hallway. When she got down on her hands and knees and started wiping up blood from the floor, the water turned red, not brown, proving her assumptions correct.

Oddly, however, while she worked her way down the hallway, her mind shuttered out all worries about the bothersome Burkes, the rebellious chickens, the rogue panther, two meddlesome but lovable elderly women, and the elusive owner of Hill House. Instead, her mind's eye searched through her limited wardrobe so she could decide what to wear to supper with Zachary Breckenwith.

Fancy that.

16

TIME. SO LITTLE TIME!
   To save time, the moment Emma finished wiping down the upstairs hallway, she stored the pail of dirty water and cleaning cloths in a corner of her bedroom instead of taking them all the way downstairs. She quickly changed into her favorite woolen gown. With a delicate lace collar, long sleeves, and slim skirts, the deep green wool and simple lines of the gown complemented her pale coloring and slender figure.

She did take the time to rebraid her hair, coil it at the nape of her neck, and hold it in place with a tortoiseshell comb that had belonged to her mother.

Before going downstairs to join the others for supper, she ventured one final glance in the mirror. Her hair and gown looked fine. Her dark blue eyes were clear but perhaps a bit too bright. Whether the flush on her cheeks was from embarrassment at facing Zachary Breckenwith, who assumed she had invited him to supper, or from anticipation at seeing him again was a question she could not answer.

Without the luxury of time to ponder the matter, she took a fringed shawl from the trunk at the foot of her bed and draped it around her shoulders when a sudden thought quieted her racing heartbeat.

Other than Emma, Mother Garrett and Aunt Frances were the only ones who knew that Zachary Breckenwith had been invited to supper as part of the older women's matchmaking scheme.

For his part, hopefully, Zachary Breckenwith should not suspect a thing. Coming to Hill House to meet with Emma to discuss legal or financial matters was nothing out of the ordinary. He had also mentioned wanting to meet with her soon, although he had specifically said he wanted them to meet to discuss more personal issues—a point of fact Emma had not mentioned to her mother-in-law for obvious reasons.

Given the fact that he had moved into his office to accommodate the many townspeople who were living temporarily in his home, meeting with her here, instead of at his office, did make perfect sense, and since he had told Mother Garrett he wanted to meet with Emma, she could only assume, and hope, he actually had business to discuss with her.

For her part, Emma could take this opportunity to ask his advice about properties she might want to investigate in the meantime, which she had already promised to do, should she be forced to find somewhere else to live.

She took a deep breath and smiled as she opened her bedroom door. For now, despite Mother Garrett's and Aunt Frances's intentions, Emma would simply act as if having Zachary Breckenwith here as her lawyer was nothing out of the ordinary. After supper, to reinforce that very notion, she would ask him to meet privately with her in her office, rather than adjourn to one of the front parlors with the others.

Problem solved.

She was ready to shut her bedroom door behind her when she remembered that she had yet to remove Orralynne's soiled gown and cleaning supplies from her office. Retracing her steps, she returned to her room. She used the private staircase that led from her bedroom to her office to retrieve what she had forgotten to remove and carried it all back to her room, where she stored it in the corner next to the pail of water and cloths she had used to wipe up the hallway.

To add credence to her plan, she gathered up her guest register and the sample book Mr. Lewis had given to her and took them back down to her office, where she laid them on top of her desk. Satisfied with her efforts, she paused for a moment to catch her breath before making her way from her office, through the library, and out into the center hallway. She peeked into the dining room and saw Liesel setting plates of molasses cookies on either side of the frosted cake already sitting on the sideboard.

The young woman hurried toward her, wiping her hands on her apron. "I'm so glad you're downstairs," she gushed. "Mother Garrett said she couldn't hold supper much longer. It's getting late. She wanted me to check on you once I set out the cookies."

"You can tell Mother Garrett that I'm downstairs now, and I'll announce supper and bring everyone to the dining room. What about the Burkes? Have their supper trays been taken upstairs?"

"Not yet. I'm going to do that next."

"You shouldn't have any trouble this time," Emma offered, fairly certain Orralynne would not create a disturbance.

Liesel nodded, then looked at Emma with a good bit of a twinkle in her eye. "You look right pretty tonight, Widow Garrett," she whispered before grinning and scampering back to the kitchen.

Emma shook her head and dismissed the notion that Liesel believed her employer had taken extra pains with her appearance tonight because of Zachary Breckenwith as ludicrous. Purely ludicrous.

Unless Mother Garrett's and Aunt Frances's matchmaking plot had been discovered by Liesel and probably Ditty, as well.

The moment Emma entered the parlor, all conversation stopped. Reverend Glenn and Aunt Frances each greeted her with a smile. Zachary Breckenwith, however, stood up to greet her, and her heart started to race. He was wearing a dark gray frock coat and looked particularly dashing tonight. Although she might consider his smile to be just a dimple past professional, his gaze and his demeanor were very lawyerly.

"I've brought some papers along we need to review, perhaps after supper," he suggested.

"As a matter of fact, supper is ready now," she announced in response, not quite certain if she was more disappointed or relieved that he had interpreted her alleged invitation to supper as nothing more than an invitation based on their professional relationship.

———

Fortunately, there seemed to be little interest in discussing the topics of matchmaking or courtship during supper, although Emma noted that Anson Kirk had eyes only for Mother Garrett, and Reverend Glenn was being particularly attentive to Aunt Frances. Everyone was too interested in listening to Zachary Breckenwith as he recounted the most recent news from town about the efforts to restore Candlewood back to rights while they dined on Mother Garrett's chicken vegetable soup and pumpernickel bread still warm from the oven.

While Liesel and Ditty cleared away the dessert dishes, Solomon shared his news about the plans to locate and eliminate the panther and the danger the animal presented to the townspeople. "Mayor Calloway divided the town and the outlying areas both east and west of the canal for a good five miles or so into sectors and assigned one to each group of volunteers," he announced.

John Ammond, the elder of the two brothers, nodded. "We'll all be meeting Monday down at Gray's Tavern at dawn. The groups assigned to the outlying areas will be setting traps."

"We can't do that in town, of course, so we'll just take turns in pairs patrolling the streets, just to make sure everyone is safe until we catch that animal," his brother Micah noted.

When Judith's gaze grew worried, Solomon smiled at his wife. "Don't worry. We'll catch it."

"Patrolling about town while the panther is free could be dangerous."

"Not as dangerous as ignoring the problem," John offered.

"We didn't see hide nor tail of the panther

when we went to town, so we never did have to use our umbrellas to chase it off. If you ask me, it's long gone," Aunt Frances suggested.

"Besides, Monday I'll be right here helping Mr. Kirk and Steven to build a new pen for the chickens, remember?" Solomon reminded his wife.

"And by Tuesday, we'll probably have caught the panther," Mother Garrett offered, "and everything will be back to normal."

"That's true enough, especially with the bounty being offered," Mr. Breckenwith said.

"There's a bounty?" Emma asked.

"Actually, there are two," Solomon explained. "The mayor posted a five-dollar bounty to the man or men who kill the panther. Gray offered ten."

"Why did Mr. Gray offer one?" Judith asked.

Zachary cleared his throat. "Apparently Gray thinks chaining the animal up in the yard in front of the tavern for a spell would be good for business, so he's offered a ten-dollar bounty to anyone who can catch the panther alive and deliver it to him."

Reverend Glenn let out a sigh. "There's no excuse for mistreating an animal. Any animal. Even a dangerous, wild one."

"Let's hope common sense eventually prevails," Zachary suggested. "I tried to convince Gray that having men risk being mauled to death to capture the animal alive or chaining it up for other folks to view is an invitation to disaster we can ill afford at any time. Unfortunately, he turned a deaf ear. He may yet change his mind, even if that only happens later, assuming the animal is actually delivered to him."

"If anyone can convince him to act reasonably and responsibly, I'm sure you can, Mr. Breckenwith," Mother Garrett offered with a smile.

"And with that in mind," Emma suggested as she rose from her seat, "I hope you will all excuse us. Apparently I need to meet with my lawyer in my office to discuss some pressing matters. Shall we take a look at the papers you brought with you, Mr. Breckenwith?"

He nodded, rose from his seat, and walked around the table to escort her from the room. When he took her arm and smiled at her, any and all thoughts of discussing her legal affairs with him scattered like snowflakes caught in a whirlwind.

The moment they reached her office, he took several papers from his coat pocket and handed them to her. "I've taken the liberty of writing down the names of several men I think would suit your needs."

She cocked a brow, tightened her hold on the papers, and took her seat behind the desk, urging him to sit down in one of the two chairs facing her. "I'm afraid I don't recall asking for such a list," she ventured and set the papers down on top of the desk. "The last time we talked about my situation, you mentioned that I should be looking for another property, in the event that I'm not able to keep Hill House. I was even hoping we might discuss the matter tonight. May I assume these are the names of men, perhaps, who have property for sale that you think might interest me?"

He drew in a long breath and locked his gaze with hers. "No, they're not. The men on that list are all lawyers, and they're all right here in Candlewood."

She furrowed her brow. "Lawyers? But why would I need—"

"Because in all honesty, Widow Garrett, I don't believe I can or should continue to be your lawyer."

17

ZACHARY BRECKENWITH looked straight into Emma's eyes and restated his words, as if repeating them might evoke some response from her. "Although it's no longer feasible for me to be your lawyer, I'm quite certain you'll find adequate counsel with any of the five men I've included on the list you're holding in your hands."

Dumbfounded, Emma stared back at him for several long moments. She could feel the heat slowly rising up her neck to her cheeks. Her heartbeat skipped straight to triple time, and she could feel her pulse in the tips of her fingers. Given their long-standing professional relationship, she was shocked by his statement, but she was also incredibly embarrassed that she had thought he might have been interested in having a more personal relationship with her, since he seemed to be dismissing her outright. Apparently she, as well as Mother Garrett, had misconstrued his intentions toward her, and she was grateful he had no idea that either of them had been so very wrong.

She drew in a long breath and prayed she might somehow retain a modicum of dignity during the next few very awkward moments. Drawing on her years of experience as a businesswoman, she set aside her embarrassment and disappointment to focus on the impact his decision would have on her legal affairs instead of her personal life.

After clearing the lump in her throat, she glanced down at the list before folding it in half again. Her fingers trembled as she laid the paper on top of the desk, but her voice was steady when she spoke. "Given my long professional relationship with your uncle before his passing and the five years you've been handling my legal and financial affairs, I must admit that I find your decision to no longer represent me a surprise. To do so now, when my legal affairs are in such disarray, is more than problematic. To my mind, it's unconscionable and unprofessional," she noted calmly. "And yet, in the past, you've never proven to be a man driven by self-interest or questionable ethics."

When he attempted to speak, she silenced him with a shake of her head. "No, please. I . . . I have no intention of arguing the point with you. If you no longer wish to work on my behalf, even now, when I am relying on your professional help more than ever, then so be it. But I do believe I'm entitled to some sort of explanation—one that makes sense to me, one that does justice to the man of principle and solid character I've come to know you to be. Now that your aunt has passed on, are you . . . are you moving back to New York City permanently to practice law there, perhaps?" she prompted, asking the most obvious of the questions creating a logjam in her mind.

He let out a long sigh. "I'll be making a number of trips to New York City in the coming months, but no," he replied. "I'm not planning to move back there permanently, at least not at this juncture. It's just that I'm—"

"You're angry with me for not actively seeking out other business opportunities, just in case I'm unable to purchase Hill House again. Angry enough to simply sever our professional relationship?"

He cocked a brow as he sat back in his seat. "To be angry with you would imply that I expected you to follow my advice," he noted gently. "It seems to me that anger would be both inappropriate and unwarranted. I'm neither surprised nor concerned that you haven't begun to look at alternative opportunities. During the five years I've represented you, I've come to know you well enough to expect that you'd ignore my advice as often as you'd follow it."

She grimaced, although his assessment of

her was fair and accurate, then stared at the list for a moment. "I suppose you haven't failed to mention that I'm a difficult client to the men you've recruited to consider representing me, either."

He stiffened. "Recruited? Hardly," he argued. "I would never, ever approach another lawyer to ask him to consider representing one of my clients without speaking to that client first."

"Which you're doing now," she murmured. "I'm sorry. I didn't mean to imply you had been unethical or unprofessional."

He grinned. "You didn't imply that at all. By your own words, you said so and also assumed I had already spoken to those men," he noted with just a bit of a twinkle in his eyes.

"And you have the annoying habit of playing lawyer and engaging in verbal warfare whenever we launch into a . . . a discussion," she countered. Yet in spite of herself she smiled as memories of their professional association flashed through her mind's eye.

"Perhaps a better way to say it," he suggested, "is that I often argue . . . semantics."

Her eyes widened. "That's not how I remember our very first discussion, which concerned how to settle the account books at the General Store."

He laughed out loud. "You're right. That was definitely verbal warfare. Semantically speaking, there's not much room to argue the differences between forgiving a debt and collecting one or deciding which debtors deserved one or the other action. You were rather adamant about forgiving most of them and quite convincing . . . in the end," he said, his gaze softening. "I must admit I'd never represented anyone in business in New York City as forgiving as you are—then or now."

She smiled. The memory of her victory that day was still sweet. "If I'm not mistaken, that was our first meeting together after you took over your uncle's practice when he fell too ill to continue."

"Even with his favorite client, which you were."

"Indeed?"

He nodded. "His affection for you was something I kept in the forefront of my mind even after he passed on, especially on those occasions when you dug in your heels and absolutely refused to listen to reason, if not my professional advice."

"You're no doubt referring to when I sold the General Store and bought Hill House," she whispered and swallowed hard.

"In point of fact, I was actually thinking about the time you decided to sell one of your very valuable parcels of land some miles from town to a rather unpopular young couple . . . Sampson . . . Simpson . . ."

"Simmons. Matthew and Lily Simmons," she offered, nearly grinning when she thought about her victory that day. "Despite the fact that I expected you to do as I instructed without question in the matter, which you rarely ever did anyway, once you were able to convince me that you considered lawyer–client privilege to be inviolable, I seem to recall I shared my reasons with you for wanting to help the Simmonses."

"Adding generosity to the list of your qualities and a good dose of humility to mine," he concluded.

Emma realized that their reminiscing had taken them far afield from his stated purpose for their meeting today. She folded her hands on her lap and locked her gaze with his. "Before we go further astray, perhaps we should set aside the colorful aspects of our professional relationship in the past to concentrate, more appropriately, on the present. Can you at least tell me exactly why you're no longer willing to be my lawyer? With the issues surrounding Hill House still unresolved, I think you'll agree I deserve to know why."

He sat up a bit straighter but held her gaze. "To be frank, it's a matter of being pragmatic. On the one hand, as I suggested earlier, I have professional obligations in New York City that will require me to travel back and forth between Candlewood and the city from now to the end of April.

"Unfortunately," he added as his gaze softened, "these are obligations I cannot avoid, which means I could be away and unable to be of any assistance to you should the legal owner of Hill House arrive during that time. I feel duty bound to make sure you have guaranteed access to the legal advice you'll need. By Wednesday, when I'll be leaving, you should have chosen one of the men I suggested to represent you."

She dropped her gaze for a moment, took a deep breath, and looked up at him again. "And on the other hand?"

He cleared his throat and moistened his lips. "On the other hand, your mother-in-law's matchmaking efforts today came just a tad too late. You see, I had been wrestling with the idea of courting you for some time, but unfortunately—"

"Wrestling? Did you say you'd been wrestling with the idea?" she blurted, the words tumbling out of her mouth before she had the wherewithal to stop them. "Forgive me, Mr. Breckenwith, but regardless of Mother Garrett's meddling, which has been beyond my control now for a good three decades, I sincerely doubt I have ever considered that a man would openly admit to me that he found the notion of courting me so difficult that he had to wrestle with the very prospect." She huffed and sat ramrod straight in her seat.

He chuckled. "I'm quite certain Mr. Langhorne had no such dilemma last summer and fall. He was quite committed from the start to courting you for the very—"

"For the very despicable goal of taking control of my fortune," she snapped. "At least he had the decency to pretend to be interested in marrying me. Without any equivocation, I might add."

"And you spurned his offer rather forcefully," he noted smugly. "Or so I've been told."

"Absolutely. But before—"

"Before you launch into exploring another of your one-sided, misguided assumptions and wind up regretting it, perhaps you'd consider letting me finish one of my statements before interrupting me," he cautioned.

Emma clenched her jaw. If he wanted to explain why he had had to wrestle with the idea of courting her and ultimately reject it, only to decide to sever their professional relationship, as well, then she would let him—before she shoved his list back into his hands and showed him to the door. "Please continue."

"As I was trying to explain," he began, "I had been considering the idea of asking to court you when Mr. Langhorne suddenly appeared in Candlewood and set his sights on you. Once I was convinced you were astute enough to see his proposal for what it was, you were knee-deep in solving the problem with the Leonards and grappling with the very disturbing news that you did not have legal title to Hill House."

Zachary paused, took a deep breath, and smiled. "While I do have legitimate business in New York City that will require my presence there for the better part of the next few months, I have a more pragmatic reason for asking you to have another lawyer represent your interests, although I will leave the decision as to whether or not I will continue to represent you in any capacity in the future entirely up to you."

Emma nodded for him to continue, although she was afraid she might not be able to hear him because her heart was pounding so hard.

"Widow Garrett, I don't believe it is either ethical or practical to court a woman who is my client. To be frank, after my wife died, I never thought I'd be interested in marrying again. And I hadn't been . . . until I came to know you."

"Oh?" she managed, having heard him quite well despite the accelerated beat of her heart.

"Given the opportunity to choose between continuing to represent you on a professional basis or having the honor and privilege of courting you—with the express purpose of marrying you, should you find it within your heart to be able to share any sincere affection with me—I very much wish to court you."

"Oh," she repeated, and her heart skipped

one beat and then another before beginning to race again.

"Naturally, that would mean arranging for you to have new legal counsel, at least in the interim. Given my obligations for the next few months, any serious consideration about beginning a courtship, however, would probably have to wait. But do you . . . do you think you would be willing to discuss the idea more seriously over the next few months when I manage to get back to Candlewood from time to time?"

Unable to find her voice, she blinked several times and tried to swallow the lump of emotion that swelled in her throat. He wanted to court her.

He wanted to court her?

Her mind struggled with the concept that he did, indeed, want to develop a very personal relationship with her.

He wanted to court her!

"You're surprised?" he asked.

Emma nodded, still unable to find her voice and battling a swell of tears that blurred her vision.

"But not offended that I've taken the liberty to suggest that you might want to consider the idea, I hope."

She shook her head so fast she nearly spilled a few tears before blinking them back. She cleared her throat. "At the moment, I . . . I'm not sure what to say or do. I haven't been in this position for quite some time, and I never actually thought I'd ever seriously have to consider being courted or to actually marry again before . . . before now. Before you," she admitted, taking a leap of faith and following his lead by being as honest with him as he had been with her.

"Then say yes. Say you'll spend some time with me over the course of the next few months when I'm in Candlewood to discuss the prospect that we might begin an official courtship and marry. I will defer to you, of course, in the matter of how private or how 'personal' you would want our association to be."

She hesitated less than a single, rapid heartbeat before smiling at him. "Yes," she whispered as she slipped her hand into her pocket to find and finger one of her keepsakes—a piece of the dress she had worn when she had married her sweet Jonas—forever grateful for the love and affection and companionship she had shared with him.

"Yes," she repeated, trusting in His guidance as she contemplated beginning the journey to love again . . . with Zachary Breckenwith. "I do have one request," she cautioned, determined to convince him that she would be capable enough to watch out for her own legal interests until April, when he would return to Candlewood for good.

18

THE TIME HAD COME to share secrets, not keep them.

With Zachary Breckenwith on his way home and the residents and guests tucked in for the night, Emma climbed the center staircase in the dark. She wore a shawl to guard against the late-night chill of a winter evening that followed her up the stairs. She paused on the landing and waited as the grandfather clock struck the tenth hour before proceeding to Mother Garrett's bedroom.

She smiled when she spied the light filtering through the crack beneath her mother-in-law's door. As she approached it she heard hushed voices inside the room, but she hesitated for only a moment before she rapped. "Mother Garrett, it's me. Emma," she whispered as loud as she dared for fear of disturbing the others who were already abed.

The voices stilled. Slow, heavy footsteps

approached. The door creaked open a notch.

Wearing an old-fashioned nightcap on her head, Mother Garrett poked her face out the door. "Is he gone?"

Emma chuckled softly. "Yes, he left some time ago. I stayed downstairs to do some paper work for a while before I locked up for the night."

The door swung wide open. "Then do come in. Frances and I were hoping you'd stop in to see me before taking to your bed," Mother Garrett whispered.

As soon as Emma slipped into the bedroom, Mother Garrett gently shut the door again. In stark contrast to the guest rooms, Mother Garrett's bedroom was just as tiny and plainly furnished as Emma's, with a single bureau with a small oil lamp, a bed, a footstool, and a rocking chair. Aunt Frances was sitting in the rocking chair—the very one Emma's grandmother and mother had used and passed on to Emma, who had rocked each of her three sons in it.

Aunt Frances tugged at the heavy afghan wrapped around her shoulders. She smiled and patted the footstool nestled between her and the single bed covered with a rumpled patchwork quilt where Mother Garrett had apparently been sitting while chatting with her friend. "Sit, Emma dear, sit. I hope you'll forgive a pair of old busybodies, but we've been waiting here for some time. We were wondering if you and that nice Mr. Breckenwith were having a good visit together like Reverend Glenn and I had tonight. Did you?"

Emma eased herself down onto the footstool and nodded. "We had a good meeting," she offered, fidgeting a bit to get the list of prospective lawyers out of her skirt pocket. She handed it to Mother Garrett, who had sat back down on the bed.

"What's this?" her mother-in-law asked as she unfolded the paper.

"Mr. Breckenwith gave it to me. It's a list of lawyers he suggested I consult."

Mother Garrett stared at the list for a moment, shrugged, and handed it back to Emma, who stored it away again. "I can't see why you'd need another lawyer when you already have one."

"Isn't one lawyer enough for you?" Aunt Frances asked.

"Ordinarily, I should hope so," Emma replied. She quickly detailed her lawyer's plans to be traveling back and forth between Candlewood and New York City for the next few months. Anxious to end the secrecy that had undermined her relationship with her mother-in-law since last fall, she took a deep breath. "Under the circumstances, he felt it best for me to have another lawyer familiar with my . . . my legal problem so there's no delay should I have an opportunity to resolve it in his absence."

Mother Garrett frowned. "Legal problem? What legal problem?"

Emma reached out and took her mother-in-law's hand. "I've had a very serious problem since last fall. I . . . I didn't tell you about it because I didn't want to alarm you . . . or disappoint you. Unfortunately, I haven't been able to resolve this problem and it may be some time before I'm able to do so." She blinked back tears of regret.

"I'm sorry. I realize now I shouldn't have kept this problem a secret from you or Reverend Glenn or you, Aunt Frances," she added, glancing over at the elderly widow. "You're part of our family at Hill House now, too, and I can't have you planning on returning to us in the spring for the tourist season when I'm not even sure any of us will be here then."

Aunt Frances smiled and patted Emma's shoulder, but Mother Garrett's tug on Emma's hand drew her attention back to her mother-in-law. "This secret of yours. The legal problem. This is why you haven't been yourself," she managed, her voice husky with emotion.

Emma swallowed hard, both ashamed and humbled to have to confess how wrong she had been. "I thought I could keep you from worrying and tell you about all this later, after I'd solved the problem. But . . . but I'm not sure when that's going to happen or even if I'll be able to resolve it in my favor.

"I need to tell you that Hill House does not belong to me," she admitted. Slowly and carefully, pausing often to answer the two women's questions, Emma detailed the events that had brought her to this point: her first meeting with the lawyer representing the estate of the deceased owner of Hill House and the interests of the heir, as well; Zachary Breckenwith's advice to fully evaluate her plans to sell the General Store, which had been in her family for three generations, to purchase the abandoned property; then the discovery that the other lawyer had absconded with the purchase money before filing the title. She ended with the news that she was currently waiting for the heir to arrive to inspect Hill House and decide whether or not to sell it to Emma.

When she finished, she let out a sigh. "I know you urged me not to rush into buying Hill House, and as it turns out, you were right, which means you get to say 'I told you so' as often as you like."

Aunt Frances clucked and shook her head. "Poor dear. She'll do no such thing, will you, Mercy?"

Mother Garrett tightened her hold on Emma's hand. "You're a good woman, Emma. Smart too. But you're also a bit headstrong and willful at times, which makes you just as human as the rest of us. Nevertheless, I love you just as you are. I've told you so before and I suppose

I'll just have to tell you over and over for whatever days I have left on this earth. We can face anything, as long as we do it together."

"There. That should make you feel better," Aunt Frances crooned. "There's no sense fussing and fuming about something you can't change about the past."

"I know," Emma murmured, glancing from one elderly woman to the other with tears that blurred her vision. "What would I do without either one of you?"

"You'd starve yourself into an early grave if you had to rely on your own cooking," Mother Garrett quipped as she sniffed back her own tears, obviously secure in her place as the cook in Emma's household.

"I'm sure you'd manage to get along just fine without me," Aunt Frances insisted.

"Not without the benefit of your friendship and wisdom," Emma countered.

"And not without those beautifully embroidered linens you design," Mother Garrett added with a twinkle in her eyes. "Just how long do you think it'll be before that heir—that owner or whatever—gets here and makes up his mind about selling or not selling Hill House to you?"

"I have no idea," Emma admitted. "Mr. Breckenwith seems to think that since the heir doesn't seem pressed to collect his inheritance, he might wait at least until the canal reopens in the spring to come to Candlewood. But Mr.

Breckenwith is also afraid the heir might be unpredictable. He could appear on our doorstep
literally any day."

Mother Garrett huffed. "Then again,
maybe he won't. I doubt he'd travel all this way
in the heart of winter. The weather is too mean
and the snow is usually too deep—not that
we've seen much snow so far. What did you say
the man's name was?"

Emma shrugged. "We only have the name
of the lawyer currently handling the estate, a
Mr. Mitchell from Philadelphia. Apparently the
heir prefers to remain anonymous, at least for
now."

"Then how are you supposed to know he is
who he says he is when he does eventually show
up?" Aunt Frances asked.

Mother Garrett nodded. "Yes, how?"

"Mr. Breckenwith tells me the heir will have
a letter with him from Mr. Mitchell, which we
can match to the correspondence he's received
from Mr. Mitchell. Mr. Breckenwith has them
in his office, at least for now," Emma noted.

Mother Garrett nodded. "Then that's why
you need another lawyer—to have that correspondence on hand in case this heir arrives
while Mr. Breckenwith is away."

Emma pulled the list of lawyers from her
pocket again, grinned, and tore the paper into
quarters and held them in one fist. "Actually, I
don't believe I'll be using another lawyer. Mr.

Breckenwith will continue to represent me until he leaves on Wednesday. I've asked him to bring any and all letters and documents he has concerning Hill House to me. If the heir arrives, I can easily compare signatures to determine if he's the man he says he is. If he elects to keep Hill House for himself, then I don't need another lawyer at all. I'm sure I can negotiate with the heir for a reasonable period of time to allow me to find a suitable place for all of us to live.

"*All* of us," she insisted and gazed directly at Aunt Frances. "I might not be needing your help here at Hill House, but wherever we are, whatever venture I decide to embark upon, I hope you'll still come and stay with us each spring and summer."

"If I wouldn't be a bother . . ."

"You're family, remember? You could never be a bother. Never," Emma insisted.

"But we all might be able to stay at Hill House," Mother Garrett argued.

"Yes, assuming I'm permitted to buy Hill House again. That's when I'd definitely need a lawyer," Emma replied.

Mother Garrett rolled her eyes. "Then why did you tear up that list of lawyers from Mr. Breckenwith? What are you going to do if that heir does show up tomorrow or next week or next month and Mr. Breckenwith is away?"

"Yes, Emma dear, what will you do?" Aunt Frances added.

"I'll ask the heir to have his lawyer draw up the proper paper work and forward it all to a lawyer here. Hopefully Mr. Breckenwith will be back by then. If not, the paper work will just have to wait."

"Oh, I can imagine how much Mr. Breckenwith fancied those ideas of yours," Mother Garrett noted wryly.

Emma cringed. "He wasn't entirely pleased with my plans," she admitted, "but after a rather lengthy discussion, I was able to persuade him to accept them. In the meantime, he'll be in Candlewood, at least for short spells from time to time. If I'm given the opportunity to buy Hill House and he's here at the time, we can decide then whether or not it would be appropriate for him to represent me and handle the sale or not."

Mother Garrett rubbed her forehead with the tips of her fingers and sighed. "I'm old and I'm tired, so forgive me, but didn't you just say you weren't getting another lawyer because you were keeping Mr. Breckenwith?"

"Only in a manner of speaking," Emma said with a smile. "You see, our business meeting ended up becoming a visit—a lovely visit. It seems Mr. Breckenwith has an ethical dilemma, one we hope to resolve over the next few months."

Aunt Frances frowned. "Although I haven't known him as long as either of you, I do know Mr. Breckenwith's character is above reproach.

I can't fathom he'd ever be faced with a question of ethics he couldn't resolve rather quickly."

Emma grinned, got up from her footstool, and sat down on the bed next to her mother-in-law. "This particular dilemma is different. It seems he finds it problematic to court one of his clients. Naturally, I—"

Mother Garrett gasped. "Court? Did you say court?"

"Yes, Mother Garrett. I did. Mr. Breckenwith suggested that I should use the next few months, when he's in town from time to time, to decide whether or not to allow him to court me and ultimately, I suppose, to marry. Obviously, it's not a step I'd take lightly, and I'd want your blessing if I decide—"

Mother Garrett hugged the words right out of Emma's throat. "Of course. Of course you'd have my blessing," she crooned.

Emma eased away and cupped her mother-in-law's face with her hands. "No one will ever take Jonas's place in my heart, but I . . . I think I have room in my heart for . . ."

"It's time, Emma," Mother Garrett whispered. "Frances and I both know it's time."

"Yes, we do," Aunt Frances murmured. "I think Reverend Glenn does, too."

"I haven't accepted his proposal. I've only agreed to consider it over the next few months," Emma reminded them. "And I think it would be best for now if we kept this between the three of us," she cautioned, ever mindful of Mother Garrett's struggle to keep secrets of any kind. "Mr. Breckenwith and I both agreed to keep our discussions about this private for now, although I did insist on telling you both. There's a great deal to consider, not the least of which is whether or not Mr. Breckenwith is prepared to accept my family as part of our lives together. I also want to talk to the boys when they're here for a visit in April before I make a decision as important as this one."

Aunt Frances dabbed at her eyes. "What about Reverend Glenn?" she asked, bringing the subject closer to home.

"He's family, too. I hope I can talk to him about this tomorrow morning before we leave for services."

Aunt Frances beamed, along with Mother Garrett, before both of the elderly widows gave in to healthy yawns.

Emma stood up. "I think I've kept you both from your beds long enough. We can talk more tomorrow," she suggested and gave each of them a kiss good-night before walking to the door. She turned around to face them again. "Thank you both for loving me and for not being angry with me for not telling you about not owning Hill House."

Grinning, Mother Garrett looked from Emma to her friend and back again. "You're easy to love, Emma. Besides, any woman who finds a man willing to wait to be a spring suitor instead of a winter one is a very special woman."

"Well, we both know Emma is special," Aunt Frances added.

Emma chuckled, opened the door, and stepped out into the dark hallway. With her secret about Hill House and about possibly being courted come spring now unburdened, she almost floated her way to her bedroom. She slipped into her room, changed into a nightgown in the dark, and unpinned her hair. She left her clothes lying atop the trunk at the foot of her bed. Shivering in the cold, she eased along the length of her bed to the middle and dropped down to her knees. Her nightly prayers tonight took a bit longer than usual, and by the time she finished and pulled down the quilt atop her bed and slipped beneath it, she was chilled to the bone. Huddling under the covers, she yanked her pillow closer before plopping down and letting her head hit the pillow.

Simultaneously, she heard an odd cracking sound and felt a gooey substance saturate her hair and scalp.

An egg!

There was an egg . . . on her pillow!

"Faith!" she cried, leaped out of bed, and lit the oil lamp on her bureau. She glanced at the bed, and sure enough, bits of brown eggshell littered the top of her pillow amid the scrambled contents of the egg that had not stuck to her hair.

"Obviously someone left the door to the root cellar open," she grumbled. She looked around the room for the chicken, but the animal was nowhere to be seen. She looked everywhere—under the bed. Under the bureau. Behind the trunk. She was about to check under the bed again when a scream coming from the direction of the hall that led to the rooms where the Masseys and Orralynne Burke were staying sent her across the room to a peg on the wall. She grabbed her robe, slipped it on, and charged out into the hallway.

When she passed by Mother Garrett's room, both Mother Garrett and Aunt Frances were standing in the doorway. Emma stopped and showed them her egg-drenched hair. "It's just the chickens. One or both of them must have gotten out of the cellar and laid an egg on my pillow before wandering off to another room. I'll let you know as soon as I find the culprit. In the meantime, I'll try to decide if you should start making chicken stew tonight or wait until morning," she snapped, then continued on her way to determine which of her guests had been gifted with a late-night visit from one or both of the chickens.

19

THE FOLLOWING MORNING Emma over-slept clear through breakfast and did not wake up until she was nearly too late to attend Sunday services.

She charged out the front door and through the front gate to the waiting carriage. Giving a quick wave to the driver, Tom Adams, who brought a carriage from the livery to Hill House every Sunday, she climbed aboard and promptly collapsed onto the seat across from Mother Garrett and Aunt Frances.

"I'm so sorry I've kept you waiting," she gushed as she pulled her cape tighter to keep out the cold. Nothing, however, seemed to ease the dull ache that stretched in a tight band across her forehead.

"Don't bother yourself. We'll be right on time for services," Mother Garrett insisted as the carriage began to rock them toward church.

"You had a late night," Aunt Frances murmured. "But don't worry. We took care of all the guests at breakfast, even Orralynne. She still seemed a bit testy when I took her breakfast to her room, but I suppose that's not too unusual. Most folks wouldn't take sharing their bedroom with a pair of chickens well. She insisted I take breakfast to her brother, as well. Apparently he's not feeling well, but I couldn't say for sure. He had me leave the breakfast tray outside his door."

"You're right. I had a very late night, but I shouldn't have slept so long," Emma grumbled. "By the time I had corralled both chickens, got them out of Orralynne's room and back into the root cellar, then sat with Miss Burke until she settled herself back to sleep, it was nearly three o'clock. I'm still not sure why the chickens had to choose her room to roost, unless mine wasn't good enough," she added.

Mother Garrett grunted. "I still don't understand why the chickens weren't sleeping at night."

"I don't know," Emma said. "Maybe they got disoriented after spending so much time in the root cellar, where it's dark. I just wish they hadn't chosen to escape on the one night when Liesel and Ditty are at home with their families so they weren't here to help me."

"Well, at least none of the other guests suspect a thing about what happened. Apparently they all slept through it."

Mother Garrett sighed. "I don't know how they did that. Orralynne has a scream that can curdle the milk in every cow for miles."

Emma held on to the seat as the carriage descended down the steep hill to Main Street and realized the seat next to her was empty. "Wait! Where's Reverend Glenn?" she asked, miffed with herself for sleeping late and missing the opportunity to talk with him before breakfast.

"He left early today with the Masseys. They wanted to stop by their home before going to church. He was going to have breakfast with Reverend Austin and his wife before services. He's also going to spend the day with them, if I'm not mistaken," Aunt Frances offered.

"You can talk with Reverend Glenn tonight," Mother Garrett said.

Aunt Frances sighed. "This is the first Sunday since the explosion and fire. Apparently Reverend Austin thought it would be helpful to have Reverend Glenn with him. There's bound to be an unusually large number of people at services today, and some folks might want to stay awhile to talk to them."

"Tragedies have a way of bringing people to their knees. That's how Reverend Glenn put it," Mother Garrett added.

"Very true. Very true," Emma whispered, haunted by the grief and pain she had seen etched in the faces of so many townspeople touched either directly or indirectly by the tragedy at the funeral services less than a week ago.

Aunt Frances caught Emma's gaze and held it. "I was wondering . . . I'm hoping both Andrew and James are at services today with their families. Do you think they might be able to come back and visit with me for a while at Hill House?"

"I think they should all join us for dinner," Emma insisted. "Will that be all right, Mother Garrett? Would we have enough to serve everyone?"

Mother Garrett smiled. "My mother taught me well, Emma. I can stretch most any meal, even when my larder is getting low, which it is at the moment, thanks to those chickens you insist on keeping in the root cellar. By the way, I didn't start up making stew this morning because you overslept, and I was waiting on you to tell me to go ahead. Instead, I've got a nice ham that'll do for dinner today."

Emma let out a long sigh. "Tomorrow's Monday. Since Steven is bringing the supplies from the General Store to build a strong pen and Mr. Kirk has stayed behind to help him, I thought I'd give the chickens one more chance."

"Another chance? To wreck Hill House or frighten your guests?" her mother-in-law argued.

"To redeem themselves," Emma countered. "They'd have to lay a dozen golden eggs every day from now to Judgment Day to do that. To my mind, there's only one way for those chickens to redeem themselves, and that's in my stew pot."

———————

Sunday services were inspiring but bittersweet. As good as it was to have so many people packed into the church, Emma could only think about those who had gone Home or were unable to attend services today because they were lying in sickbeds at the hotel.

Reverend Austin's sermon touched everyone's heart, but it was seeing Reverend Glenn stand to give a brief sermon of his own that left Emma's face glistening with tears. Drained and exhausted by the time services ended, she did not mind that it took a good while for people to exit the building. In gentler months, members of the congregation often lingered to chat in the churchyard, but the harsh January cold sent everyone back to their carriages and others rushing back home on foot.

Aunt Frances rode back to Hill House with her two sons and their families, leaving only Mother Garrett and Emma to ride home together. Emma helped her mother-in-law into the carriage, but before she could climb aboard herself, Zachary Breckenwith approached her.

Smiling, he tipped his hat. "I was hoping to speak with you before you left. As you know, I'll have to leave on Wednesday. Is there any chance you might have time to meet with me before then? Tomorrow, perhaps?" he asked as he helped her into the carriage.

She took her seat next to Mother Garrett but hesitated before answering him. Although she was surprised he was leaving again so soon, she also felt hesitant to begin this new aspect of their relationship. "Tomorrow isn't a good day, I'm afraid."

"Tuesday?"

"I . . . I'm not sure."

Mother Garrett poked her head around Emma to address him. "Tuesday will be fine. If you come for dinner at one o'clock, you'll be able to see whatever you need to see with the warmth of the afternoon, such as it might be. These old bones of mine tell me snow is coming soon."

Emma cast her mother-in-law a hard glance. Obviously, if she did decide to allow Mr. Breckenwith to court her, she would have to set up some rules at home with Mother Garrett and probably Aunt Frances, as well. The time to set those rules appeared to have come a whole lot sooner than later, but she did not want to embarrass her mother-in-law by counter-manding her suggestion in front of the man.

She turned away from Mother Garrett to face him and smiled. "Tuesday, then. At one."

He grinned. "I'll be bringing a mount for

you, so dress well for cold weather. You might want to save those golden trousers you wore riding last fall for another time. They're not nearly heavy enough for this time of year," he stated before waving to the driver to begin taking the two women back to Hill House.

Stunned, she leaned back against the seat and closed her eyes to ease the pounding in her head that had started up again the moment he mentioned the time she had gone riding with the Mitchell sisters. "He's taking me riding? In the dead of winter? With a panther lurking about? Has the man no sense at all?" she groaned.

Mother Garrett patted her knee. "You'll enjoy riding again. You'll do just fine."

Emma poked one eye open. "Fine? The last time I went riding, I was sore for a week. And I wasn't riding out in the bitter cold, either. And what about the panther?"

"You won't be riding alone. You'll have Mr. Breckenwith with you as your protector. But just to ease your worries, I'll be generous and loan you my umbrella."

———

Sunday dinner was raucous, reminding Emma of the meal they had all shared together to celebrate the Leonard brothers' reconciliation last fall. For whatever reason, Orralynne did not mention the midnight visitors to her room last evening, for which Emma was grateful, although she did have the opportunity to remind everyone to make sure their doors were closed and securely latched at night.

Andrew Leonard agreed to return for his mother in two weeks, weather permitting. Both Andrew and James, along with Andrew's four sons, made quick work of hauling away all the spoiled food in the root cellar back to their farms and even managed to keep the two chickens from escaping again in the process.

By late afternoon, the boardinghouse had quieted down again. Along with Mother Garrett and Aunt Frances, Judith Massey was upstairs resting while her husband, the Ammond brothers, and Anson Kirk went into town to help finalize the plans for tomorrow's panther hunt. Orralynne and Lester Burke had come to dinner, along with Mr. Lewis, then retired together behind closed doors in the library.

Left on her own, Emma went up to her bedroom. Although she was still tired from her late-night misadventure, she decided against taking a nap in favor of spending a little time looking back at her life before she could look ahead and seriously consider Mr. Breckenwith's proposal.

Late-day sunlight filtering through the single window in her room added even more warmth to the pale yellow walls. Kneeling, she opened the trunk at the foot of her bed. She lifted out the several gowns she kept stored there, laid them neatly on top of the quilt on the bed, and glanced at the collection of personal treasures she had saved from her parents and grandparents, along with others she had accumulated during her life as both a wife and mother.

She reached into the far-left corner to trace the outline of the first account book her grandmother had kept after opening the General Store. Next to the book, a brown paper wrapper protected her grandfather's glass harmonica. She closed her eyes for a moment and cocked her head. The memory of sitting on her grandfather's lap after supper while he played his harmonica or told her tales of how he had brought his family to this area, one of the first families to call Candlewood their home, came to her.

Emma took a deep breath, opened her eyes, and turned her attention next to the items from her parents that she had stored away after giving most of them to her sons to treasure. In her reticule she still carried the pocket watch her mother had used while operating the General Store, but kept the well-worn work apron her mother had used for years here, where it rested next to the comb her father had used to groom his beard.

Next she studied the center of the trunk where she kept a small box filled with mementos from her beloved husband, Jonas. She took hold of the box, leaned back on her haunches and cradled the box on her lap. She did not have to open the box. She knew the contents too well.

The words on the many little notes he had written to her and left on her pillow or in the cash box at the General Store where she alone would find them had been inscribed on her heart for many years, along with the simple word engraved inside the slim silver wedding band she had worn as his wife: *Blessed.*

"Blessed," she murmured as visions of their lives together flashed quickly through her mind. Their work, side-by-side, at the General Store. Their three sons, now grown with families of their own. Their easy companionship. Their laughter. Their love.

"Our lives together were truly blessed," she whispered. Without the blessings of her marriage to Jonas, she would never have the courage to contemplate marriage to anyone else.

While Jonas and Zachary Breckenwith were two very different men, in looks and temperament and avocation, they did share many good qualities that she considered essential in a spouse. Like Jonas, Zachary Breckenwith was a decent, honorable man. Even more important, he was also a man of faith who embraced the Word.

Though her life with Zachary Breckenwith

would be far different than it had been with Jonas, she suspected she would find that marriage to him would bring her the very things she had missed during her widowhood: the friendship and companionship one could only pray to find with a loving spouse.

She gripped her box with both hands and bowed her head. "Dearest Lord, now I must come to you again to ask for your guidance. This time I need help that I might make the right decision—for Zachary Breckenwith, for me, and for all those I love. Amen."

Lovingly, she put the box back into the trunk, replaced her gowns, and closed the lid. She was scarcely back on her feet when she heard a series of crashes and a cry of distress coming from the first floor.

She grinned as she walked to her bedroom door. "Ditty must be back. Poor thing. I wonder if she'll ever grow into those feet of hers," she murmured as she left her room. When she reached the hall and heard Ditty's voice, along with another she did not quite recognize, her suspicions were confirmed. She proceeded directly to the center staircase, prepared to find almost anything by way of an accident downstairs.

When she reached the top of the stairs and glanced down to the hall below, however, she gasped, gripped the banister with one hand, and clapped the other to her heart. As much as she knew and accepted Ditty's clumsiness, and as much as her imagination might allow, she was totally and absolutely unprepared for the vision of pure catastrophe that lay waiting for her at the bottom of the stairs.

20

Paint. Paint. And more paint.

Red. Blue. Yellow. Orange. Purple. Emma gave up trying to determine how many colors had splashed onto the floral carpet runner she had had designed especially for the main hall at Hill House and rushed down the steps as fast as she could.

Ditty was rooted in the center of the mess, and the young woman's gown wore enough paint to serve as an artist's palette. Surrounded by upended tins of paint the size of an ordinary butter crock, Malcolm Lewis was merely standing in the hallway in front of Ditty. He was wearing a well-stained artist's coat, looking rather dazed and stupefied.

His narrow face mottled red with embarrassment the moment she stepped, albeit very carefully, into the disaster zone. "I'm sorry. Oh my. I'm so sorry, Widow Garrett. Forgive me. Oh my. Oh my, do forgive me," he pleaded as he approached her, his voice a bit shrill with despair. "I shouldn't have opened up all that paint and brought it out here. I simply shouldn't. I know better. I truly do."

Emma was half tempted to strap on her skates to make her taller and keep her skirts from touching the floor and getting paint on them, but she would probably just slip and fall anyway. Instead, she used both hands to lift her skirts and tiptoed around a puddle of sunflower yellow paint and a tin of orange paint that had miraculously landed upright. She sighed when she noted that there were several areas on the walls that had not escaped ruin, but the massive oak coat rack near the front door appeared to have been spared. "Whatever happened?" she asked as soon as she reached him, making sure she was in a clear spot before letting her skirts drop back into place.

"*He* tripped, and the paint he was carrying on a tray flew everywhere," Ditty offered, almost triumphantly.

Emma scowled at her by way of reprimand.

"Well, I didn't trip. I didn't make this mess," the young woman argued. "I'd just gotten home when Mr. Lewis—"

"I did. I tripped. I'm not sure how it happened, but apparently I must have simply tripped over my own two feet," he offered in support of Ditty's explanation. "It's all my fault.

This poor girl only had the misfortune of arriving home just in time to become a victim of my own clumsiness."

"Are either of you hurt?" Emma asked, looking from one to the other.

"I'm fine," Ditty insisted, looked down at her paint-splattered skirts, and shook her head. "I'm afraid I can't say the same for my skirts, but at least I had already taken off my cloak and hung it up before the paint flew. There's no real harm, I suppose. This is just an ordinary work gown, after all. A few splashes of paint won't matter when I'm scrubbing floors."

"Nevertheless, I'll pay whatever it costs to replace your gown. I insist," Mr. Lewis added. He paused, looked down at the paint dripping from the hem of his trousers, and shrugged. "Other than a well-deserved stab to my pride, Widow Garrett, I'm not injured. But I still don't understand how this happened. I've been in at least a hundred homes over the years, and I've never, ever once created such a mess."

He looked directly at Emma and swallowed so hard his Adams apple bobbed in his skinny neck. "I know that it is little consolation to you, and I truly do apologize."

"We all have accidents from time to time," she offered. After last night's chicken fiasco, she was not about to point blame at the man for having an accident, but she could not shake the nagging feeling that this accident may not have been his fault.

"Whatever were you doing carrying a tray of opened paint tins into the hallway? I thought you were busy in the library with the Burkes," she said, glancing at the hallway carpet and floorboards while searching for any evidence that might prove that her nagging feeling was well-founded.

"Miss Burke only stayed a short while to discuss what she might wear for her sitting before retiring to her room. Mr. Burke was quite emphatic about her wearing a gray gown, although I'm not certain Miss Burke is very happy about that. He was going to double-check the measurements for the suit he's tailoring for me, but within half an hour he had to stop. I'm afraid he wasn't feeling up to the task and retired to his bedroom," he stated quietly.

Emma nodded, silently confirming that she recalled the artist's earlier conversation with her about Lester Burke's poor health.

Mr. Lewis cleared his throat and continued. "Since I had the afternoon free and the boardinghouse seemed rather deserted, I thought I might move the paints from the library up to my room. Then I thought maybe I should just bring some of my paints out to the hallway. The daylight here is less filtered than in the library. I was hoping to choose a combination of colors for a stencil I had in mind for you."

When she tried to object, he held up his hand. "I know you haven't had time to decide whether or not you even wanted me to design a stencil for the hallway, but I thought if I made a sample, with just the right colors that would be pleasing to you and match the colors in the carpet runner . . ."

He let out a sigh. "I'm sorry. The very last thing I wanted to do was create trouble for you."

"Your intentions were good," Emma replied, then spied something behind him that caught her attention and made her stomach drop.

"I'll help you clean this up," Ditty offered, "if you tell me how. I've never had to clean up wet paint before."

Emma scarcely heard the conversation that ensued. She was too focused on walking around him to get closer to the section of carpet behind him. The moment she saw the telltale stains, she stopped, walked back to the staircase, and noted the same stains on several of the posts below the banister. Hoping against hope she might somehow be wrong, she turned and looked back over her shoulder. "Did you have any black or white paint on the tray, Mr. Lewis?" she asked, interrupting his conversation with Ditty.

"I beg your pardon?"

"The paint tins you brought into the hallway—did you have any tins containing black or white paint?"

"No, but I'm not sure I understand why—"

She let out a well-deserved sigh. "Come take a look," she insisted, quite prepared for another "I told you so" from Mother Garrett.

He made his way over to where she stood near the base of the staircase, along the route he would have taken when he left the library. When he drew close, she pointed to the black and white stains. "I believe those are chicken droppings. In all fairness, I don't think you tripped at all, Mr. Lewis. You probably walked through these droppings and lost your footing, which surely absolves you from any blame."

His eyes widened. "Chicken droppings? Here? In this very hallway?"

Emma swallowed her pride and quickly detailed the events that led to keeping the chickens in the root cellar, including last night's escape. "What happened here is decidedly not your fault, Mr. Lewis."

"Apparently not," he murmured. His shoulders squared and his backbone straightened a bit with the news.

She moistened her lips. "Naturally, I'll replace the carpet, but I'll most assuredly need your help in restoring the floorboards and some areas on the walls."

"I can do that for you," he assured her.

"And perhaps you might want to draw up

that sample of the stencil design you had in mind for the hallway," she added in an attempt to assuage her guilt. She set aside her previous concerns about not having the right to change Hill House in any way until the question of ownership had been resolved. By offering Mr. Lewis the opportunity to earn a fee, Emma also hoped to compensate him for this awful experience.

He nodded, thanked her, and recruited Ditty to follow him to secure the necessary agents to clean up the floorboards and walls before the paint dried.

In their absence, Emma walked to the far end of the hallway, got down on her knees, and started rolling up the carpet runner in the hopes of shoving it outside to the front porch when she finished. "Why, oh why did Mr. Lewis have to step in those droppings?" she complained. But when she thought that someone else might have slipped and fallen, like Mother Garrett or Aunt Frances, whose aged bones were very fragile, or Lester Burke, who was already troubled by his deformed foot, she decided to be grateful. At least Mr. Lewis was young enough and healthy enough to keep his balance and not fall and injure himself.

She rolled up several yards of carpet, stopped to catch her breath, and glanced down the hallway to the entrance to Hill House. If the heir and rightful owner of this boardinghouse walked through that front door right now and discovered this mess and how it had happened, he would probably evict her before the sun set.

Hopefully, he would not arrive in the next several days, which was long enough to get the hallway restored to some semblance of order. Even better, if he did not arrive for several weeks, there would be a lovely stencil on the walls to welcome him, which was the only benefit she could imagine might come out of this whole episode.

Emma was halfway down the hall, where the damage to the carpet was the greatest, when she heard a carriage pull up outside the front yard. Fearful that her thoughts about the heir might actually have conjured up the man's appearance, she froze in place—until she heard Butter barking.

Spared her worst fear, she then fretted that Reverend Glenn and Butter would soon be entering the house through the front door, unaware of the disaster lying in wait for them. With horrid visions of the retired minister slipping on wet paint or the dog tracking paint throughout the first floor, she started rolling the carpet as fast as she could.

She ignored the wet paint flecking back toward her, but she was still a good ten feet from the door when she heard the retired minister's footsteps on the front porch. She stopped and leaned back on her haunches again, waiting for just the right moment.

"Stop!" she shouted the moment she saw the knob begin to turn.

"Emma?"

"Yes. Please stop. It's not safe to come inside yet. We have a bit of a spill in the hallway. I need a few more moments to make it safe for you to enter," she explained.

"We'll wait."

At this point, the carpet roll probably weighed as much as she did, but she managed to roll up the last ten feet and used the last of her strength to shove the entire roll far enough away from the front door to let the elderly man and his dog inside.

She stood up, stretched to ease the kink out of the small of her back, opened the front door, and led the two of them past the barrier to the west parlor. "I just need you to keep Butter in here until we get the paint off the floorboards," she explained, grateful the dog usually stayed close to his master.

While she carried Reverend Glenn's coat and hat to the oak rack in the hallway, he settled himself into one of the chairs facing the fireplace with the dog plopped faithfully at his feet. "When I asked Reverend Austin to bring me home in time for supper, I had no idea I'd be in the way."

"You're not ever in the way," she argued, quickly explaining what had happened last night and just this afternoon. By the time she finished, he was chuckling, and so was she.

"Forgive me, Emma. Since the tragedy, it seems some days, like today, are very difficult, but the good Lord always seems to find a way to add a bit of laughter. I didn't mean to laugh at your expense."

She chuckled again. "If I don't laugh about this, I might be tempted to cry."

"Some folks might get themselves into a snit over what happened," he said.

"Being angry never solved anything."

He smiled. "Being home with you all at Hill House is good for my spirit. I hope you know that."

She nodded but swallowed hard. Unable to sit down for fear of smearing wet paint on any of the furniture, she stood beside his chair and placed her hand on top of his. "Home is more than just Hill House. It's wherever we are. To-gether," she murmured. "There's something I need to talk to you about," she began and poured out the same tale of mistakes and dis-appointments she had shared with Mother Gar-rett and Aunt Frances last night.

He listened patiently and without judgment, as always. When she finished, he turned his hand over to clasp hers. "You've carried a heavy burden alone all these months."

She nodded. "I didn't want to worry anyone else."

"Worry never solved much of anything," he prompted with a smile. "Unfortunately, I've had to remind far too many people of that these last few days."

She nodded. "I do have some good news," she shared, and this time, as she detailed the proposal she had received from Mr. Brecken-with, her mind was more peaceful and her heart beat just a little faster.

21

I CAN'T DO THIS."

At midmorning on Tuesday, Emma repeated her statement for the third time as she paced back and forth in the kitchen.

And for the third time, Mother Garrett simply continued stirring the barley soup she would be serving for dinner and ignored Emma.

"I've given this a lot of thought over the past few days, and I've decided I'm just going to have to be honest with the man, speak my mind, and get the matter settled right now."

Mother Garrett let out a sigh. "Which man? The one who has turned the library into the messiest tailor shop this side of the Atlantic? I've only had a peek inside, but that was enough for me."

Emma stopped in her tracks and scowled. "No. I've already spoken with Mr. Burke. He's agreed to let Liesel and Ditty into the library to clean tomorrow, and I'll be there to make sure he doesn't mistreat them," she added, then resumed pacing, troubled by the man's deteriorating health as well as his mood.

"Then you must mean the man who has made it nigh impossible to use the center hallway without risking life and limb," her mother-in-law prompted.

Emma paced faster. "I had no idea Mr. Lewis would have to erect some kind of makeshift scaffolding just to sketch a bit of the design he's created, but I'm hardly in a position to complain. He's been very understanding about what caused his mishap in the hallway."

"And almost as pleased as I am that those chickens of yours are safe and secure outside again," Mother Garrett quipped. She took a taste of the soup and added more salt to the pot before stirring again. "If it's not Mr. Burke or Mr. Lewis, that leaves a few other men here at Hill House, but I doubt they've done anything to set you to pacing back and forth in my kitchen like that poor panther that's tied up in the tent Mr. Gray put up in front of his tavern."

Emma stopped again. "Encouraging folks to spend twenty-five cents to see that pathetic creature when there's so many people in Candlewood in need—or to use the panther to lure people into the tavern to spend more money on refreshments—is a disgrace." She drew in a long breath but was unable to stem her outrage. "To allow people to throw stones at the animal or to poke it with poles is uncon-scionable. I have no qualms about confronting Mr. Gray . . . which I fully intend to do when I have the time, the opportunity, and an appro-priate escort. And I'll say the same to Mr. Guenther and his cronies who managed to cap-ture the animal to collect Gray's bounty."

Emma shook her head. "It's Mr. Brecken-with I need to speak to," she admitted.

Mother Garrett sighed and laid her spoon down on a small plate next to the stove. After taking a seat at the kitchen table, she pulled out a chair and patted the seat next to her. "Come. Sit yourself down next to me."

Emma hesitated. "I'm not sure I can sit still for very long. I'm too unsettled."

"Then try. Otherwise, you're going to wear yourself out, and you have a busy afternoon planned."

Emma sighed her way to the chair and sat down. "I do have a busy afternoon, which is ex-actly my point. Mr. Breckenwith is coming to dinner in precisely three hours."

"He's come for dinner before."

"As my lawyer. This time is different," Emma argued and slipped her hand into her pocket to hold her keepsakes. "When he asked me to see him over the next few months to de-cide whether or not I would allow him to court me, I was very flattered and happy . . . and I said yes."

"But now you've changed your mind?"

Emma bowed her head for a moment. "I . . . I think so, yes. But I'm not sure. I'm confused."

"I see," her mother-in-law murmured, placing her hand at the nape of Emma's neck and gently massaging the tenseness from the muscles there. "Would you like to talk about it and tell me why?"

"I just don't like how I'm feeling," Emma offered, leaning back and savoring the comfort of her mother-in-law's touch. "For the first day or so, I was certain that I welcomed Mr. Breckenwith's interest in me. I've known him for over five years. He's a good man. He'd make a good husband."

"Agreed."

"But then I began to think about how much my life would change if I eventually did marry him. What would that mean? Would I give up Hill House—assuming I get to buy it again, of course—or would I have to give up whatever venture I choose instead? There are simply too many uncertainties."

"Isn't that precisely what you two would be discussing over the next few months?" Mother Garrett asked.

"I suppose."

"You've had any number of meetings and discussions with him over the years. Have you ever found him to be domineering or unreasonable or calculating?"

Emma managed half a smile. "He can be forceful in his opinions, yet he listens to me and hears me out when I disagree with him. But we were always discussing possible investments or legal matters, not building a life together. I'm not even certain I remember how to have a conversation that isn't related to business when I'm alone with a man."

She paused and fingered her keepsakes. "Maybe . . . maybe I should just be content with the life I have. I have wonderful memories of being married to Jonas. My children and grandchildren are coming this April, and I'm looking forward to spending time with all of them again. I have you and Reverend Glenn and Aunt Frances with me. My life is full, albeit a tad unsettled at the moment, and all Mr. Breckenwith does is complicate my life."

"'Complicate,'" Mother Garrett said and dropped her hand away. "You should reconsider using that word. It's a little harsh. Try *enrich* or *fulfill.*"

"They don't mean the same thing at all!"

"Don't they? Think about it, Emma. Until your recent legal troubles, your life was decidedly uncomplicated. It's better here at Hill House than it was at the General Store, I'll grant you that much. But even though you've only had the boardinghouse open to guests for two years, those guests come and go from spring through fall, and you spend all those months, season after season, working so hard you scarcely have a moment for anything but work. When winter comes, we're all holed up here waiting for spring to come and the cycle to repeat itself." She put her arm around Emma's shoulders.

"I know, but—"

"You won't have me or Reverend Glenn or Frances here forever, either. At our ages, we're grateful every morning just to wake up and be here for another day. I can't speak for the others, but I can tell you that I don't want you to be alone like I've been for all these many years. I want you to have a husband, a companion, someone who will enrich your life and make it more fulfilling for you as a woman—just a woman, not a woman of business. That usually means your life gets more complicated."

Emma leaned toward her mother-in-law. "I don't want to be alone, either," she whispered. "It's just hard to think about courting again. I'm going to be fifty-two years old in a few months, but the very notion of being courted makes me so anxious I wonder if I can do it at all. It would be a whole lot easier to just forget about the whole notion and be content remaining a widow. At least, that's how I feel one minute; the next, I'm looking forward to it."

"Marrying is serious, complicated business," her mother-in-law noted. "Just remember that it's better to be alone than it is to marry the wrong man. I think that's something you should be thinking about over the next few months. Is Mr. Breckenwith the right man or isn't he? You must think he might be or you wouldn't have given his offer any more thought than you gave to Mr. Langhorne's."

Emma chuckled, looked up at her mother-in-law's beloved face, and found the woman's eyes twinkling. "He was a cad, wasn't he?"

Mother Garrett grinned.

"Cad? Who was a cad?" Aunt Frances asked as she walked into the kitchen.

Emma straightened up and grinned at Aunt Frances. "We were talking about Mr. Langhorne."

"Hmmph. He was a cad, a charlatan, and a fool for thinking he could set himself up as a country gentleman on land he tried to force from my boys. Not when we had you to help us. But I'm willing to forgive the man, considering he eventually found land a good ten miles from my boys," she added with a smile. She settled into the rocking chair near the fireplace and looked back directly at Mother Garrett. "I thought I'd better tell you that we'll be having another guest today for dinner."

Mother Garrett rose and went back to stir the soup still simmering on the cookstove. "There's plenty," she said before tasting the soup and adding more salt. "Who's coming?"

"Anson Kirk."

Mother Garrett scowled. "And I thought you were my friend. You invited Anson Kirk here? For dinner?"

"No, Reverend Glenn invited him yesterday when Mr. Kirk said he wanted to stop back to check on the chicken pen he helped the others build. I just plumb forgot to tell you."

"Wasn't Reverend Glenn home all day yesterday? I don't remember Mr. Kirk stopping by," Emma noted as she rose to get the afghan for Aunt Frances's shoulders.

"Reverend Glenn went out for an hour or so in the afternoon with Reverend Austin. The members of the church vestry called a special meeting and wanted both ministers to be there, probably to thank them both for all the hours they spent helping members of the congregation after the fires and such. I'm not sure, though. Reverend Glenn didn't really say what the meeting was about when he got home. We were so busy chatting about other things, I never thought to ask him."

"I don't remember him leaving," Emma countered as she handed the afghan to her aunt-by-affection.

"Thank you, Emma dear. You were probably busy upstairs at the time. Wasn't it Monday when Miss Burke was demanding your attention for some reason or another?"

Emma shivered. It had taken her several long hours to convince Orralynne she did not look like an elephant in the voluminous gray gown her brother insisted she wear when she began sitting for her portrait. "Yes, I believe that's where I was."

"Remind me to have a chat with Reverend Glenn after dinner," Mother Garrett snapped, sloshing a bit of soup over the rim of the pot.

"Matchmaking must be contagious these days, although Mr. Kirk doesn't seem to need any persuasion to be interested in a certain person who just happens to be stirring soup at the moment."

Mother Garrett cast a hard glance in Emma's direction. "Please don't make me remind you to respect your elders, namely me. Anson Kirk is just a winter suitor. Nothing more. Which means I have no intention of paying any mind to that man." She huffed. "All he does is complicate my life."

Emma raised a brow. "'Complicate'? You should reconsider using that word. It's a little harsh," she teased, tossing the woman's very words back at her.

"He's a winter suitor, Emma."

"Don't be a ninny, Mercy. That's just a schoolgirl idea of ours and you know it," Aunt Frances countered. "He's a very nice man."

Mother Garrett sniffed. "Then you talk to

him at dinner," she suggested before stirring the soup again.

———

Emma managed to eat only a slice of bread spread thick with butter for dinner. She was too anxious to eat much, although Zachary Breckenwith seemed to be quite at ease. She was also too entertained by Anson Kirk's antics as he attempted to gain favor with Mother Garrett to be distracted by food, although Mother Garrett ate even more than usual.

By 2:30 Emma was outside of the gate to the front yard, ready to begin her outing with Mr. Breckenwith. She was astride the same gentle mare from the livery she had ridden last fall, and she was well-dressed for a winter ride. Beneath her heavy wool cape, she wore an old pair of men's trousers under the flannel skirt Aunt Frances had altered for the occasion. Thick leather gloves protected her hands, and a sturdy bonnet kept her head warm while she waited for Zachary to mount his horse. Fortunately, since the panther had been captured and posed no danger to her, she had no need to bring along the umbrella Mother Garrett had offered to her some days ago.

Once he was in the saddle, he nodded toward the hill that led down to Main Street. "We can ride through town, should you want to stop at any of the shops along the way, or we can skirt around the back of Hill House. Either way suits the destination I have in mind."

She brightened, grateful for the opportunity to act on the idea that had been simmering in her mind ever since she had heard about the panther's capture. "Actually, there is one stop I'd like to make first before you take me to this surprise of yours."

He waved her to proceed. "Let's get started, then."

When she urged the mare toward the hill, he rode alongside her. "Is your stop a surprise, as well?"

She shrugged. "Not at all. Since I have both the time, the opportunity, and a suitable companion this afternoon, I thought we might stop at Gray's Tavern." Emma was prepared to match wits with the opportunistic Mr. Gray, but she had no idea how she was going to convince the man to stop showcasing the animal.

Zachary slowly let the air out of his lungs and shook his head, although he did not rein up. "If I didn't know you as well as I do, I'd suspect you were merely curious and wanted to see the panther for yourself."

"But you do know me well," she offered with a smile.

"Indeed," he grumbled. "Indeed."

"And you're still willing to accompany me?"

He cocked a brow, and the muscles along his jawline tensed. "As your lawyer, which I still am until I leave tomorrow, I have no other choice but to go along to protect you against yourself."

"And as a man who would be my suitor?"

He grinned. "I look forward to the occasion."

She grinned back.

He just might be the right man after all.

22

FIFTY YEARS AGO, Candlewood could boast only three struggling business establishments. All three lynchpins had survived the town's transformation from a fledgling settlement into the thriving town it was today, but not all were faring equally well.

The General Store, owned and operated initially by Emma's grandmother, now had its fifth owner, Mr. Atkins, a newcomer to town. Thomas Adams had purchased the blacksmith and livery some ten years ago to become only the second owner. Gray's Tavern, however, was the only one of the three businesses to stay in family hands and the only one to be experiencing economic difficulties.

Following the construction of the Candlewood Canal and the subsequent growth of the town, the tavern's role within the community had shifted significantly. The influx of travelers as well as easterners on holiday who arrived by canal vastly outnumbered the few traveling by coach. These folks demanded more, if not finer sleeping accommodations than the small tavern could offer. The Emerson Hotel, as well as a number of boardinghouses like Hill House, easily lured away their business.

Struggling to survive, Gray's Tavern had become a haven for the hungry, thirsty men who worked in the factories nearby, many of whom were single and lived together in boardinghouses considered less reputable by other visitors. Consequently, the atmosphere in the tavern had changed into one considered unseemly for women and children.

Emma kept all of this in mind as she looked ahead and saw a number of shoppers lured out into the sunny afternoon to visit the numerous shops and businesses that lined the planked sidewalk on either side of Main Street. In the far distance, workmen were busy repairing shingled roofs on several of the factories that hugged the east side of the canal nearest the now-destroyed match factory. The sound of hammers hitting nails and saws chewing through wood was heavy here in the north end of town, as well, as friends and neighbors helped one another repair the homes damaged by fires carried to their roofs by the gusting winds that tragic night.

When Emma and Mr. Breckenwith rode past Banfield Lane, she reined up and pointed to her left. "Isn't the Burke cottage down there?"

Zachary stopped his mount. "As a matter of fact, I believe it is."

"I'd like to see it. Would you mind? I don't want to go through it, obviously, but I would like to see the damage for myself."

With a nod of his head, he urged her to turn down the lane and followed along behind her. "Having second thoughts about having the Burkes for an extended stay at Hill House?"

"No, but I'd feel better if I could see how extensive the damage is and to gauge for myself how long it might take for that damage to be repaired," she explained as they passed a number of small homes that appeared to have sustained no damage at all. "Unfortunately, I haven't been to the cottage for years."

"It's up ahead on your left. If you look carefully, you can see a portion of the charred roof just above that large oak tree."

She looked up at the roof but waited until they reached the front of the small, rustic dwelling before commenting again. The shingles on the cottage had darkened with age to the color of burnt gingerbread, and the property was badly overgrown with vegetation, but there did not appear to be any other damage than to the roof and the garret below it. The walkway to the front door, however, was clear so that anyone coming here for tailoring work could reach the front door.

"The roof looks bad enough that the whole thing has to be replaced," she noted.

"That's what I understand."

She turned in her saddle to face him. "You've heard talk?"

He shrugged. "A bit of gossip here and there."

She cocked a brow.

He let out a sigh. "Word has it that the roof needs to be replaced, but no one has been willing to start work because they don't want to be on the receiving end of one of Mr. Burke's infamous lawsuits."

Emma groaned. "Please tell me Mr. Burke hasn't filed more lawsuits."

"He hasn't filed them yet, but he's got his usual lawyer in town making it plain that his client is prepared to file suits against the owner of the match factory, the town itself for not putting out the fire in a timely manner, and the three families who refused to keep the Burkes after the fire unless he receives a fair settlement, which is unlikely."

"He must have spoken to his lawyer before he came to Hill House. He hasn't seen him since," she countered until she realized he could have met with his lawyer in her office without anyone else knowing he had a visitor. "Why do you think he won't be able to collect a settlement?"

"The owner of the match factory had no insurance and left town a few days ago, penniless. The town is immune from lawsuits like this, and none of those families have either the ability or the obligation to pay Burke anything."

"Why didn't you tell me this before now?" she questioned, concerned that she might be added to Mr. Burke's list—a development that could bring to light her current legal difficulties concerning ownership of Hill House.

"Because Mr. Burke has no legitimate grounds for a lawsuit and no hope of recovering a single coin. More important, I have it on good authority that Judge Cheshire has instructed the town clerk not to file any lawsuits on the matter from Mr. Burke or anyone else until the dust settles, so to speak. That won't be for several months, by which time I'll be back in Candlewood permanently and I'll be able to look out for your interests, assuming I have the opportunity. You may have another lawyer by then," he added with a bit of a grin.

Emma shook her head, turned her mount around, and headed back up the lane. "Sometimes I wonder if that man has any heart at all. He seems absolutely determined to turn everyone in town against him."

They rode in silence until they reached the crossroads and turned left toward the tavern.

When they were riding side-by-side again, she found Mr. Breckenwith studying her. "Is there something you wanted to ask me?"

"No."

She furrowed her brow. "Then why are you looking at me like that?"

"Like what?"

She rolled her eyes and tightened her hold on the reins. "Never mind," she murmured, wondering if she might survive this prelude to courtship, let alone courtship itself.

Looking ahead, Emma saw the tent in the front yard of the tavern. The tent, however, was not a tent at all; rather, walls of canvas stretched between posts in four corners, with the top open to the elements. A flap of canvas covered a single opening that allowed folks inside.

She glanced at her companion and noted that his expression had hardened. "Progress hasn't been kind to all," she offered, thinking of how much Candlewood and its residents had changed since the construction of the canal as three men lined up outside the makeshift tent went inside together.

"In the end, most people profit one way or another," he noted.

"Everett Gray has every right to pursue profit. I just think misusing an animal, even a wild one, is an obscene way to do it."

"Granted, but not everyone would agree with you. To be fair, the panther is admittedly a curiosity in these parts. Most people have never seen one," he suggested as they approached the tavern and drew to a halt.

She shivered with the memory of her close encounter with the panther. "That doesn't give anyone the right to poke and prod the animal or give Mr. Gray the right to profit from the animal's misery."

He helped her to dismount and tethered the horses to a nearby post. "Appealing to the man's sensitivities might not be very successful," he cautioned when he returned to her. "I've already tried that. Do you have a specific approach in mind that you'll use when you talk to him?" he asked, offering her his arm.

Emma accepted his arm and smiled, but she decided not to tell him about the small purse secreted in the pocket of her cape. "Not yet, but I'm sure I'll think of something. Before I see Mr. Gray, I'd like to see the panther for myself," she suggested as the three men left the canvas structure and proceeded into the tavern itself.

He frowned. "I rather suspected you might."

When they reached the entrance, there were no sounds coming from the animal. A young boy of ten or eleven, with more freckles than fair skin on his face, was standing there protecting a coin box sitting on top of a wooden crate, with a stack of long poles lying on the ground next to a small saw sitting at his feet.

Shivering, he wore a coat far too thin and

threadbare for winter, and he had no hat to cover the unruly auburn curls on his head. He picked up the coin box and looked up at them. "Twenty-five cents to get inside. Ten cents for a pole. For another five cents, I can sharpen the pole real good."

"Just the viewing fee. No poles," Mr. Breckenwith replied.

When he reached into his pocket, Emma placed her hand on his arm. "Just a moment. Please."

Once he dropped his hand away, she turned her attention to the boy. "Has business been good?"

He nodded, shuffling from one foot to the other. "Not so much right now, but once the factories let out at six, it'll pick up again 'til about ten."

"Will you be working outside until then?" she asked.

"I gotta. My pa can't work. He got hurt in the explosion. My ma can't work. She's home takin' care of him and my five brothers and sisters," he offered, straightening his narrow shoulders. "I'm the oldest, so I'm doin' what I can to help."

With her heart heavy, Emma took a deep breath. "If I might ask, how much is Mr. Gray paying you?"

The boy shrugged. "He's not payin' me nothin', but he said I get to keep whatever I can make by sharpening the poles. Are you gonna let me sharpen up one for you? I'm really good with the saw. My pa taught me."

"What's your name?" Emma asked.

"Charles. Charles Schmidt, ma'am."

Emma smiled. "My name is Widow Garrett, and this is Mr. Breckenwith, my lawyer. I own Hill House. Do you know it?"

He shrugged again. "I don't think so. We just moved here a month ago. We're probably gonna have to move again, once Pa gets better."

"How much have you made since you started?"

He grinned. "All told, thirty-five cents."

She reached into her pocket to get her coin purse, counted out several coins, and handed them to him. "Here are three dollars, which is much more than you could expect to make in the next several days. You may keep them on one condition," she cautioned as he set down the coin box and shoved the coins into his pocket. "You must leave here now. Your work for Mr. Gray is done for good."

He glanced down at the coin box before grinning up at her again. "Yes, ma'am. Thank you, ma'am. But I still gotta charge you to see the panther."

She chuckled and thought she heard her escort chuckle, as well. "Of course."

While Charles waited for the coins, the boy's smile suddenly drooped into a frown. "I gotta give the coin box back to Mr. Gray. He's not gonna be happy about me leavin', especially in the middle of the day."

Zachary Breckenwith reached in front of Emma and handed the viewing fee to the boy, who quickly added it to the box. "I'll see to it that Mr. Gray gets his coin box and tell him you had to leave," he promised.

Charles hesitated for a moment before handing him the box. "You bein' a lawyer and all, I guess that'd be okay," he offered, looked at the entrance to the makeshift tent for a moment, and then up to Zachary Breckenwith. "You gonna stop Mr. Gray from lettin' people hit the panther?"

"Yes, I believe we are."

"Good," the boy said softly before scampering off with his newfound wealth jingling in his pocket.

"Thank you," Emma murmured.

Zachary cast a questioning look her way.

"For not interrupting me or trying to stop me."

He chuckled. "I wouldn't dream of it. You realize, of course, that Gray will probably have another boy here to replace young Charles in a matter of hours," he cautioned.

"Not if I have my way," she insisted and silently offered a prayer she might prevail as easily with Mr. Gray as she had with young Charles Schmidt.

23

THE MOMENT EMMA stepped onto the dirt floor inside the makeshift tent, she nearly gagged. The air was thick with the rancid stench of animal waste, blood, and the soul-wrenching smell of needless suffering and man's capacity for cruelty and greed.

The chain attached to a stake in the center of the canvas room and the panther's neck was so short the animal was virtually pinned to the ground. When she studied the animal that she had sighted in the back yard at Hill House only last week, her eyes filled with tears.

With its eyes closed, the panther lay very still, although muscles in its thin body twitched nervously. One of its hind legs lay at an unnatural angle. Caked with blood and fur, the chain was nearly embedded in the animal's neck.

Overwhelmed by evidence of the brutality the animal had endured, she turned away. "I've seen enough," she whispered and slipped past

Zachary Breckenwith to go back outside.

He followed her, let the flap fall back into place, and stood beside her, still holding the box of coins. "I'm sorry. If I had had any idea of the condition of that poor animal, I never would have agreed to let you—"

"I needed to see it," she insisted and swiped at her tears. "Why didn't someone stop this before now? Couldn't Sheriff North do something? Anything?" she asked, looking up at him.

"What Gray is doing here isn't illegal. Immoral, perhaps, but not illegal, which he quickly pointed out to me. To be fair, Sheriff North probably hasn't even seen the animal. He's still pretty busy," Zachary said gently.

When he locked his gaze with hers, she saw the same glint of anger that was making her heart beat faster. Then his gaze softened. "I can't be sure, but I doubt the animal will last much longer than another day or two."

"Which is another day or two of needless suffering and abuse," she countered as she glanced away and channeled her anger into determination. "I must see Mr. Gray."

The coins in the box he held jingled as he shifted it from one hand to another. "So do I. In all truth, I'd much prefer to see Gray again by myself, if only to have the satisfaction of forcing him to destroy the animal immediately without worrying about offending you."

She cocked her head. "Please. I'd like to try

speaking with him first. If he won't listen to me or I'm convinced I need your help, I'll ask you."

Reluctantly, Zachary handed her the coin box and deferred to her wishes. "I won't stop you, but I'd really prefer that you didn't go into that tavern. At least permit me to ask Gray to step outside where he won't have an audience and he won't feel obliged to dismiss your concerns in order to save face in front of his customers."

She hesitated for a moment before acquiescing. "Perhaps you're right."

"If he becomes agitated and treats you with disrespect of any kind, I'm not going to wait for you to ask for my help," he cautioned.

"Agreed."

His eyes widened ever so slightly. "Agreed? Without an argument?"

She smiled. "I'm not thoroughly unreasonable."

"Only occasionally," he retorted with a laugh and left her to enter the tavern to find Mr. Gray.

———

Half an hour later, Emma was chilled to the bone. Her feet were numb. So were her hands, despite the leather gloves she wore. She had spent the first twenty minutes waiting outside of the tavern, sending away two potential customers who wanted to see the panther.

The last ten frustrating minutes, however, she had spent arguing her concerns with Mr. Gray. A massive man, he towered over her, and his girth matched his impressive height. He probably would have taken the box of coins, spewed his outrage at her audacity for having dismissed the boy he had hired, and sent her away without a second thought, had it not been for Zachary Breckenwith's very lawyerly presence, although he had kept his word and held silent.

"In sum, madam," Mr. Gray concluded, "while you might disagree with me from now until Judgment Day, there's little you can do to stop me. I paid the bounty. The animal belongs to me. No one has the right to stand in a man's way to earn a profit, as long as he's within the confines of the law," he snarled, casting a disgusted look at Zachary Breckenwith before staring down at Emma again.

She held his gaze and stood her ground, refusing to be intimidated by his size or his glower. "Even if that profit comes at the expense of a helpless animal?"

"Profit is profit," he spat. "When a man's family is hungry, he has to feed them."

"And exactly what profit do you expect you might lose in the next day or two, which is probably all the time that animal has left?" she asked in a steady voice.

His eyes began to glitter. "Between viewing

fees and the like, not to mention the tendency of the curious to come inside the tavern for a bit of refreshment and to hear tales of the animal's capture . . ." He scratched the side of his head with one of his fleshy fingers. "I suspect I might earn thirty dollars. Hard cash."

She swallowed hard. The sum was outrageously exaggerated, and she had no way near that amount in her purse. "I'll pay you fifteen dollars if you'll agree to sell the animal to me."

Mr. Gray tightened his hold on his coin box. "Fifteen dollars? In hard cash?"

She nodded.

"The panther is yours."

She held back a smile and turned toward her escort. "Mr. Breckenwith, I wonder if I might ask for your help."

He edged closer.

"I need to get to the bank to make a withdrawal. While I'm gone, would you be kind enough to draw up a bill of sale for the panther?"

"Yes, of course, but I wonder if Mr. Gray would be willing to accept a note for fifteen dollars, payable no later than tomorrow. I'd be happy to deliver the funds for you before I leave. You'd find that acceptable, would you not, Mr. Gray, out of deference to Widow Garrett, who has been standing out in the cold for a considerable period of time."

"I . . . I would. Naturally, I would," the man sputtered.

"Thank you. I'll meet you inside in a few moments and we'll take care of the necessary paper work."

Without another word, Mr. Gray turned and went back inside the tavern.

Zachary Breckenwith smiled at Emma. "I shouldn't be very long. Will you be all right waiting here in the cold again, or would you rather I take you back home first?"

"I'd like to come inside with you," she countered. "While you're drawing up the papers with Mr. Gray, I think I should see if I can recruit some of the men inside to destroy the panther and take it back to Hill House, where I can be assured it's been buried properly; otherwise, I'm afraid that poor animal will be exploited, even after death, with any number of people willing to pay for a piece of fur or something," she explained.

"Think about what you just said," he urged. "Your plan has some merit, but in the end it's self-defeating."

"My plan is perfectly good, but your objection is self-serving. You're just bound and determined to keep me from going into that tavern."

He stepped aside. "Enter as you wish, although I caution you to consider something first. The men you might recruit inside to bury the animal, which is going to be no easy task with the ground frozen, are the very men who would be tempted to return later to dig it back up to get any sort of morbid treasure they might want from the carcass. That's why your plan is self-defeating."

Deflated by his argument and miffed she had not fully thought through her idea, she had no choice but to admit he was right. "I assume you have a better plan."

He smiled. "In point of fact, I might, but I'll need your help and I'll need to know more about where you think you might bury the panther back at Hill House."

———————

As they had planned together, Emma waited for Zachary Breckenwith in the woods behind Hill House near a narrow trail where it crossed the northernmost end of Main Street just beyond the town limits. In the distance, beyond the stark, barren woods, softened only by copses of candlewood and other evergreens, the frozen canal waited for spring.

Directly behind her, the woods were thicker with candlewood trees, which created a barrier between the roadway and the gazebo centered on the grassy plateau nestled at the base of the rose gardens that bordered the granite steps that led up to Hill House.

Shivering, she looked up at the thick gray cloud cover that blocked the late-afternoon sun.

The temperature had dropped significantly since midday. The air was still and expectant.

Snow was coming.

Both blessing and curse, snow was definitely coming.

Emma hugged her gloved hands together at her waist and walked back and forth behind a pair of massive candlewood trees to keep warm. In the several hours since she had parted company with Zachary Breckenwith, she had returned her mount to the livery and made her withdrawal at the bank before heading for home.

If she had not stopped at the General Store to have a chat with Mr. Atkins and warm up a bit, she never would have been able to withstand the cold for so long. She never would have gotten a tidbit of news that was bound to both gladden and irritate the two elderly matchmakers waiting for Emma at home, either.

Grinning to herself, she was not sure which tidbit to announce first—Mr. Atkins' news or the tale of how the panther had come to be buried at Hill House.

The moment she heard a rider approaching from the north, she stopped in her tracks. She peeked around one of the trees, recognized him immediately, and hurried into view to wave to him. "Over here. The trail is over here!"

Zachary Breckenwith headed directly toward her with a smile on his face. Behind him, a shovel rested on top of a long, narrow canvas sack that straddled the horse's rump. The closer the man got, the more she could see evidence that he had been able to carry out the initial phases of the plan they had devised together.

The front of his winter coat and his trousers were filthy, his gloves and boots caked with dirt. Though his shoulders slumped, his gaze, however, was sharp and alert.

When he was but a few yards away, he reined up, dismounted, and brushed what he could from his outerwear.

"Did you have any trouble?" she asked.

"I wouldn't describe the crowd this whole affair attracted as troublesome—just curious. Digging the first two graves in frozen ground wasn't easy. I do hope you were serious about that dry creek bed. I'm not sure I can dig another hole."

"You dug two graves?" she asked a bit incredulously.

"The first one is just south of the old toll collector's cabin. For good measure, since I convinced Gray to sell me all of the canvas he had, I had enough to fashion three sacks and rode a little farther south to dig another hole. Then I crossed the canal, skirted west around town, and crossed the bridge over the canal just north of here."

He stopped and grinned. "I doubt anyone

who tried to follow me will have the energy to get past that second grave. If they do, they'll continue looking south, not here."

"I hope so. If you'll come with me, I'll show you the way to the creek bed," Emma said, anxious to be done and back inside out of the cold. Zachary walked alongside her, holding the reins so the horse followed behind him. "At least I had the opportunity to warm up a bit. You must be frozen." Remembering the money she had withdrawn from the bank, she handed it to him.

He slipped the money into his pocket. "Not really. Between the physical work of digging as much as I did and riding a good ways, I'm fairly comfortable. I'll see that Gray gets his money on my way home," he promised and looked up at the overcast sky. "There's a snowstorm coming. That should help keep our tracks covered and the real grave hidden for a good while."

"Snow usually accumulates fairly quickly. You may have to delay your trip," she noted as they followed the trail back toward Hill House.

"I hope not. In any event, if I leave at first light and head south, I might be able to outride the worst of the storm before heading east."

Emma knew him well enough not to argue, but she decided to press him on another matter. Curious about his original plans for their outing today, she smiled up at him as they continued walking along the trail. "Can you tell me where we were going before we got sidetracked at the tavern?"

He shrugged. "I could, but since I'm still planning to take you there, I don't believe I will."

"Then it's a secret," she offered, growing more curious.

"No," he countered, "it's a surprise."

She stepped over a branch that had fallen into the trail in front of her. "There's hardly a difference between one and the other."

He chuckled. "I beg to argue, but there is. It's a surprise because I'm the only one who knows where I wanted to take you today. If it were a secret, we'd both know, but no one else would."

She pursed her lips. "I should have known you'd enjoy yet another opportunity to play with my words. You're not going to tell me where we were going, are you?"

"Not today. It's a surprise, remember?"

She sighed, spied the outline of the see-through tree that stretched a good thirty feet into the air, and pointed to her left. "If we leave the trail up ahead by that see-through tree, the creek bed isn't far."

"A see-through tree?" he questioned.

"The oak tree that appears to have two trunks. That's the see-through tree. I suppose it's hard to see from this angle," she explained. When they got closer, she hurried ahead and around to the right side, where she waited for him. "See? It's one single trunk. There's just a huge hole in the center, like a window. From this direction, you can literally see through the tree."

He poked his head inside the opening, glanced around, and shrugged. "I'm surprised the tree can survive like this, but I can imagine any number of critters who might want to hole up here in a storm."

"Probably," she agreed, wondering if the chickens had found this hideaway when they had escaped from the panther. Anxious to get to the task at hand, she led him off the trail and through the woods. When they reached the place she had in mind, she stopped and drew in a long breath. Beneath the canopy of barren branches and evergreen candlewood trees overhead, pine needles and broken tree limbs littered the dry creek bed. The air was laced with the heady scent of timber and pine. "Will this do?" she asked.

"This will do," he murmured. After tying up the horse, he made quick work of clearing a section in the creek bed, untied the canvas sack, and laid the panther's body in place. When he started breaking up the frozen soil along the creek bed to cover the canvas, he nodded toward a number of dead tree limbs. "If you could collect some of those, along with some pine needles, we can cover the dirt."

She did as he asked and lugged several tree limbs over to the site while he finished shoveling the dirt. While he positioned the tree limbs, she used her cape as an apron and filled it several times with pine needles she dropped on top of the branches.

By the time they finished, there were so many pine needles stuck to her woolen cape, she was not sure she would ever get them all out. Her gloves were stained with dirt, but working hard had helped to warm her up. She glanced at the panther's final resting-place with a heavy heart.

"What's wrong?" Zachary asked as he moved to face her. "I can't imagine that anyone will be able to tell there's anything buried here."

Emma sighed. "I can't help thinking that this was all my fault. If I hadn't rushed outside that night, I'd never have seen the panther. And I never would have sounded the alert if I had had any inkling of the suffering that poor animal would have to endure."

"You had to alert everyone," he said. "That animal posed a very real threat. Someone could have been killed or badly hurt."

"That's what I keep telling myself," she whispered. When she looked up at him, she found his gaze was both gentle and understanding. "I'm so grateful for your help today, and I really should apologize. I'm afraid I quite spoiled the plans you made for our outing today."

His gaze became so tender, he almost took her breath away. "I wanted to spend my afternoon with a spirited but very kind and very good woman," he countered. "And I did."

She held his gaze but a moment before she dropped her eyes, warmth filling her cheeks.

"There will be other days and other outings we'll share together as soon as I return," he promised.

Silently, Emma made a promise to herself to hold him to his word . . . if only to discover whether or not she could spend the rest of her life with this spirited, very kind, and very good man.

24

AFTER ZACHARY Breckenwith left to deliver the money to Mr. Gray, Emma entered the boardinghouse through the front door. Instantly she knew that unless she literally secreted herself in her bedroom, enjoying any semblance of privacy at Hill House was a bit like trying to find peace and quiet during the Founders' Day celebrations last fall—difficult and tedious and nigh impossible.

She had scarcely shut the door behind her when she encountered the Masseys and Reverend Glenn sitting together in the west parlor. Judith Massey smiled and waved to Emma. "Did you enjoy your afternoon with Mr. Breckenwith?"

"Very much," Emma replied.

"As soon as you're able, do come and tell us all about it," the young woman urged.

"I will," Emma promised, not quite sure how much or how little she was willing to share about her remarkable outing. After removing her soiled gloves and bonnet, she stored them on the oak rack just inside the door and savored the heat coming from fires burning in the parlors on either side of her. Once she noticed all the pine needles still stuck to her dark green cape, she simply removed the garment, turned it inside out, and folded it over her arm to carry out to the kitchen for brushing.

"Widow Garrett! You're back," Malcolm Lewis noted, calling out to her from the east parlor he was sharing with the Ammond brothers. His gaze was both curious and anxious for details. "I trust your ride went well?" he asked.

"Very well," she managed, nodding to the other two men who were listening with rapt attention, "but I'm afraid I need a hot cup of tea to warm up."

"I don't doubt it. When you have a moment, I'd like to show you the hallway design. I finished sketching it earlier this afternoon."

"Mr. Burke wasn't sitting for his portrait?"

"He insisted on starting the suit of clothes he promised to make for me. Just be careful of the scaffolding in the hallway. I moved it a bit," he cautioned.

"I will," she promised. Carefully she made her way down the hallway and slowed down to skirt the scaffolding. As anxious as she was to see the contraption removed, she had yet to decide exactly how to tell the artist she could not, as a matter of good conscience and fiscal prudence, allow him to proceed with his plans to stencil the hallway without being certain she would be here long enough to enjoy it.

She cleared the scaffolding but had barely passed by the center staircase when the library door opened and Orralynne Burke poked her head out. "I thought I heard your voice. My brother and I wish to speak with you, but you seem to prefer prolonging your outing with Mr. Breckenwith instead of seeing to your responsibilities as proprietress," she noted sourly.

"As you know, I had an appointment with my lawyer," Emma retorted truthfully. He was, in fact, her lawyer, at least until tomorrow. "If you like, I can stop in the library to speak with you both once I warm up a bit."

"Yes, but don't be too long. It's close to time for supper, and my brother has needs that must be tended before we eat," she snapped and shut the door.

Ignoring the woman's rudeness, Emma proceeded to the dining room, where Liesel was busy setting the table for supper.

The young woman stopped, looked at Emma, and grinned. "Mother Garrett and Aunt Frances have been in the kitchen for over an hour waiting for you to return, but I told them you probably wouldn't be home until closer to supper. Ditty thought you might even have supper with Mr. Breckenwith at his home, but I guess she was wrong, too. Would you like me to hang up your cape for you?" she asked as she laid out the last of the silverware.

Emma shook her head. "It needs a good brushing first," she said, wishing she could dispel the notion that absolutely everyone seemed a bit too preoccupied with how she had spent her afternoon.

To be fair, Zachary Breckenwith had made no secret at dinner that they were spending the afternoon together. To be honest, she found it unsettling to find both the guests and the residents and staff so interested in the details, except for the Burkes, who typically only thought about themselves.

A loud crash overhead made Emma flinch, and she glanced up at the ceiling. "If I hadn't been proved wrong lately, I'd suspect Ditty might be having a problem upstairs."

Liesel frowned. "Actually, Mother Garrett sent her up with the warm water and linens for Mr. Burke's room. He prefers having them brought up before supper," she explained as she set out the last of the utensils. "I'm finished here. Would you like me to go up and see if Ditty needs help?"

With visions of water spilled in Lester Burke's room, Emma nodded. "Maybe you should."

"I really, really hope you had a pleasant time with Mr. Breckenwith," the young woman gushed before hurrying out of the room.

Emma drew in a deep breath, crossed the dining room, and followed the sweet aromas to her mother-in-law's domain. Prepared for a thorough questioning about her afternoon from both of the elderly women waiting for her, she opened the door to the kitchen.

Mother Garrett was standing slicing the first of three loaves of pumpernickel bread on the kitchen table, while Aunt Frances sat arranging a plate of fried apple cider doughnuts. "It certainly smells good in here. And it's nice and warm, too," Emma offered by way of announcing herself before closing the door behind her.

Aunt Frances immediately rose from her seat. "You must be chilled to the bone, you've got so little meat on you. I put water on the stove a bit ago to make you a good hot cup of tea. It won't take more than a minute or two," she promised as she hurried to the cookstove.

"Thank you," Emma replied as she walked over to a peg on the wall near the back door. She hung up her cape under Mother Garrett's watchful gaze. "What's on the cookstove that smells so good?"

"Beans with molasses and bacon."

With her mouth watering, Emma joined her mother-in-law at the kitchen table and snatched the heel of the still-warm bread. "You're rather mum," she noted before taking a nibble. "I thought you'd start peppering me with questions about my afternoon the moment I arrived."

Mother Garrett stopped slicing and narrowed her gaze while staring at Emma as she sat down. "I didn't ask you anything because I was too busy thinking."

Emma raised a brow. "Thinking? About what?"

"About how oddly you were walking," Mother Garrett replied before resuming her task.

Aunt Frances set a cup of tea in front of Emma and sat down beside her. "I don't see what all the fuss is about. To my eye, you were walking very normally," she murmured and patted Emma's arm.

Mother Garrett sighed. "Which is precisely my point," she argued and waved the knife in the air as she spoke. "After you went riding with the Mitchell sisters last fall, you were so sore you couldn't walk normally again for a week."

Emma cringed. "True."

"Which makes we wonder how it is that after spending the entire afternoon riding with Mr. Breckenwith, when you haven't been on a horse since then, you don't seem to have any trouble walking at all. That's what I think is odd," Mother Garrett explained.

Emma took a sip of tea and shrugged. "I could argue that I was gone the entire day last fall, not a few hours like today, but in all truth, I rode scarcely more than half an hour this afternoon," she offered and continued to sip at her tea.

Mother Garrett laid down her knife, glanced over at Emma's soiled cape, and frowned. "You got tossed off that horse, didn't you? I knew going for a horseback ride wasn't a good idea, and I told that man so! You don't look like you hurt yourself, but you certainly could have," she huffed. "If he wanted to take you for a ride, he should have brought a carriage, and I have every mind to make sure of it next time."

Emma sputtered and choked on her tea. "You talked to him? You actually talked to him about taking me for a ride this afternoon? When?" she asked as she caught her breath.

"While we were waiting for you to come down for dinner on Sunday," Aunt Frances replied. "He listened to Mercy's concerns well enough, but the man certainly knows his own mind where you're concerned."

"But not very forthcoming about where he intended to take you," Mother Garrett complained. "Exactly where did he take you, or is that a secret?"

Emma shrugged. "It's not a secret, but since we never actually rode far enough to get there, I wouldn't be able to tell you where we were headed."

Aunt Frances brightened. "Then it's a surprise. Did he tell you when he would be able to take you there?"

Mother Garrett scowled. "Don't let her keep changing the subject like that, Frances," she cautioned before looking directly at Emma. "Tell me how you fell off the horse."

"I didn't fall off the horse. I've never fallen off a horse in my life!" Emma exclaimed and wrapped her hands around her teacup and let out a sigh. If and when she did decide to be courted formally, there were no two ways around it—the three of them had to sit down and discuss exactly what rules each of them would follow. The first rule was that she was not going to be questioned about every moment she had spent with the man.

"If you didn't fall, how did those pine needles get all over your cape? Really, Emma. First chicken feathers and now pine needles! You should take better care of your cape. It's the only one you've got. And if you weren't riding, what were you doing all afternoon?" Mother Garrett prompted, pressing for more information.

"I wasn't riding because we had a change of plans. We stopped at Gray's Tavern, where I bought the panther from Mr. Gray and had it destroyed so it wouldn't suffer any longer," she said, much to the older woman's surprise.

Confident they were alone and would not be

overheard because the guests respected the kitchen as a domain reserved for the permanent residents and staff, she quickly explained what she had seen inside the makeshift tent. "My cape got dirty when I helped Mr. Breckenwith bury the panther in the woods behind the gazebo," she informed them, rendering both Aunt Frances and Mother Garrett speechless.

"I'll talk to Reverend Glenn and tell him the entire story, too, but I think it's wise to keep the location of the animal's grave a secret," she cautioned, all too familiar with Mother Garrett's struggle to keep a secret of any kind. "Otherwise, we're bound to have any number of profit-hungry people digging up the grounds to find the panther and plunder its body for gruesome souvenirs to sell to others. Mr. Breckenwith went to a great deal of trouble to cover our tracks, so to speak." Emma then nonchalantly took a long sip of tea.

Aunt Frances clapped her hand to her heart. "The panther is here? At Hill House?"

"The poor animal is dead and buried," Mother Garrett commented drily. "I don't suppose the two of you managed to get everything done today without garnering any attention, did you?"

Emma shrugged. "The customers in the tavern were quite fascinated," she admitted. "Obviously, since I had several tasks to tend to, I wasn't with Mr. Breckenwith when he rode down Main Street with the panther's body strapped to his horse, but I think it's fairly safe to consider he drew most folks' attention. He rode out of town to the south," she added, "just in case anyone decided to follow him."

Aunt Frances looked at Emma and frowned. "As much as I admire what you did, do you think it was wise to get involved like that? If the real owner of Hill House should arrive now and hear the gossip, he might not be inclined to let you buy Hill House again."

"I agree," Mother Garrett offered. "You did a good deed today, but the last thing you need attached to your name right now is gossip. And regardless of whether or not we keep your secret, whatever will you do if someone does dig up the grounds anyway because he suspects you deliberately tried to fool everyone and the owner arrives to find the grounds ruined?"

Emma smiled and got up from her chair. "I'll simply have to be honest, explain what really happened, and pray the owner is a man of good character and conscience. Now, if you'll both excuse me for a moment, I need to speak to the Burkes. Apparently, they have something very important they need to discuss with me."

She left them at the kitchen table, speechless again. She was tempted to turn and suggest they have a chat later about setting up some guidelines to guarantee Emma some autonomy as well as privacy in her dealings with Mr.

Breckenwith, but she decided to wait since Zachary would not be back for a good five to six weeks.

She did, however, turn around to share a bit of news with them. "Oh, I almost forgot to tell you. I stopped at the General Store to see Mr. Atkins. He has some rather interesting news for you," she teased before turning around again.

The two women were busy arguing about what Mr. Atkins' news might be when she opened the door, stepped into the dining room, and nearly collided with Mr. Lewis.

He stumbled back so quickly, he barely managed to stay on his feet. His cheeks flushed dark red and his eyes widened with embarrassment. "I . . . I can explain," he stuttered. "Please let me explain. I didn't mean to be eavesdropping."

M R. LEWIS!"
      Instinctively, Emma reached around
and closed the door behind her before Mother
Garrett and Aunt Frances discovered there had
been another set of ears listening to them. With
her heart pounding from both shock and disbelief, Emma did not know if she or Mr. Lewis
was more surprised to see the other. She was
tempted to vent her outrage that he had become
privy to her very private and personal conversation with Mother Garrett and Aunt Frances,
but the poor man looked too pathetic and too
upset with himself.

      "I'm truly, truly sorry." He dropped his gaze
and hung his head, the image of pure remorse.
"I can only imagine how angry you must be
with me. I could hear you were all having a conversation and felt uncomfortable interrupting,
but the longer I waited, the more awkward the
situation became. If I waited far enough from

the door to avoid eavesdropping, I was too far away to know when you'd finished your conversation."

He sighed and wrung his hands together as he looked up at her with tear-filled eyes. "I only wanted to fetch some water for Mrs. Massey."

"For Mrs. Massey? Perhaps you might be able to tell me why you would have been the one to see to her needs instead of her husband. He was with her in the west parlor. As I recall, you were across the hall," she countered.

He blinked hard. "Mr. Massey was with the Ammond brothers helping Mr. Burke. After I escorted Miss Burke to the west parlor, Mrs. Massey thought I might help further by getting some water for Miss Burke."

Emma shook her head several times to knock his words around in her mind, hoping they might make sense, but failed. "I'm afraid I don't understand—"

"Mr. Burke took a fall at the bottom of the staircase. Miss Burke ran into the parlor to ask for our help."

"Whatever were you thinking? Since this was an emergency, you should have interrupted and come directly to me to tell me what happened," she charged. "Depending on how badly Mr. Burke is hurt, I may need to send for Dr. Jeffers."

The man paled. "But Mr. Burke insisted there was no real emergency. He said he tripped trying to manage the first step and hurt his deformed foot. He was quite insistent the whole mishap could have been avoided had you been home earlier to make arrangements for him to turn your office into a sleeping room again so he could have all his accommodations on the first floor. He was even more adamant about not wanting anyone to send for the doctor, although reaching town to fetch him would decidedly be very difficult."

Emma's stomach clenched. "Mr. Burke told you he wants to move into my office?"

"He already sent Mr. Massey and the Ammonds upstairs to the garret to get the sleeping cot and mattress his sister used while she stayed there." He paused and lowered his voice. "I'm afraid he had a bit of an argument earlier with his sister. He was very forceful and nasty to her after his mishap, and he absolutely refused to have her tend to him. She was quite distressed," he added. "I hope Reverend Glenn was able to help her in that regard."

Emma imagined all sorts of ways the middle-aged spinster might react to Reverend Glenn's advice. She also found it rather preposterous that no one had the presence of mind to notify her immediately about what was happening, since she was the proprietress.

"And no one, not a single person, thought to send for me first before doing what Mr. Burke ordered them all to do?" she managed.

Mr. Lewis's gaze grew tender. "Since you had such a pleasant afternoon, no one wanted to spoil it," he offered meekly. "Not when you've been so kind and worked so hard for all of us. We thought you deserved not to have your day ruined by the Burkes."

Truly touched, but not placated, Emma drew in a long breath. "While I appreciate everyone's concern, I've never, ever put my personal interests above the needs of my guests, even difficult ones."

"We meant no harm."

"I know, but right now I need to see how Mr. Burke is faring, as well as Miss Burke," she said firmly. "Before I go, I must ask you in the strongest way possible not to repeat to anyone at all anything you overhead us talking about in the kitchen."

His head bobbed up and down. "On my word. I'll say nothing to anyone at all," he promised, leaned forward, and lowered his voice. "I would never forgive myself if I betrayed you and found the grounds here at Hill House dug up by opportunistic, sadistic profit-mongers or . . . or added to your worries about your current legal problem and your anxiety while waiting for the real owner to appear."

Her heart dimmed with despair that he had overhead so much and in such detail. When she went to speak, he held up his hand. "Please believe me. I'll tell no one. You have nothing to fear on my account."

"I pray not," she whispered.

"As a way of making amends, I want to stencil the hallway for you at no cost and with as little inconvenience as possible. I'll work at night, if need be."

"That's not necessary," she insisted, keeping her voice low. "As you well understand now, I don't have the legal or moral right to authorize any further refinements to Hill House."

He cocked his head and smiled. "No one, least of all the heir and rightful owner, would object to adding to the beauty of Hill House."

"Perhaps not," she argued, "but I will be the one held accountable."

"By custom, I always sign my work. Should there be any ramifications, which I most sincerely assure you will not develop, given my years of experience in hundreds of homes, then my name, not yours, will be there to take the blame."

When she remained silent, holding firm to her position, he relented. "I defer to your wishes," he said reluctantly.

"I think that would be best," she murmured, but before she could say more, Liesel scampered into the dining room with Ditty on her heels. "Excuse me, Mr. Lewis. Widow Garrett? We just finished mopping up the water in Mr. Burke's room and were coming downstairs when we saw Mr. Massey and the Ammonds moving a sleeping cot downstairs. Is it true Mr. Burke is moving? Again?"

"Apparently," Emma admitted. "For now, why don't you both see if Mother Garrett needs help in the kitchen and see that Mr. Lewis gets a glass of water for Mrs. Massey. I want to see if Mr. Burke might want to reconsider," she said and headed straight for the library to set Mr. Burke straight about who was in charge at Hill House.

————

With the heavy drapes closed to ward off the winter cold and the oil lamps burning low, the image of Lester Burke was shadowed and barely distinct as he sat in one of two leather chairs facing the fireplace.

Although he had called out after she had knocked and allowed her to enter, he made no effort to speak to her as she skirted the piles of fabric and two boxes containing the tools of his trade. She sat down in the chair next to his and noted that he had his injured foot covered and resting on a hassock someone had brought in from a front parlor.

With his face drenched with sweat that glistened in the firelight and his clothing uncommonly disheveled, he stared directly into the fire and acknowledged her presence with a grunt. "Your interest in my welfare comes too late."

"I came as soon as I was told about your fall. Do you need Dr. Jeffers to come or will you be able to care for yourself?"

"If and when I need a doctor, I'll send for one myself," he spat. "Until then, I must insist on the service, as well as the privacy, you accord to your other guests."

"I've been making every effort to do that."

"If that were true, you would have been here earlier, and I would have been able to inform you that I cannot accommodate climbing the stairs several times a day to reach my bedroom. You would have immediately moved a sleeping cot and my belongings into the adjoining office. Instead, you were obviously more interested in pursuing your own affairs. My mishap on the stairs could have been and should have been avoided."

"I had no idea you needed to change your accommodations or that you wanted to speak to me until I returned. I had an appointment today with my lawyer that unavoidably took longer than expected," she explained, annoyed that she felt obliged to make excuses for herself to this rude and pompous man.

"Given what happened while you were gone, you could very well need another."

"Another appointment or another lawyer?" she quipped.

"I care little about your choice of a lawyer."

"Then I assume you're suggesting I make

an appointment with him," she prompted. "Is that because you're planning a lawsuit against me for not seeing that you didn't trip and fall on the staircase?"

He chortled. "Lawsuits serve no greater purpose than to remind people, by lightening their purses, they should take their obligations seriously. I find my lawyer quite useful in that regard."

"Would you be going into town to see your lawyer and instruct him to file suit, or would you simply have him call on you at Hill House again by way of my office door so no one would know what you were doing?"

He ignored her questions.

She pressed harder. "Or do you expect that I will be so intimidated by the threat of a lawsuit that I would offer you a settlement—just like you expect of the others you've sued as a result of the fire that damaged your cottage?"

When he still remained mute, she folded her hands in her lap and drew in a deep breath. Last fall, she had been frightened witless when Mr. Langhorne attempted to force her hand by threatening a lawsuit. She refused to make the same mistake with Mr. Burke. Even though a lawsuit now would make her very tenuous status as the owner of Hill House public knowledge, she was almost at the point where she did not care who found out. "Unfortunately for you, sir, I am neither intimidated nor frightened by your threat to sue me," she said calmly.

He repositioned his foot and groaned ever so softly. "You overstate my intentions and understate your own position," he stated gruffly.

"You're wrong on both counts," she argued. "I did not overstate your intentions. Based on the number of lawsuits you've filed against other residents of Candlewood over the years and even recently, I believe you were very definitely implying a lawsuit would be your course of action against me. My position as owner and proprietress of Hill House and my reputation as a competent and fair woman of business are well-known and equally well-respected," she retorted.

With her cheeks growing warm, she continued. "I have a decided advantage should you decide to sue me, and I promise you that I will use the considerable funds at my disposal to guarantee that you will lose everything you own to pursue such a lawsuit, only to find that the courts will prevail on my side in the end."

He turned slightly away from her.

"As long as you remain here as my guest, I must insist that you bring your complaints to me directly and in a timely manner to allow me to accommodate you as best I can. Bullying the other guests to do your bidding without waiting for my instructions or my approval ends here and it ends now, or you will have to find other living arrangements."

This time he did respond—eventually—with a quick nod.

She was surprised by his acquiescence, but she assumed the man was simply a bully who was not accustomed to having anyone stand up to him. Or perhaps he felt too poorly to argue with her. In any event, he was still her guest—an injured guest, as well—and she felt compelled to see to his comfort. "May I assume you are now satisfied having use of my office for your bedroom?"

Another nod.

"I rode by your cottage today. The damage to the roof is extensive. Have you any idea of how long it will take to make the repairs so you and your sister can return home?"

He stiffened. "Once I've fully recovered from my mishap today, I will be certain to pursue the matter. In the meantime, I suggest you confine your interests to seeing that my sister and I are properly cared for here at Hill House."

Rather than agitate the man any further by responding, she rose from her seat. "I need to go into my office to remove some of my papers before I look in on your sister. I understand she was very distressed by your mishap."

He snorted. "My sister has lived in a state of distress for most of her life."

Emma ignored his cold, flippant remark.

"I'll have your meals brought to you for a few days so you can continue to recuperate," she offered. She made her way to her office wondering what it was that had sparked the argument between this very odd man and his sister and how that might affect the remainder of their stay at Hill House.

26

SOME DAYS, being proprietress at Hill House had its decided disadvantages.

Once again Emma stored away her papers upstairs in her bedroom, along with the rest of the contents of her desk, including the skates she had shoved into one of the drawers. When she finished, she went to the west parlor to see how Orralynne was faring and found Reverend Glenn alone, dozing on the settee. Orralynne and Mrs. Massey were gone. Even his faithful companion, Butter, was missing.

Tempted by the warm fire and the opportunity to get off of her feet, she sat down on the chair facing the retired minister to rest for a moment before going back upstairs.

Almost immediately, he stirred awake. "Emma!"

"I didn't mean to disturb you. I was looking for Miss Burke," she explained.

"I believe she's upstairs resting."

"And Mrs. Massey?"

"She went upstairs, as well. The menfolk decided to bring a good supply of firewood closer to the house and store it on the side porch before the snowstorm hits. I was just sitting here hoping you'd come and keep me company. I guess I fell asleep."

Emma glanced at the floor by his feet. "Butter is usually resting close-by. He didn't go upstairs or venture outside, did he?"

"Not when he's been invited to the kitchen for something tasty."

Emma sent a questioning look to Reverend Glenn. Mother Garrett tolerated the dog; she certainly did not spoil it.

The retired minister chuckled. "Apparently there was a spill of some kind. Frances said something about beans and molasses when she came for Butter. That dog will eat most anything that accidentally ends up on the floor," he remarked with a chuckle.

She laughed with him, knowing full well he "accidentally" dropped more than he should at mealtimes, much to Butter's pleasure. "I'm sorry. I wasn't aware of what happened with the Burkes earlier. I hope it wasn't too difficult to have Miss Burke brought to you to be consoled."

He let out a deep sigh, as if recalling the incident some years ago involving Orralynne and his late wife, Letty. "I don't believe it's my place to judge the poor woman, but I am called to forgive her. I spoke with her a short while, but I'm afraid she wasn't very receptive."

Emma was not surprised. "From what I've been told, she had some sort of an argument with her brother before his mishap."

He rubbed his left thigh. "Whatever it is they argued about surely upset her, but I spent the better part of the little time she was with me trying to help her stop weeping. Fortunately, Mrs. Massey fared better in that regard."

Emma furrowed her brow. "Are you certain? Judith Massey and Orralynne Burke were actually conversing together? Amicably?"

He smiled. "Mrs. Massey was very attentive and very sweet to poor Miss Burke."

"Judith has a good heart," Emma whispered. "I just think it's a miracle that Miss Burke actually turned to her and that Judith, in turn, would be willing to offer comfort to the poor woman," Emma said. She did recall, however, that after Orralynne's nosebleed, the woman had eventually shed her bitter shell when Emma intervened, if only for a few hours.

"Miracles abound most frequently in the common events of daily life, though we don't always notice them," he suggested.

Emma leaned back in the tapestry chair and shook her head. "I would definitely have noticed that miracle." Completely content to simply sit by the fire with Reverend Glenn, she let out a sigh. "As much as I would like to sit here with you, I should probably go upstairs and check on Miss Burke."

"Or you could let Mrs. Massey continue to see to her. Miracles take time. So does forgiveness, Emma. Perhaps you should let the two of them have some time alone. I think if Mrs. Massey needs your help, she'll let you know. I'm quite certain Miss Burke would."

"You're right, as usual," she admitted. Oddly, for the first time since she had opened Hill House to guests, she found it a relief rather than a disappointment to relinquish her role as hostess and peacekeeper to someone else. In all truth, however, she had never had guests as demanding or temperamental as the Burkes.

Given the choice, Emma much preferred enjoying Reverend Glenn's company at the moment, especially since she had had little opportunity to spend time with him since the tragedy. "Aunt Frances tells me you had a meeting with members of the church vestry a few days ago," she began, anxious to find out if Aunt Frances was right about the true purpose behind the meeting.

"Reverend Austin, as well. He was kind enough to take me with him," he replied as he bent his left arm at the elbow and repeated the motion, as if his arm had begun to tingle.

"I suppose they wanted to formally thank both of you for all the hours you spent with the victims and their families."

He laid his arm flat again at his side. "They did. I've been mulling over something we discussed at the meeting and waiting for an opportunity to talk with you about it. Perhaps now would be as good a time as any since everyone else seems busy elsewhere," he suggested.

Emma edged forward in her seat.

"I hope you know how much I've enjoyed being with you all at Hill House," he began.

He slowly explained why both he and Reverend Austin had been summoned to the meeting, and by the time he finished, she had to wipe away more than a few tears. Reverend Glenn was right. Miracles truly did happen in the everyday moments of life, but this particular miracle was almost beyond belief: Reverend Glenn had been given the opportunity to return to the pulpit.

"After my stroke, when I lost my pulpit, I never, ever thought I'd be called to service again," he murmured.

"I knew Reverend Austin was very busy since the congregation has grown considerably, along with the town, but I hadn't realized they were looking for someone to assist him," she offered. Like other women, however, Emma was rarely privy to the workings of the all-male vestry, unless they needed the women's help to raise money for the church.

"Apparently they've been considering the

idea of having an assistant pastor for some time. The great need of the congregation after the tragedy merely prompted them to consider it more seriously," he replied.

"If you accept their offer, would you have to leave Hill House to live in the parsonage?" she asked, unable to fathom how much he would be missed by all of them.

"It wouldn't be proper to live at the parsonage. Once there's an associate pastor, Reverend Austin will be riding circuit as the senior pastor, trying to visit folks who live a good distance from town, so Mrs. Austin will often be at the parsonage alone. There's a small two-room cottage in the center of town where they'd like me to live to be close at hand for the members of the congregation here in Candlewood. I'd also be available, of course, to assist Reverend Austin when he is in town."

She swallowed hard, reluctant to voice any concern that might give him reason to decline the offer. She was thrilled that he had the opportunity to resume his active ministry, but she was also fearful that the disabilities caused by his stroke would once again prevent him from tending to the flock of believers he so dearly loved. "Living alone would be difficult for you," she murmured.

His eyes began to twinkle. "But I wouldn't be living alone," he countered. "Not if Frances agrees to be my wife."

With her eyes wide, Emma clapped her hand to her mouth. Overwhelmed, overjoyed, and elated, she could not win the struggle to find her voice or to fully comprehend that she would be losing not one but two very special members of her Hill House family.

He chuckled. "Don't look so surprised! I should think it's been fairly obvious that I've grown sweet on the woman since she came to Hill House last fall, but I surely could not act on my feelings. I had no means to support myself, let alone a wife. Serving as an assistant pastor, however, I'd receive a stipend. It's small, but we could manage if we were frugal."

The expression in his eyes grew serious. "Do you think it's wise for me to consider returning to my ministry again? Or marrying again? Or am I just an old man, tricked into chasing after a foolish dream that I might serve God in a greater capacity again and have a helpmate by my side?"

"You're the wisest man I know," she replied. "We were all blessed the day you came to live with us at Hill House and every day since," Emma insisted. "I find it impossible to believe that He would present you with this remarkable opportunity only to make you appear foolish if you accept it. He isn't teasing you or tricking you. He's trying to reward you for your faithfulness."

Reverend Glenn nodded ever so slowly and

smiled. "If you hadn't been uncommonly charitable and welcomed me into your home, I'm not sure what would have happened to me after I took sick. I firmly believe He led me to you, and I thank you, dearest Emma."

She pulled her head back and stared at him. "There's no need to thank me. I've probably hounded you to help me when my faith grew weak more than anyone else at Hill House."

"You've been both daughter and friend to an old man who came to Hill House with neither, and you've given me the courage to believe He had a purpose for me in this world when no one else did, including myself."

Humbled, she bowed her head. "You're very kind."

"I'm being very candid."

She let out a long sigh before lifting her head and facing him again. "As you know, I'm not certain about my own future or what purpose I might serve. With Jonas passed on and our three boys grown with families of their own, continuing to operate the General Store did not seem to be enough. I've been waiting for months now to find out if buying Hill House was just a foolish and costly mistake or if this is where I'm suppose to be. I'm afraid Mr. Breckenwith's proposal adds yet another layer to my already confused, very uncertain situation."

"You might consider that being here at Hill House was all part of His plan. You just haven't discovered how long He intended for you to be here. You might also want to consider Mr. Breckenwith's proposal in the same way, regardless of whether you accept it or not. There are always lessons to be learned along the way," he offered.

She cocked her head. "I hadn't thought about it from that perspective."

"Prayer helps, but so does patience."

"And so do you. I'm going to miss your guidance, but mostly I will truly, truly miss you," she whispered and blinked back another swell of tears.

"I haven't left yet," he cautioned with a chuckle. "What I really need is your help to find the right time and the right place to propose to Frances without having an audience. I wouldn't mind so much if I were certain she'd accept my proposal, but I'd rather not have anyone watching if she rejects me."

"I don't think she'll do that, but of course I'll help," she said. "Why not propose in the gazebo? You and Aunt Frances spent a lot of time there last fall."

He drew back, his eyes wide with disbelief. "The gazebo? In this weather? Even if the snowstorm that's coming drops less that the usual two or three feet of snow, it's far too cold outside. By the time Frances and I both managed down all of the steps to get to the gazebo, we'd have to turn right around to get back to the house. And I surely don't want to wait until spring, nor can I. The vestry expects an answer within a month or so."

"Unless the snow interferes, Aunt Frances is going home a week from Sunday, which doesn't give us much time," she added as her mind raced through the possibilities. If Mr. Burke had not commandeered the library, that would have been her first choice. With so many guests, using one of the two parlors was also not an option, which pretty much made finding a private place for them inside Hill House a problem. "Wait. I know. I know a perfect place! There'd be no stairs involved. I'd make sure it was warm enough and cozy and private. It's perfect! I only need some time to arrange things. Just leave it up to me," she urged. "You have more important things to think about."

When he frowned, she chuckled. "You have to plan how to propose to Aunt Frances so she definitely says yes," she suggested, quite certain Aunt Fances would consider this "winter suitor" as the exception to the stereotype she and Mother Garrett had created so many years ago.

"You won't tell anyone, especially your mother-in-law, will you? I don't want Frances to know about the position or anything else until I tell her."

"It'll be our secret," Emma promised, although keeping this joyous secret, out of all the others that seemed to be floating around Hill House these days, would be the hardest of all.

27

TWO WEEKS LATER, when February was but a few days old, Emma finally had everything nearly ready for Reverend Glenn.

Despite a record four feet of snow still on the ground that imprisoned folks for miles around in their homes.

Despite day after day of pestering from Mother Garrett and Aunt Frances to reveal Mr. Atkins' secret, since they had no hope of getting into town to visit him until the snow melted.

And despite the upset surrounding Lester Burke, who had taken to his bed in Emma's office just yesterday with a fever, demanding only his sister could tend to him. Although his demand signaled a truce to the estrangement they had suffered after their argument, the nature of their argument still remained a secret between the siblings.

In the quiet moments just after dawn, Emma pulled back the heavy drapes that covered the single window in her bedroom. She peered outside to enjoy a solitary view of the grounds behind Hill House before going downstairs to start what she hoped would be a day of momentous joy.

She cupped one hand at her brow against the glare, awed by the mystery and the majesty of God's power to transform the world He had made for them, season by season.

In the distance, beyond the snow-filled woods where the panther had been buried, a solid blanket of white obscured the path of the frozen canal. Copses of evergreens, including candlewood trees, bowed to their Creator under the weight of the heavy snowfall.

On the plateau, nestled at the base of a snowdrift that covered the steps leading down from the outdoor patio, the gazebo wore a cloak of dazzling white, with icicles hanging from its roof and reflecting the rays of a strong sun wrapped by a clear blue sky.

Encouraged that the weather appeared to be improving, she had to get on tiptoe to get a good view of the patio below her window and just outside the dining room on the first floor. Snow nearly reached the top of the stone walls that enclosed the patio. Two summer chairs sat in front of the outdoor fireplace, which she had cleared, and wood for a fire was already in place. After Mr. Massey and the Ammond brothers had cleared walkways to the chicken pen in the backyard and from the front porch to the gate, she had asked them to clear some of the snow on the patio to make a winding walkway from the dining room to the outdoor fireplace. To her relief, the walkway was still intact.

"Unlike my reputation," she murmured, grinning to herself. Being considered eccentric, if not foolish—or accused of having a touch of cabin fever for wanting to use the patio in the middle of winter—was a small price to pay for helping Reverend Glenn find a private place to propose to Aunt Frances.

She turned from the window and stopped to extinguish the oil lamp on her dresser before leaving her room. Descending the staircase to the center hallway below, she knew that the heavy snowfall had proven to be more blessing than curse after all.

Because roadway travel, even by foot, was virtually paralyzed, Aunt Frances's stay at Hill House had been extended indefinitely, giving Emma more time to prepare for Reverend Glenn's proposal. Instead of worrying if the owner of Hill House might suddenly appear on her doorstep, she could simply enjoy each and every day and try to follow Reverend Glenn's advice about letting God's plan for her unfold and hope to learn the lessons He set before her as it did.

Because the storm had taken a good two days before dumping the record snowfall, she was hopeful Zachary Breckenwith had been able to ride ahead of the storm. She was also relieved Mr. Lewis had finally given up his plans to stencil the center hallway. He had removed the scaffolding yesterday.

Shivering despite the heavy work gown she wore, she hurried down the stairs to the kitchen, where she found a good warm fire burning in the fireplace and water already heating on the cookstove. Liesel and Ditty were already at work on breakfast peeling, slicing, and dicing a mound of potatoes, but there was no sign of either Mother Garrett or Aunt Frances. She greeted the two girls with a smile before closing the door behind her. "Good morning."

"It is a good morning, Widow Garrett. Did you see how bright the sun is today? Maybe now some of the snow will begin to melt," Ditty announced.

"You wouldn't say that if you'd been the one to go outside to collect the eggs. It's just as cold today as it was yesterday," Liesel argued. "I'm sorry. I forgot to say good morning, Widow Garrett."

Emma donned an apron and tied it at her waist. "How many eggs did you get today?" she asked, worried how the chickens were faring after the storm.

"One. Just like yesterday. Come spring, we're going to need more chickens or we won't have enough during the season."

Emma chuckled. "I'm not certain I can bring another chicken onto the property. Mother Garrett seems pretty set on seeing the two I already have end up in her stewing pot."

As if summoned, Mother Garrett appeared, coming into the kitchen by way of the service stairs, with Aunt Frances right behind her. "To my mind, the only good chicken is a dead one, and that's the only kind I expect to see brought into my kitchen. What you pen up outside is entirely beyond my interest. You two young ones can scoot back upstairs now. We'll take over getting breakfast ready," she ordered.

Emma agreed. "The bed linens need changing today. You can get an early start in our rooms and be done by breakfast. Afterward, you can start on the guests' rooms."

The two young women gave up their places at the table to the two elderly widows, but Ditty lagged behind Liesel when she started up the stairs. "What about Mr. Burke?"

"I'll ask his sister, but if she needs help changing the bed linens, I'll take care of it," Emma promised and noted the relief in Ditty's gaze before the young woman scampered up the stairs, tripping once on the way up.

Mother Garrett shook her head in disgust. "And to think I was under the misguided notion the girl had finally grown into her own two feet."

"She did better today. She fell twice going

up those same stairs yesterday," Aunt Frances offered, stopping her work long enough to defend Ditty.

"And twice again coming down," Mother Garrett countered and sliced her knife clear through a potato the size of her fist. "I'm not certain, but I suspect she grew into her feet, but they've simply started growing again."

Emma carried the pot of hot water over to the counter to add to the pitchers already half filled with water for the guests who would be rising soon. "As I recall, you seem to have been more patient with Ditty in the past," she remarked as she started to fill the first pitcher.

"That was before. When I didn't have so much on my mind."

For fear of burning herself, Emma kept her gaze focused on her task. "I'm sorry. I didn't realize you were troubled."

"Considering we've all been snowed in for a good while, I've had lots of time to think lately, rather than actually doing something about what's on my mind. Not that you'd notice lately. You've spent the past few days convincing guests to help you dig a walkway through the snow on the patio so you can sit outside this afternoon in the middle of winter to enjoy a fire when we have more fires going inside the house than there are people. And just to set the record straight, I didn't say I was troubled. I said I have a lot on my mind."

Emma prompted, feeling oddly left out of the conversation.

Mother Garrett stared at her.

"Mercy, give that girl what she wants and stop being so fussy."

"One tin of oatmeal cookies, but not today. I promised Mrs. Massey I'd make her some apple dumplings. Since she's hoping to move back home a day or so after the snow melts, I need to do that first. I'll make your oatmeal cookies tomorrow."

Emma did not try to hide her grin. "Tomorrow is good. In return, you can each have two questions."

"What? We only get to ask two questions?" Mother Garrett protested.

"You already know the answer to the most important question: Has Mr. Atkins found someone he's interested in courting? The answer, obviously, is yes," Emma admitted. "You two matchmakers just want to know who she is, so I'll let you each have two questions, and I'll give you hints for an answer. Fair or unfair?"

"Fair," the two elderly women replied in unison.

"Think carefully. You only get two questions apiece," Emma reminded them, leaned back against the counter, and folded her arms across her chest. Giving the two of them hints about the young woman who had caught Mr. Atkins' attention might just give them both enough fodder for conversation this morning to keep them too busy to notice the final preparations Emma would be making so Reverend Glenn could finally propose to Aunt Frances after dinner.

The two friends haggled back and forth for a few moments before Mother Garrett addressed Emma. "Was the young woman in question born in Candlewood or did she move here later with her family?"

"She was born here."

Mother Garrett smiled. "That's gonna make it easier to narrow down the list of prospects."

"Maybe for you. I haven't been living in town like you have," Aunt Frances complained before giving her attention to Emma. "Does she attend services on Sunday?"

Mother Garrett sniffed her displeasure. "Don't answer that, Emma," she insisted before gazing at her friend. "What difference does that make?"

"It makes all the difference," Aunt Frances argued. "Mr. Atkins shouldn't consider courting anyone who doesn't have a good strong faith in God or attend church on Sundays."

"I know that. I mean, what difference does that make to us? We only had three questions left, and you wasted one of them with that one."

"Maybe we saw her at services. That would help us, wouldn't it?"

"That's clever thinking," Mother Garrett

admitted. "Go ahead, Emma. You can answer Frances's question."

"Yes and no."

Mother Garrett heaved a sigh. "That's not an answer."

Emma grinned. "Yes, she regularly attends services, but no, she wasn't at services the last time we were there."

"Oh dear. I think I did waste a question with that one," Aunt Frances admitted.

"We'd better think about this, Frances. We only have two left now," Mother Garrett cautioned.

"Don't think too long," Emma warned. "I'll be sorting through some of the boxes up in the garret most of the morning, and I'm planning on enjoying a good fire outside on the patio right after dinner."

"That's nice," Mother Garrett quipped. "Frances and I have a full day planned, too."

"You do?" Emma asked, alarmed that her plans for Aunt Frances to spend time with Reverend Glenn this afternoon might be undone.

"We do?" Aunt Frances echoed, batting her eyes in confusion.

"We do," Mother Garrett insisted. "We just have to decide whether we want to go sledding down the hill behind Hill House toward the woods or down the hill in front of Hill House toward Main Street."

Emma gasped. "You're not serious. You two

can't go sledding! Not at your age!"

Her mother-in-law tilted up her chin. "I don't see why not."

"You're both bound to get hurt, for one thing."

"And you're bound to wind up with lung fever if you don't change your plans about sitting outside in the snow on the patio for the afternoon. The snow is so high, we wouldn't even be able to watch to make sure you don't freeze solid in one of those chairs," her mother-in-law countered. "Of course," she added with a gleam in her eyes, "I sure would be willing to reconsider if you'd agree to do the same."

"Reconsider? Not a chance."

Mother Garrett turned to her companion. "We'd better hurry up and ask Emma our last two questions. This time tomorrow, she'll be too sick to answer them."

"And probably too sick to eat any of her cookies, too," Aunt Frances noted solemnly.

Mother Garrett scowled. "What a pity."

28

WITH DINNER concluded, Mr. Lewis was the last guest to leave the dining room to seek out ways to spend another snowbound afternoon. Since Emma was the last resident or staff member there, she used the opportunity to speak to him privately before carrying out her own plans for the afternoon.

"Before you leave, I'd like to have a word with you," she suggested as he approached the door to the center hallway.

He turned and walked back to where she was standing. Before responding, however, he looked around as if making sure they were alone. "May I hope you've reconsidered my offer to stencil the hallway?" he whispered.

"I'm afraid not."

The sparkle in his eyes dimmed. "How can I help you?"

"The Burkes have been taking their meals separately from us for several days now, ever since Mr. Burke took ill. His sister is either tending to him or staying in the library . . ."

"I've started painting her portrait," he explained.

Emma nodded. "They've isolated themselves rather completely. In all truth, although my bedroom is connected to the office with a staircase, I really can't overhear anything that is happening because the door is closed. We leave their trays at the library door at mealtimes, as well as fresh water and linens. They won't even allow us inside my office or the library to clean or to change his bed linens anymore. Orralynne does that now," she informed him.

"You're the only one who has contact with them now on a regular basis, and I'm concerned about Mr. Burke's well-being. Has he recovered from the fever that sent him to his bed?"

Mr. Lewis swallowed hard enough to set his Adam's apple bobbing. "He hasn't stirred from the office to sit for the finishing touches on his portrait or to work on my suit of clothes for a good while. Since I haven't seen him at all for the past few days, I believe he's still ill."

Troubled, Emma furrowed her brow. "You spend the majority of your days in the library with his sister. Hasn't she said anything to you about her brother's health?"

He shook his head. "I tried asking, but Miss Burke has an uncommon ability to make one reluctant to do anything she finds objectionable a second time," he said tactfully.

"I see," she murmured, reluctant to overstep her bounds as proprietress. "If I may speak freely and in confidence, I'm concerned that Mr. Burke might not be well enough to dictate the course or the matter of his treatment or that his sister might be too intimidated by her brother to defy him and ask for the doctor to be summoned."

He nodded. "If it's any help, you should know that I believe she's also concerned."

When Emma cocked her head, he smiled. "Her eyes. I can see it in her eyes."

"Yes, of course," she replied, acknowledging his gift as an artist to see emotions and details that others might miss. "Will you tell me, please, if Mr. Burke improves or if you think his condition has worsened and requires the attention of Dr. Jeffers?"

"Most definitely," he assured her. "Is there anything else? I asked Miss Burke to be ready to begin about now for another session, and she doesn't like to be kept waiting."

"No. Thank you."

He turned on his heels and left the room.

After offering a quick prayer for Mr. Burke's health, Emma set aside these concerns in favor of happier ones. Without wasting time to fetch her cape, she quietly but quickly made her way to Reverend Glenn's room and rapped on the door. "Reverend Glenn? It's me. Emma.

It's time," she whispered.

When the door creaked open, he greeted her wearing a heavy coat, a hat that did not quite cover his overlarge ears, and thick gloves. Butter was right by his side. "Are you sure no one is about?"

She nodded and smiled. "We have to get you outside. They're bound to finish up in the kitchen very soon."

Although they were slow going, they made it from his room next to the kitchen to the patio without being discovered. The sun was high and bright in a sky of blue, but without her cape, Emma was shivering. The air was cold but not unduly frigid, since walls of snow lining the winding pathway blocked what little wind existed.

Emma's heart raced with anticipation as they walked arm in arm. Surprisingly, Butter was ahead of them, both energized and excited by the snow.

"I do trust you, Emma, but I'm afraid I'm a bit concerned about sitting outside for too long in the cold."

She urged him to go around the final bend and stopped. As Butter edged around them and headed directly to the fireplace to plop down in front of the fire, she nodded toward a clearing in front of the outdoor fireplace that measured a good six feet square. "I don't think you'll be cold here," she suggested, savoring the warmth from the fire on her chilled body.

The elderly man tightened his grip on her arm and stared straight ahead. His eyes widened with wonder and amazement, and he was speechless.

Even Emma was impressed as she moved them closer to the fire and surveyed her handiwork. The two outdoor chairs were lined with fur coats she had found stored up in the garret and sat side-by-side in front of a cozy fire that had lured the dog away from its master. Beneath the chairs, to help keep the couple's feet warm, Emma had spread an old floral rug that had once been in a guest room. Walls of snow provided privacy for anyone sitting there.

"We have to get you seated so no one can see you," she urged and helped him into one of the chairs.

"I can't quite believe it, but it's actually warm sitting out here," he offered.

"Too warm to expect the snow not to melt," she added, noting the water that had begun to collect on the stone floor along the edges of the clearing. "I'll be back with Aunt Frances as soon as I can," she promised and raced back to the house.

Shivering with cold again, she let herself into the dining room, where Mother Garrett was waiting for her. "I . . . I forgot my cape," Emma offered.

Mother Garrett smiled. "I was just on my

way to check on Ditty. She's polishing the furniture in the parlors. Your cape is in the kitchen
where you left it after you finally managed to
brush out all those pine needles."

Emma nodded and turned to exit the dining
room.

"It's hanging on the peg right next to the
sleds Mr. Massey was kind enough to bring
down from the garret," her mother-in-law
added.

Emma braced to a halt. Tempted to turn
around, she decided she had no time to take the
bait on Mother Garrett's hook this time and let
herself into the kitchen. She spied her cape,
noted the two wooden sleds leaning up against
the wall, and grinned at Aunt Frances, who was
storing away the last of the pots from cooking
dinner.

"Have you changed your mind yet about
spending the afternoon on the patio?" Aunt Frances asked hopefully.

"Not exactly," Emma replied and walked
past her elderly friend to snatch her cape off the
wall.

Aunt Frances glanced at the sleds. "I do
wish you'd change your mind. I think Mercy
might be serious about the two of us going sledding, just to prove she's as stubborn as you are."

"You're not going sledding," Emma argued
as she searched the back wall. "Where's your
cape? It was hanging here before dinner."

"It was in the way. Ditty took it upstairs for me to make space for the sleds."

Emma groaned. She would have given her own cape to Aunt Frances to wear, but the cape would be too long for this tiny woman. "I'll be right back. Don't leave. Just stay put," Emma insisted, worried that a long delay might give the fire too much time to melt the snow.

By the time she scampered up the service staircase to Aunt Frances's room, found the cape, grabbed a bonnet as well as a pair of gloves, and rushed back downstairs again, she had a stitch in her side. "Here. Put these on," she said as she handed Aunt Frances her outerwear and donned her cape.

Aunt Frances held her garments at arm's length. "Emma dear, I'm not sure what you're—"

"Do you trust me?" Emma asked.

"Yes, but—"

"Then get dressed. Quickly. I have something out on the patio I want you to see."

Without further argument, Aunt Frances put on her cape, but she was just trying the ribbon on her bonnet when Mother Garrett charged back into the kitchen. "I won't be a moment, Frances. I just have to get dressed so we can go sledding."

Emma looped her arm with Aunt Frances's, smiled, and started for the dining room.

"Where are you going?"

Aunt Frances looked back over her shoulder. "I'm not sure. Emma said—"

Emma turned to face her mother-in-law. "I'll have her back in no time. I'd invite you to come along, but I know how opposed you are to my plans for the afternoon," she quipped and left Mother Garrett standing there, mouth agape and eyes wide with disbelief.

Getting Aunt Frances outside onto the patio and along the winding pathway was easy. Convincing her to go around the final turn on her own was more difficult. "You go on ahead," Emma repeated. "I have to go back to the house for a moment. I've forgotten something I should have brought along."

"I'll go back with you."

"Don't be silly. I won't be long," Emma promised and turned back toward the house.

"I'm afraid I don't quite have my bearings. I don't want to be out here all alone," Aunt Frances said in a trembling voice.

When Emma turned around, Aunt Frances had started walking back toward her—until Reverend Glenn came around the corner and called out, "Frances?"

The elderly woman turned to face him.

"You won't be alone," he said gently and held his hand out to her. "You don't ever need to be alone again. Come. Be with me."

With her throat thick with emotion, Emma quickly backed away and returned to the house, ever respectful of the couple's need for privacy and ever mindful of the blessings of affection and companionship waiting for Reverend Glenn and Aunt Frances within the sacred bonds of marriage.

When she got back inside, once again Mother Garrett was waiting for her. This time she was dressed for winter from head to toe and her expression was remorseful.

"Where are you going?" Emma asked and pressed her back against the patio door.

"I was coming out to the patio to see you."

Emma's heart dropped down to her feet and back up again.

"I came to apologize. Once I saw Frances going with you, I realized I'd been a foolish, stubborn old woman. If all it takes to make you happy is a place to sit outside in the snow in front of a fire, then I have no right to stop you. You're a grown woman with a good mind and more sense than most folks. You wouldn't do anything to get yourself sick."

"And you weren't really serious about going sledding, were you."

Mother Garrett scowled. "I'm not dumb. Just stubborn. I thought I could threaten you into changing your mind."

Emma chuckled.

"Where's Frances? You didn't leave her out there in the cold all alone, did you?"

"She's not cold," Emma argued, took her

mother-in-law's arm, and guided her back through the dining room. "There's a good fire going. Once she saw how cozy and private it was, she didn't say a word when I left. I thought maybe I should fix some tea," she said, quickly ushering Mother Garrett through the door and into the kitchen. "Why don't you set some water to boil. I'll fix the teapot."

"We just had tea with dinner."

"I'd like more," Emma argued and took a tin of tea from the larder. She tried not to panic, but keeping Mother Garrett away from that patio now was going to be nearly impossible.

"Stop. Put the tea back. You're wasting my time as well as yours."

Emma gripped the tin harder and stared at her mother-in-law. "I am?"

"Yes. You are. You don't want tea right now any more than I want Anson Kirk to show up here again as soon as the snow melts to pester me."

"He's a nice man," Emma countered, hoping to sidetrack and prolong their conversation long enough to let Reverend Glenn propose before Mother Garrett charged her way out to the patio.

"You're changing the subject."

"I am?"

"Yes, which tells me you don't really want that tea."

Emma shrugged, feigning innocence.

"You're stalling. You don't want me out on that patio, do you? I'm not sure why you don't want me there, but you're definitely stalling."

"I am?"

"Emma, if you say, 'I am?' one more time, I have a good mind to lash you onto one of those sleds, push you right down the back hill, and watch you slide straight through the woods to the canal."

Emma baited a hook of her own. "If you do that, then you'll never have a chance to discover my secret."

The elderly woman pulled back. "Secret? What secret?"

"The one out on the patio," Emma murmured and measured out a good amount of tea before putting the tin back into the larder.

"You have a secret out on the patio?" Mother Garrett asked, removing her gloves and bonnet to get a pot for the water. "Why does Frances get to see this secret of yours before I do?"

Emma managed to keep Mother Garrett guessing for a good twenty minutes. By then, the tea was steeping in the teapot, and Emma was running out of ways to stymie her mother-in-law. She no sooner said a silent prayer begging for divine inspiration when Reverend Glenn and Aunt Frances walked into the kitchen, hand-in-hand, with their aged faces beaming. Butter, as always, tagged along.

Mother Garrett went directly to her friend. "It's about time you wandered back inside, Frances. Emma should never have left you ... alone ... on ... that ... patio," she said, slowing her words and widening her eyes as she spoke. "You ... you weren't alone," she murmured, staring at the couple's joined hands.

"No, I wasn't alone, and we want you and Emma to be the first to know that Reverend Glenn and I won't ever be alone again."

Speechless, Mother Garrett looked up at Reverend Glenn, whose smile came straight from his heart. "Frances has given me the honor of accepting my proposal," he said proudly. "We'll need to speak to her sons, Andrew and James, of course, but with your permission, Emma, we'd like to be married here as soon as possible."

Emma's heart soared. Her eyes filled with tears that spilled down her cheeks. "I would consider it a great privilege," she managed, and her mind raced ahead, impatient to begin planning the first-ever wedding at Hill House.

29

IN YEARS PAST, Candlewood slept through most of the winter under a heavy patchwork quilt of bitter cold and heavy snow. With the construction of the Candlewood Canal, however, the strong winds of commerce had grown warmer year by year, slowly waking the town after each heavy snowfall for a spell until another storm forced the town back to sleep.

Several days after Reverend Glenn proposed to Aunt Frances, excitement and commotion seemed the order of the day. At midmorning on Tuesday, an odd assortment of travel bags and other paraphernalia on the floor wound from the oak rack in the center hallway into the west parlor. Baskets of food bound for several different destinations rested on the dining room table, while guests and residents alike scurried from one room to another.

Emotions ran the gamut from high to low, and the only areas of the boardinghouse insulated from the chaos and commotion were the library and Emma's office, where the Burkes remained in virtual seclusion.

"They're here!"

Liesel's cry, announcing the arrival of two horse-drawn sleighs, drew everyone to the front of the house. While the drivers, Mr. Massey and Mr. Lewis, loaded up the many bags and baskets, Emma bid farewell to the travelers, starting with Judith Massey, now in her final month. She hugged the younger woman to her. "Please don't forget to send word when your little one comes."

Judith blinked back tears. "I won't. I . . . I don't know how to thank you for everything you've done for Solomon and me."

"You've both been a joy to have at Hill House. Truly," Emma replied as she walked the very expectant woman to the front door.

Judith stopped and glanced down the hall toward the library. "I'd like to stop and see Miss Burke during the day once her brother doesn't require such constant care. I . . . I still remember how difficult it was to leave my sister's bedside when she was so very ill," she murmured, shaking her head sadly. "Do you think she'd like it if I came by with Solomon now and then?"

"I think she'd like it very much," Emma replied and handed Judith over to her husband, who was anxious to take her home. Deeply concerned that Lester Burke's health was apparently not improving, Emma was also awed by the odd friendship that had apparently developed between Orralynne and Judith. "Liesel should be right down," she offered and bid the Masseys a final good-bye. She watched the young couple through one of the two glass panels on either side of the front door as they slowly crossed the front yard and prayed they would soon share the great joy of welcoming a healthy, strong babe into their home.

Liesel came charging down the center stairs and raced toward Emma. "Ditty's upstairs crying. She's awfully sad she can't go home, too."

"It's too far. She understands that."

"I feel bad for her."

"She'll be fine. I'll talk to her," Emma assured her.

Liesel still hesitated. "Are you certain it's all right for me to stay home for a few days?"

Emma nodded. "You haven't seen your family for weeks. Now hurry. Mr. Massey is anxious to get his wife back home again. Since you didn't want to leave earlier with the Ammond brothers, and Mr. Massey offered you a ride, you shouldn't keep him waiting," Emma cautioned.

Liesel needed no further encouragement and nearly got to the sleigh before the Masseys did. Chuckling to herself, Emma walked to the east parlor and poked her head inside. "You're next. Sleigh's waiting!"

With Butter on one side and Aunt Frances on the other, Reverend Glenn started walking toward Emma immediately. Mother Garrett followed reluctantly behind them, along with Mr. Lewis.

"We'll only be staying with Andrew for a few days. We don't want to be stranded so far from town with the next snowstorm," Aunt Frances offered.

Reverend Glenn looked less confident. "I might need more time than that to convince those boys of hers to give us their blessing, but we'll be back for Sunday services."

His future wife looked up at him and patted his arm. "You'll have their blessings as fast as you had mine."

Emma hugged them both. "I know everything will be fine," she offered and turned them over to Mr. Lewis to escort them outside.

When Butter tried to follow his master, Reverend Glenn patted the dog's head and shook his own. "You can't go with me on this trip. Behave for Emma, now," he warned.

The dog turned, walked over to Emma, and plopped down at her feet.

While Mr. Lewis helped the elderly couple to the sleigh, Mother Garrett made one last plea to remain behind at Hill House. "I don't see why it's necessary for me to go along. The idea that the two of them need a chaperone traveling back and forth from here to Andrew's farm is ludicrous."

"They're going to be married. They don't want folks to gossip about them," Emma argued.

Mother Garrett scowled. "So I get to be chaperone to a couple whose combined ages add up to more years than we've been a country, but you get to stay here at Hill House with not one single man under your roof, but two. That's proper? You don't think people might gossip about that?"

Emma laughed out loud. "One of those single men is so sick he can't get out of his bed, and his sister has to tend to his every need. Mr. Lewis, as you well know, is going with you now as far as the hotel to make arrangements to sleep there each night. For propriety's sake," she added.

"That's all well and good. Until another storm hits and he can't leave Hill House to get back to the hotel one night."

"You'll be back by then," Emma countered.

Mother Garrett sniffed. "Have your way. But don't complain a single word to me when I get back."

"What would I have to complain about when you get back?" Emma asked, gently guiding her mother-in-law to the front door, with Butter tagging along.

"You're going to spend the next few days

here alone with that dog on your heels and only Ditty to help you. I cooked up enough food to last while I'm gone, but what food one of them will invariably drop or spill on the floor, the other will devour faster than you can remember I said 'I told you so.' And then you'll all starve to death."

Still laughing, Emma pressed a kiss to her mother-in-law's cheek. "I love you. I'll miss you. And I promise we won't starve. Now go," she insisted and opened the front door.

Mother Garrett looked out at the sleigh, took Emma's hand, and pressed a kiss to it as Mr. Lewis returned to escort her. "I love you, too. Just say a prayer the sleigh doesn't tip over."

"You're worried about traveling by sleigh? You? The woman who said she was going sledding just recently?"

"I'm old enough to know my sledding days are long gone, thank you, but I haven't forgotten how to sled. That driver out there doesn't look old enough to drive nails, let alone a sleigh," she grumbled. "I'm glad either Andrew or James will bring us back. I know I can trust them," she added and waited for a moment until Mr. Lewis was close enough to offer her his arm.

"Godspeed," Emma murmured and closed the door. Butter stayed with her while she watched through the glass again as the sleigh disappeared from view. She patted the dog on the head and turned around to face an unusual hush of silence within Hill House.

Slowing her steps a bit to allow the old dog to keep up with her, she went straight upstairs to the room Ditty shared with Liesel and knocked on the door.

Ditty opened the door with one hand while swatting at the tears still trickling down her cheeks with the other. "I'm sorry, Widow Garrett. I didn't mean to stay in my room for so long."

"I feel very badly that your family lives so far from town that you couldn't go home to see them," Emma offered.

Ditty rubbed one of her eyes with the back of her hand. "Me too."

"I really do need a few things from the General Store. It's too bad I didn't think of it before so Mr. Lewis could bring them home for me. I'm not certain I want to risk slipping and sliding down the hill to get to Main Street."

With her reddened eyes wide, Ditty perked up. "I could go to the General Store for you."

Emma feigned concern by furrowing her brow. "You'd end up slipping and falling all the way down, too."

"Not if I use a sled! I could borrow one of the sleds Mr. Massey put back up in the garret to get down the hill. When I get to the General Store, I could load up what you needed and pull the sled back home."

"You wouldn't get hurt sledding down the hill?"

Ditty squared her shoulders and straightened up to her full height, barely an inch or so now shy of six feet. "I can sled better than most anyone."

Emma suppressed a grin and relented. "All right, then. I'll make up a list and meet you in the kitchen."

"I'll have whatever you need back here in no time," Ditty promised, rushing past Emma to get to the stairs that led up to the garret.

"There's no hurry. I certainly wouldn't object if you wanted to stay in town a bit today. I assume there might be other young folks anxious to test their skills with their sleds. You might want to stop and see if Liesel wants to go sledding, too."

Ditty stopped and spun around so fast she nearly tripped, but caught herself. "Really?"

"You and Liesel have been punished long enough. It's time for both of you to start earning back the trust you lost."

"We won't disappoint you. I'll be sure to be back in time for dinner to help you, too," Ditty said before scampering away.

Emma looked down at the dog, who had plopped down to the floor again. "No more excitement. No more commotion. We have a very quiet, very peaceful few hours facing us," she murmured, and she knew exactly how she wanted to spend those hours.

With a joyful heart, she went directly to her bedroom to get her writing box and the letters she had received recently from her three sons. She also grabbed a needle and thread and a scrap of fabric. Once she had the fabric added to her keepsakes, she wanted to reread the boys' letters and pen a reply to each of them so they would hear from her before making their final plans to come home in April for her birthday.

Within twenty minutes, Ditty had left for town and Emma was sitting in a rocking chair enjoying a cozy fire in the kitchen. Butter was curled up at her feet. Her sewing notions rested on top of her sons' letters lying on her lap. Her keepsakes were still in her pocket.

Using tiny stitches, she hemmed the dark brown piece of fabric and set it down. She tugged the collection of keepsakes from her pocket and smiled as she stitched the hemmed fabric to the back. She had taken the brown fabric from the split skirt she had worn the day she had gone riding with Zachary Breckenwith to Gray's Tavern.

Whether the fabric would be more a reminder of the panther they had rescued or her first outing with the man who wanted to court her still remained to be seen. Satisfied with her handiwork, however, she stored her keepsakes back in her pocket, but thoughts of Zachary

Breckenwith were not quite as easy to tuck away.

If he had outridden the storm, he would have spent the past several weeks in New York City and should be returning to Candlewood soon. But he could just as easily have been caught by the storm and only now en route to his original destination. She let out a sigh. The timing of Zachary's return to Candlewood was as unpredictable as the arrival of the legal owner of Hill House, although she was quite certain she would be happier to see the former than the latter.

Before she had an opportunity to reread a single one of her sons' letters, she tensed with the odd feeling she was not alone.

She looked up, saw Orralynne standing in the doorway, and immediately knew that the peace she had coveted had ended. The only question in Emma's mind was what kind of excitement or commotion Orralynne's arrival might announce.

30

EMMA COCKED her head. "Orralynne?"

"I waited as long as I could. Have all the others gone?" the woman asked but remained standing in the doorway with her shoulders drooped. Exhaustion dulled her gaze and bleached out the little color she once had in her pale features, and her gown hung loosely on her frame.

"It's just me and Butter left, at least for a spell. I expect Ditty and Mr. Lewis back for dinner," she replied, setting aside her letters and leaving her seat in front of the fire. She approached the woman, both curious and anxious to know why Orralynne needed to speak to her alone. "Would you like me to fix something for you to eat? Or some tea, perhaps?"

"No. Nothing. I can't stay that long. I have to get back before Lester wakes up again," she insisted while gazing over her shoulder for a moment. When she looked at Emma again, her gaze was steady and determined. "I need to know if it's true," she whispered, as if she might be afraid her brother could hear her.

Emma lifted a brow.

Orralynne tilted up her chin. "You've been to town since the explosion and fires. Although you have a reputation as a woman who does not engage in gossip, you can't avoid hearing it. My brother tells me he's filed a number of lawsuits against . . . against a number of people because of the fire that damaged our cottage. I want to know if that's true."

"In a manner of speaking," Emma admitted, disappointed that Orralynne was apparently as self-concerned and greedy as her brother.

"I've lived with my brother long enough to know that lawsuits are either filed or they're not. Which is it?" Orralynne argued, though the hush to her voice softened her words from a demand to more of a plea.

Emma hesitated for a moment. Since Lester Burke had obviously discussed his plans with his sister, she felt no need to keep her conversation with him about the lawsuits private. She did, however, decide to edit some of what Zachary Breckenwith had told her, if only to avoid involving him. "The last time I spoke with your brother, he admitted meeting with his lawyer here at Hill House to discuss the lawsuits."

"They met here?"

"Apparently in my office."

Orralynne narrowed her gaze. "Before my brother's mishap," she murmured.

"Yes. When I was in town, just before the snowstorm, I heard that his lawsuits hadn't actually been filed at that point. The court has been rather inundated with many other issues since the tragedy."

Orralynne shook her head and frowned. "The court is always clogged. Lester never let that stop him before."

Emma was fairly confident that she had convinced the man not to file a lawsuit against her. She bridled at the notion he would proceed against the others, as well as his sister's apparent support of that action, pitting neighbor against neighbor.

"You should know that the likelihood of collecting a settlement of any kind from the owner of the match factory is unlikely. He's already left town. Penniless," she stated.

Emma could not find it in her heart to love either of these two mean-spirited people, but she did want to follow Reverend Glenn's advice and treat them as she would any other guest. She walked over to the larder, took out a crock of butter, a jar of jam, and a hunk of bread left from breakfast and set them on the table.

"That's only one of the lawsuits," Orralynne countered, cocking her head as if straining to listen for her brother. "There are several others."

Emma arranged the bread on a plate, took a knife from the drawer in the cupboard, sliced the bread into bite-size chunks, and started buttering them. "The lawsuit against the town will be just as useless as the first one. Your brother might recover something from the Andersons, the Morgans, and the Hoffners, but they can ill afford to lose any of the little they have."

Orralynne huffed and her cheeks flushed deep rose. "I'm not a party to any of those lawsuits. I'm not involved at all," she protested.

Emma shrugged, wondering if naming the three families who had each taken in the Burkes for a single night had pricked Orralynne's conscience. "You'll certainly benefit from anything your brother recovers in a settlement," she countered. While she added a dollop of mulberry jam to each buttered chunk of bread, she wondered why Orralynne was staying so long to talk after insisting she did not have time for a cup of tea.

"Judith told me she knows all of the families quite well. She says they're good people," Orralynne murmured.

Emma paused and looked over at Orralynne. "You discussed them with Judith? I didn't think you left your brother long enough to—"

"She usually stopped by my room late each night to see how I was faring. She wasn't comfortable sleeping, so we'd chat awhile. She . . . she understood how hard it was for me because she was very close to her sister and helped to care for her when she was very, very ill."

Emma dropped her gaze. She had been so happy to have the Burkes isolated and out of the way, she had never made the effort to stay up until late at night to speak to Orralynne herself. Embarrassed that one of her guests had done what Emma had not thought to do, even a bit ashamed of herself, she carried the plate of jellied bread to Orralynne and handed it to her. "Here. Take this with you. In case you want a snack before dinner."

Orralynne looked from Emma to the plate and back to Emma again. "You don't need to be nice to me or my brother. He told me he's decided not to file a lawsuit against you because of his mishap."

Emma extended the plate farther. "I try to be attentive and kind to all of my guests. I'm sorry I haven't seemed to have done that for both of you."

"We're used to having people treat us . . . differently. I . . . I need to go. I've stayed away from my brother for too long," she whispered and promptly left.

Feeling quite unsettled and a little perplexed by Orralynne's visit, Emma returned to the rocking chair. Instead of giving her attention to her sons' letters, she folded her hands on her lap and bowed her head.

She used her feet to set the chair into

motion. Rocking back. Praying. Rocking forward. Praying. Simply praying.

————————

Emma tossed and turned all night. When
she was not dreaming of the owner of Hill
House arriving and oddly demanding that she
leave wearing only the clothes on her back and
those old skates of hers on her feet, she was
wide awake, staring at the ceiling and listening
to every creak and night sound that echoed in
the very empty boardinghouse.

She was just drifting off to sleep again when
she heard someone rapping at her door. Concerned that Ditty might have been having a fit-
ful sleep, since Liesel was staying with her family, Emma slipped out of bed. Shivering in the
cold and dark, she grabbed the dressing robe
she had left at the foot of her bed and put it on
as she stumbled across the short distance to the
door and opened it.

No Ditty.

The rapping came again. "Emma!"

She turned, realized someone was rapping
at the door at the top of the staircase that led
from her bedroom down to her office. Now
fully awake, she heard soft groaning sounds
over the pounding of her heart as soon as she
opened the door.

With light behind her coming from the office below where Lester Burke had his sick-

room, Orralynne's features were shadowed, but her voice was low and desperate. "We need Dr. Jeffers to come. Please send for Dr. Jeffers."

"What's wrong?"

"My brother. He's burning with fever. He's delirious. He's . . . We need Dr. Jeffers."

"I'll fetch him," Emma promised, although she was not quite sure how she was going to manage that feat. The doctor lived all the way on the other side of town. Traveling by day over snowpacked walkways was difficult. Attempting to get to the doctor's home in the middle of the night would be almost impossible. According to Ditty, who had gone back into town after dinner to meet Liesel to go sledding again, the afternoon sun had melted the top layer of snow, which Emma was certain had frozen into a solid sheet of ice.

"Please hurry. I don't want my brother to die. He can't die. He has to—"

"I'm sure the doctor will be able to help your brother," Emma said reassuringly, although she suspected the poor woman was overreacting simply because she had been exhausted meeting her brother's demands for the past few weeks. "Go back downstairs and sit with your brother. I'll wake Ditty and have her bring you some fresh water and cloths. Keep him as comfortable as you can until I get back."

Emma was dressed and fully armed to begin her mission of mercy half an hour later.

Once again the storage boxes in the garret had proven to be invaluable. Wearing one of the fur coats she had used on the patio to line the chairs made better sense instead of her cape, which might tangle up and cause her to fall. She wore several layers of men's work shirts and a pair of men's trousers beneath her riding skirt. Heavy boots on her feet and a woolen cap on her head completed her transformation from genteel woman to middle-aged urchin.

She cared little about what anyone might say about her apparel or her decision to leave for Dr. Jeffers' house now instead of waiting for full daylight. She had given serious thought to using the road that eventually led from the side of the house into town, but that route would take twice as long. The one sure way to get to town quickly was to use the brick lane that led down the hill in front of the house, although she was admittedly anxious about the sled she held in one hand and the skates she held in the other.

Ditty had the good sense to simply offer Emma some last words of advice. "There's a good bit of moonlight to guide you. Remember to put the skates under you when you lie down on the sled. You'll never feel them with all you're wearing."

"I will."

"Once you start down the hill, stay on one

side or the other. There'll be less ice there. Lean hard on the opposite side of the sled to keep yourself to the side. Once you get near the bottom, steer closer and closer to the snowbank. You'll stop in time to avoid any traffic on Main Street."

Emma cringed. "I'm not worried about riders or wagons on Main Street. It's not even dawn. I'm worried about slamming into a snowbank at full speed and breaking my neck."

"I told you I'd go," Ditty reminded her.

"So you can break your neck? Despite your talent, I doubt you've had any experience sledding in the middle of the night. Thank you, but I'd rather not have to explain to your mother and father how you broke your neck."

Ditty sighed. "All right. Now, once you're at the bottom of the hill, all you have to do is strap on the skates. You'll be at Dr. Jeffers' house in no time, as long as you don't skate in the middle of Main Street. Too many ruts," she explained.

"I'll do my best," Emma murmured. Going sledding was daunting enough. Skating down Main Street, day or night, was paramount to inviting a disaster only her good intentions and a lot of prayers might avoid. "I know you're not overjoyed to be left here alone with the Burkes, but—"

"I'll be fine. Mr. Burke is too sick to be rude to me, and Miss Burke isn't so terribly nasty anymore," Ditty said softly. She helped Emma carry the wooden sled through the house to the front door. "You can still change your mind and let me go."

"Not really," Emma gritted and opened the door.

In all truth, by the time Emma arrived at Dr. Jeffers' home, she was rather proud of herself. She had sled down the hill to Main Street almost without incident, save for her rather pitiful landing at the end when she flew in one direction, clutching the skates, and her sled went in another. Other than sliding on her tummy for a few feet until she landed face-first in a snowbank, she survived relatively unscathed.

After retrieving the sled and storing it on top of a snowbank at the base of a tree, she strapped on her skates and only fell once when she hit a rut in the roadway and ended up facedown on the ice again.

She was relieved to find the doctor at home and willing to venture out to treat one of the more miserable of his patients. She was doubly thankful he had a carriage and insisted on taking her back to Hill House with him by way of the road that led to the side of Hill House, thereby avoiding that steep, icy hill in the front.

They left the horse and carriage at the edge of her property and trudged through the snow to reach the side porch and outer door to her office. "Mr. Burke is right through that door. His sister should be with him. I'll walk around front and go in that way. I'll be waiting in the kitchen with Ditty if you need anything," she prompted.

He nodded and knocked on the door. "Dr. Jeffers here," he announced and let himself inside.

When dawn broke, Emma sent Ditty to bed. The poor young woman had run herself ragged, twice carrying hot water and cloths back and forth from the kitchen to the sickroom. She had even gone outside once to get a bucket of ice the doctor had requested.

Once Emma set a third pot of water to boil and set out more clean cloths just in case the doctor needed them, she picked up the teapot, then set it down again. She had had three cups of tea already. Exhausted and anxious to know if the doctor would be able to help Lester Burke through this crisis, she was tempted to sit down and rock by the fire. She rejected that idea, too. She was too tired and would probably fall asleep—like Butter, who was asleep by the fire despite all the commotion.

She stood next to the kitchen table and arched her back. Overtired, she could barely focus properly. Her muscles were starting to ache a bit now that she had warmed up from her late-night sledding and skating, and the skin on her face felt a bit taut, probably from being exposed to the cold for so long.

"I'll walk and pray," she whispered, hoping to stay awake and do something useful. She scarcely completed a simple walk around the table when Dr. Jeffers entered the kitchen.

Though he was a young man, some fifteen years Emma's junior, he had thinning black hair that scarcely covered his head. Concern for his patients had etched permanent creases in his forehead but also softened his dark eyes. "Mr. Burke is resting more comfortably now," he offered, walked closer to her to study her, and frowned. "Did you say you fell once or twice tonight?"

"I fell once. Slid once," she admitted.

"Hmm." He grabbed a clean cloth from the counter, went to the back door, and disappeared outside for a moment. When he returned, he handed her a cloth filled with a handful of snow. "Your one eye is swelling a bit. I suspect you'll be sporting a good bruise in no time. Have a seat at the table. This should help."

She sat down, pressed the cold compress to her eye, and winced, more at the thought of explaining what happened to Mother Garrett than from pain. "I thought I was just too tired to focus properly."

"You should have sent for me days ago to tend to Mr. Burke."

Emma swallowed the lump in her throat. "I'm sorry. He was quite insistent otherwise."

He let out a sigh. "I'm afraid Mr. Burke has no greater enemy than himself." He paused and glanced at the teapot still sitting in the middle of the table. "Would there, by chance, be any tea left?"

"Of course. Forgive me. Have a seat. I'll get a mug from the cupboard for you," she gushed, but he urged her back into her seat.

"You sit still and keep that eye covered," he insisted and got the mug himself. He set it down on the table and poured tea into the mug before taking a seat across from her.

"I have honey or sugar and cream—"

"No, thank you." He took a sip and let out a sigh. "I've talked with Miss Burke. She understands what to do now."

"Is Mr. Burke's condition worsening, as his sister fears?"

"Unfortunately, I'm fairly limited in what I can tell you about his condition, since he's not a member of your family. His sister is quite adamant that I not discuss any aspect of her brother's treatment or the nature of his illness with anyone."

Emma set down the snow-filled cloth, unhappy that she had not thought to be concerned that Mr. Burke's illness might spread to anyone else. "At the very least I should be told if his illness is contagious. I've had many guests staying here. I have a staff—"

"Rest assured, the man's illness poses no risk to anyone but himself."

"How can you be so sure?" she demanded as the faces of her Hill House family flashed through her mind. "I need to know why you're so sure."

He clenched his jaw for a moment. "I lanced an infection in his foot. Unfortunately, that infection has spread throughout his body."

"I see," she murmured and recalled how Lester Burke had begun to favor his deformed foot shortly after arriving at Hill House, how she had found blood stains in the hallway upstairs, and how Mr. Lewis had come to her worried about the man's health.

"I can't tell you any more than that. In fact, I've probably said more than I should, but I believe I can rely on you to hold what you know in strict confidence." He paused to clear his throat. "I also feel compelled to warn you of what lies ahead, at least for the next few days."

Skin prickles covered her arms and traveled up the back of her neck. Her heart began to pound. "Is this infection that serious?"

Dr. Jeffers nodded, his eyes growing very sad. "I've done all I can, but I'm afraid Mr. Burke's condition is now irreversible."

Her eyes widened. "Irreversible? Are you absolutely certain?"

He drew in another long breath. "There's

little to be done now except to see that he is kept as comfortable as possible. He's dying, Widow Garrett."

She caught her breath and held it for a moment, unable to fully process what he had just told her. Orralynne's fears were real after all. Her brother was dying.

"You mentioned on your way here that you'd be alone for the next few days until the other members of your staff return," he said.

"Mr. Lewis is here during the day, and I have Ditty with me," she managed.

"I'll stop each day, as well."

She nodded, but all she could think about was that Lester Burke was dying. That poor wretched, unhappy man was dying.

31

LIKE AT BIRTH, the time of anyone's death is a mystery known only to the Creator.

Only the gentle sounds of hushed footsteps and quiet whispers could be heard within the walls of Hill House for the next two days as the body of Lester Burke grew weaker and his soul yearned to begin the final journey Home.

On Thursday morning, while Reverend Austin waited in the east parlor with Mr. Lewis, Emma escorted Dudley Larimore to the library. She rapped on the door just as the grandfather clock struck the nine-o'clock hour.

Orralynne opened the door, greeted her brother's lawyer with only a solemn nod, and stepped aside to let him enter.

"The doctor will be here later this afternoon again, but Reverend Austin is here. He wanted me to ask you—"

"Please don't ask again. I've told you. My brother said no. No minister. Just the lawyer and the doctor," she said and shut the door.

Emma sighed, deferring to the Burkes' wishes again, although she kept praying Lester Burke would change his mind about seeing the minister before dying. She had not been able to convince Miss Burke to let them move her brother into a guest room where he might be more comfortable and Orralynne would definitely have more room to care for him. Emma had also failed to change Orralynne's mind about refusing to let Emma or anyone else sit with the dying man to relieve Orralynne, as women traditionally did for one another.

As she walked back to the parlor, however, Emma was troubled most by her failure to help Reverend Austin minister to Mr. Burke before his passing.

With his gaze hopeful, the minister stood up the moment Emma entered the parlor.

She shook her head. "I'm sorry. Not today."

He let out a sigh. "I'll come back again tomorrow. Should Mr. Burke send for me, I'll return. Day or night."

"Thank you. Let me help you get your coat," she offered.

"You look tired, Emma. Take care of that eye of yours," he urged. "Why don't you sit a spell with Mr. Lewis? I can get my things and let myself out," he insisted and took his leave.

She sat down on the end of the settee closest to the fire, where Mr. Lewis was standing with one hand resting on the mantel. "Is there anything I can do for you?" he asked.

She chuckled softly. "If you bring any more firewood to the side porch, I'm afraid it might collapse. The sun has melted what little snow was left on the walkway you shoveled across the front yard and off the patio, as well as the front porch. I can't possibly think of anything you might get for me at the General Store. So unless you can think of a way I could be rid of the bruise on my eye, perhaps with a bit of paint, I should think you deserve a free afternoon."

Although the swelling had gone down, she still sported a bruise the same deep shade of purple as the violets that used to grow in her grandmother's garden. She also knew, as the mother of three active boys, the bruise would soon become a kaleidoscope of garish yellows and blues that would eventually fade—but not before Mother Garrett returned home.

"I wish I could help," he replied. "At times like this, I find it easier if I keep busy."

"Your portraits are done, then?"

"Only Mr. Burke's. I still have some work to do on his sister's," he said and glanced down at the fire. "You've been unusually accommodating to the Burkes, as well as to me and so many others displaced by the tragedy in town."

She stared at her lap and pondered his words aloud. "When I bought this property and restored it, I prayed Hill House would be a special place, a source of comfort and hope to travelers and a home filled with contentment for myself and those who depend on me," she said. "For most, I believe Hill House has been that special place, but I fear I've failed some of my guests, like the Burkes."

"How so?" he asked. "From all I've observed, you've done everything they've demanded of you."

"To a point," she countered. "I didn't precisely leap at the opportunity to offer them a place to stay when they first needed one. I'm afraid I needed a lot of convincing, mostly from myself," she admitted.

"Despite my rather pleasant experiences with them, I've heard and seen enough to know how uncommon that is. Most people I've encountered have nothing good to say about the Burkes."

"Unfortunately that's true."

"Then why did you bring them to Hill House? You'd already taken in so many others."

She looked up at him. "Because they had nowhere else to go. I felt if I didn't offer them a place to live, my hopes and dreams for Hill House would shatter with hypocrisy, along with my faith."

He pressed his lips together and narrowed his gaze for a moment. "Have you considered what you'll do if you lose Hill House?" he asked, reminding her that he had become one of a very few people who knew the secret about her legal problems.

She swallowed hard. "I don't know. I honestly don't know."

"But you'd stay in Candlewood."

She blinked hard. "Stay? Of course. Candlewood is my home. I'm not sure where I'll live or what business venture I'll pursue, but I'd never consider leaving this area. What are your plans?" she asked. "Will you continue to stay with us here at Hill House for a spell?"

"Only long enough to finish Miss Burke's portrait." He paused and smiled at her. "I've been meaning to head south to Pennsylvania to visit with relatives and take care of some pressing family matters. I'm thinking that now might be a good time to do that. I'll stay here, of course, through the . . . through the funeral, most especially because I wouldn't want you to go through all this alone. Unless you think your family might return within the next day or so."

She shook her head. "I have no way of knowing exactly when they'll be back. The weather has warmed and cleared so well, I suspect they might prolong their visit at most until Saturday. Reverend Glenn assured me they would all be home in time for church on Sunday," she replied.

"Widow Garrett?"

Startled by the sound of another man's voice, she turned. Mr. Larimore was standing just outside the parlor in the center hallway. She rose immediately. "You're leaving already?"

"I have several errands and paper work to prepare."

"Is Mr. Burke resting comfortably?"

"I didn't see the man today. Miss Burke is my client, too. I came to see her. I should be back within an hour or two," he said curtly, turned, and let himself out the front door.

———————

Puzzled all through dinner by the question of why Orralynne needed the services of a lawyer, Emma got no answer from Mr. Larimore when he had returned later that afternoon. Or when he summarily left after spending an hour with his client. Mr. Lewis rode back into town with the lawyer to save himself a long walk, but she doubted the lawyer would tell the artist much of anything, either.

To keep busy, Emma sat on one side of the dining room table with Ditty on the other, a bolt of black bunting spread between them. It was a sad but necessary task to make mourning drapes for the front porch and door.

Hill House was not Mr. Burke's home, but with his cottage still waiting to be repaired, Hill House would be the home where he spent his final hours on this earth. Hill House would also be where Orralynne would receive mourners before they carried her brother to the cemetery and laid him to rest.

Surrounded by the sadness she carried in her heart, Emma worked with Ditty without sharing a conversation, each of them lost to their individual memories of other times when they had used the long, sorrowful hours waiting for the death of loved ones, friends, and neighbors in much the same way.

When a knock at the front door interrupted them, Ditty started to get up, but Emma waved her back into her seat. "I'll go. It's probably Dr. Jeffers," she said and hurried to let him inside.

When she opened the front door, Dr. Jeffers was there, but he was not alone.

"Mrs. Massey asked if she might ride with me to visit with Miss Burke, with her husband's blessing," he explained as he held the very pregnant woman by the arm.

Zachary Breckenwith tipped his hat and smiled. "I only returned home this morning. I came as soon as I heard."

Both surprised and elated, Emma ushered them into the house and stored their winter garments on the oak rack. She nodded to Zachary. "While I take Dr. Jeffers and Mrs. Massey to the library, why don't you warm up by the fire in the parlor. I won't be long," she promised.

When Orralynne opened the library door this time, her expression brightened the moment she saw Judith Massey. "I was so hoping you'd come, but I didn't dare think you'd venture back here," she said and opened the door wider.

The doctor entered immediately, but Judith turned to Emma first and smiled. "My husband will be coming for me in a few hours so I can spend the afternoon with Miss Burke. I hope that's not an inconvenience."

Touched by the young woman's goodness, Emma blinked back a tear. "I'll fix supper to save you the bother, and you and your husband can eat with us before you go home. Please let me know if there's anything I can do for you all in the meantime."

Judith nodded. When she took a step to go into the library, she stopped and pressed her hand at the base of her spine for a moment.

"Are you all right?" Emma asked.

"I'm fine. It's just a little twinge in my back. I've been sitting too much today," she said with a weary smile before she entered the room and closed the door.

As she walked back down the hallway, Emma silently said a prayer offering praise and thanksgiving to Him for sending Judith to Hill House.

She found Zachary Breckenwith facing the fire in the parlor. "I was hoping you'd outridden the storm."

He turned around and grinned at her. "I

fared well, although it appears you were less fortunate."

She blushed and gently touched the bruise on her face. "I'm afraid I'll live to be ninety but still not outlive this tale."

"And I hope to be with you to hear it," he murmured, his gaze softening. "For now, I thought perhaps I could help you. I understand this is an especially difficult time, particularly for the Burkes."

"Come. Sit with me. There's so much I need to tell you," she offered.

He spent the next hour with her, listening, talking, and offering her the understanding and support she had longed for him to give. When she finished, he shook his head. "I'm terribly sorry. When I asked you to have the Burkes move here temporarily, I never thought it would end like this."

"No one could have known," she argued. "The poor man has had trouble with that foot since birth, but who would have thought that foot would one day be the instrument that would lead to his death?"

He narrowed his gaze. "Has Dr. Jeffers offered any explanation of what happened? Until now, Lester Burke has enjoyed reasonably good health, I believe, despite the defect in his foot."

"The doctor is bound by the same ethics as you are," she reminded him. "Since I'm not a member of the family, he can't and won't offer any explanation. He only told me enough to satisfy my concerns that Mr. Burke's illness wouldn't spread to anyone else. I'm hoping he'll speak with me again before he leaves today, though."

"What can I do to help?"

"Pray. For Lester and his sister," she suggested. "I'm so worried about what will happen to her after her brother dies. She met with Mr. Larimore yesterday."

"Indeed?"

"He wasn't one of the lawyers on the list you gave me," she noted with a bit of a smile.

"He's handled Mr. Burke's legal affairs for some time now. He'll do well enough for Miss Burke. Did you perhaps have a change of mind while I was gone and engage the services of a lawyer to represent you?"

She shrugged one shoulder. "I haven't needed one. The owner of Hill House hasn't shown up on my doorstep yet."

He drew in a long breath. "Then I suppose my question should be whether or not I should expect to once again represent your interests."

She smiled, knowing full well his true question was whether or not she was willing to consider his proposal. "I think not."

His smile touched her heart, easing the heavy burden of sadness she had been carrying for many days now.

When Dr. Jeffers entered the parlor, she and

Zachary Breckenwith both stood up. "How is your patient?" she inquired.

"Which one?" he asked, looking a bit frazzled.

"Is Miss Burke ill now, too?" Emma asked, worried that the poor woman had finally collapsed from the strain of caring for her brother for so long.

"No, but as you might expect, she's quite overwrought. Her brother has slipped into a coma, a circumstance she has allowed me to share with you. I'm afraid I had to tell her not to expect she'll have the opportunity to speak with him again, although it's not entirely impossible that he could rouse for a moment or two."

He paused and took a deep breath. "Mrs. Massey, on the other hand, is about to deliver her babe."

Emma clapped her hand to her heart and remembered Judith had complained of back pain. "She's not due for some weeks yet. Now? She's going to deliver now?"

"Soon. Very soon. I need to ask if there's a room downstairs where she might be more comfortable giving birth. It would be better for Mr. Burke, as well, if she didn't remain in the library."

Emma's mind raced ahead to all that needed to be done. "Reverend Glenn's room is next to the kitchen. We need to send for the midwife. And summon Mr. Massey!"

"I saw Mrs. Freeman late yesterday. She said she'd been called out to the Radcliff farm and didn't expect to be back in town for several days." He paused for a moment and grinned. "She also didn't expect the Massey babe to make an early entrance into the world," he added.

Zachary Breckenwith started toward the hallway. "I'll get Mr. Massey."

"I'll show you the room, and we'll enlist Ditty's help along the way," Emma suggested as her emotions shifted yet again from sadness to utter excitement and joy before descending into worry. She prayed that the sad history of Hill House might not be repeated again this night.

32

U NDER ANY CIRCUMSTANCES, the birth of a newborn child is always a miracle. This night the birth of the Massey baby was a beacon of God's goodness that multiplied the miracle of his birth many times over.

Isaac Jeremiah Orrin Massey, named to honor both Reverend Glenn and Orralynne Burke, entered this world at candlelighting on Thursday evening, just as the chill of early evening chased the last rays of sunshine over the horizon. A fine-boned boy, with tiny wisps of dark, curly hair atop his head, he had a good strong pair of lungs he used to announce his unexpected arrival.

To add to that miracle, Judith Massey had safely delivered her first child. Though she was exhausted from the rigors of a hard but short labor, she was recovering quite to the doctor's complete satisfaction. She also put to rest, once and for all, the sad history that had haunted Hill

House since it had been built.

Still, the miracles continued, gently flowing through the hearts and spirits of all who tempered their joy this night with the sorrow of Lester Burke's impending death.

After tapping on the door and announcing herself, Emma slipped back into the room where the miracle of birth had just taken place several hours ago. By the gentle light of an oil lamp, she could see Judith had finally fallen asleep, her face still aglow with contentment and happiness. Her husband was due back shortly, after returning to their home to pack a bag for them since they would be staying at Hill House again for a few days until Judith was strong enough to travel.

Orralynne was sitting in the rocking chair Ditty had carried into the room from the kitchen, and she was holding the sleeping newborn babe close, crooning as she rocked.

She had surprised everyone earlier when she asked Mr. Lewis to stay with her comatose brother so she could stay with Judith. Emma had witnessed firsthand how Orralynne had held Judith's hand and offered encouragement during the younger woman's labor. Orralynne had also flatly refused to leave after the baby's birth in order to stay and help change the bed linens and assist Judith into a fresh nightgown Emma had given to her.

Even so, the vision before her now was

nothing shy of a most amazing miracle. Orralynne's features had softened and gentled. She
looked younger. The bitterness in her gaze had
melted to awe—raw, unadorned, and innocent
awe.

Overwhelmed by the woman's total transformation, Emma swallowed the lump in her
throat, reluctant to interrupt and deliver the
news she carried. She feared, however, that this
news could not wait. "Mr. Lewis thought I
should summon you," Emma whispered as she
approached her.

Orralynne glanced up from the babe. "Has
my brother. . . ?"

"No. He's still comatose, but his breathing is
getting very, very shallow," she murmured. "I'll
stay here with Judith and little Isaac so you can
go to your brother."

Orralynne bowed her head and pressed her
lips to the baby's forehead before handing him
up to Emma. "When Judith wakes up, she'll
want to nurse him again," she whispered as they
exchanged places.

When Orralynne started for the door,
Emma called out to her in a whisper. "Mr.
Lewis said he would fetch Dr. Jeffers if you
think he should."

Orralynne stopped but did not respond before slipping quietly from the room.

A short while later, Emma handed Isaac over to his proud father. Unable to find Mr. Lewis in either of the parlors, she headed directly to the kitchen, where she found him with Ditty having a late supper.

"I'll fix something for you to eat," Ditty offered.

"Sit, sit," Emma urged. "I'm too worried about Orralynne and her brother to eat much of anything."

"Dr. Jeffers said we shouldn't expect Mr. Burke to last much longer," Ditty said quietly.

Emma nodded, both relieved the man's suffering would soon end and saddened that Orralynne's grief was just beginning.

"Mr. Lewis?"

All heads turned toward the sound of Orralynne's voice.

The woman was standing in the doorway. "Please summon Reverend Austin. Quickly, if you will," she urged and promptly disappeared from view.

Without comment, Mr. Lewis left his supper on the table and headed for town again. Emma's first thought was to offer a prayer of thanksgiving that Mr. Burke had not only roused to wakefulness but had also changed his mind about seeing the minister. Her second thought was to add a prayer for Orralynne, that she would remain strong through the difficult hours ahead.

She silently offered both prayers, headed up to her room, and quietly opened the door to the staircase that led below to her office. For too long, she had let her own feelings about the Burkes justify the fact that she had left them alone and allowed them to isolate themselves from her as well as her guests.

Judith Massey, however, had shown Emma how to truly love her neighbor.

With that lesson tucked deep within her spirit, Emma did what she would have done for any other guest who was facing the death of a loved one alone.

She descended the staircase slowly, one step at a time, using the very dim light in the office to guide her. She heard no sounds coming from below, other than the hush of shallow breathing. When Emma was halfway down the steps, she sat down and folded her skirts around her legs. "I'm here, Orralynne," she whispered. "You shouldn't be alone right now. Would you like me to come down and sit with you?"

She heard a slight rustle of fabric, as if Orralynne stirred, but the woman uttered no response.

"I'll just sit here, then," Emma suggested. She prayed, waited, dozed now and again, only to wake and start the cycle again. Then Orralynne's plaintive yet insistent cry startled Emma awake.

"God will punish you, for all eternity, unless

you confess and ask for forgiveness. Please, Lester. You've done a terrible, terrible wrong. You can't leave this world without making your peace with God."

Emma could not hear the dying man's response, if indeed he made one at all. She felt incredibly awkward, as if she had intruded on an intensely private moment, especially since she did not have Orralynne's express permission to stay. Even though Orralynne had lowered her voice now and Emma could hear only muffled sounds, she could hear enough to know the brother and sister were having some type of conversation and felt obligated to leave.

She held on to the wall with one hand and stood up. She was easing the kink in her knees and arching her back to stretch the taut muscles before turning to go back upstairs, when Orralynne appeared at the bottom of the stairs.

"I don't know what to do. Reverend Austin still isn't here. My brother needs to . . . He has to . . . I don't know how . . ."

"I'll try to help," Emma offered and descended the stairs as quickly as she could. The light in her office was so dim she could only make out Orralynne's silhouette, as well as the dying man's as he lay ever so still on his deathbed.

"I think he wants to confess, but . . . but he's failing so quickly now, I don't know what to do. May God forgive me, I don't know what to do."

With her heart pounding, Emma took Orralynne by the arm and knelt with her at Lester's bedside. At first, the man was so still, she thought he had already passed, until she heard him take a gasp of air.

"Take his hand," she urged.

"He can't even manage a word," Orralynne whispered as she placed her hand over her brother's.

"God will hear the words in his heart that he can't say aloud," Emma assured her.

"How can I be sure? How will I know he's saying enough?"

"You can speak for him and ask him to nod, to let you know he agrees with what you're saying, if that would make you feel better."

"You do it," Orralynne argued. "God will listen to you."

When Lester Burke gasped for air again, Emma swallowed hard and knew there was no time to convince Orralynne that God heard the prayers of anyone and everyone who turned to Him. "Mr. Burke," she began, "are you sorry for all the wrong you have done and all the good you have failed to do in this life? If you are, say so with your heart and simply nod to let us know that you understand what I'm saying."

One nod. One very slow, very deliberate nod.

Emma blinked back tears. "And do you seek

forgiveness from God, the Father who created you, and from His Son, who gave up His life that you might claim eternal life, and from His Spirit, who waits to welcome you Home?"

Another nod.

A single gasp.

And then, on the very day little Isaac Massey entered this world, there was a hallowed silence as the soul of Lester Burke passed from this world and through the gates of heaven, free from suffering and free from sin.

Weeping, Orralynne turned toward Emma, who opened her arms to embrace the woman in love, without reservation and without hesitation.

She held the grieving woman until Reverend Austin arrived. When he left some time later, Emma went into the library, where the minister had been talking with Orralynne. The oil lamps in the library were also set low, but the fire added enough light for Emma to see the grief and sorrow etched on Orralynne's face.

Looking forlorn and utterly drained, Orralynne sat in one of the two leather chairs near the fire. Emma sat down in the other chair but offered only her presence as comfort.

After many long, quiet moments, Orralynne sighed. "Reverend Austin said there's no sin too grievous that God would not forgive. Even if that's true," she whispered as she stared into the fire, "even if he's right, and Lester's soul is in heaven now, there's no place I can lay his body to rest where people won't see his tombstone and read his name and remember what he did . . . what a terrible, terrible thing he did."

"People's memories are shorter than you think," Emma argued, assuming Orralynne was referring to the lawsuits her brother had planned to file against so many people after the fire. She also assumed that those potential suits ended with the man's death. "Today's gossip quickly fades with tomorrow's," she added. "In time, people will forget—"

"In time, everyone will find out what he did, and I will be the one to bear the brunt of their disdain."

Emma swallowed hard. "I'm afraid many people already know about the lawsuits."

Orralynne sniffled and shook her head. "I'm not talking about the lawsuits. I've already spoken to Mr. Larimore about them. There won't be any lawsuits now," she whispered, solving the mystery of why she had met with the lawyer.

"Then what has you so troubled?" Emma asked gently.

"I'm talking about what Lester *did*, not what he was planning to do," she countered. "If Dr. Jeffers doesn't know for certain, he surely has his suspicions. He's not a stupid man. Mr. Larimore knows for certain because he told me as much, which means Lester's secret will not be buried with him."

Thoroughly confused about what Lester

Burke might have done, Emma shook her head. "Even if they know whatever it is your brother did, it's not like either man is simply keeping a secret he might be tempted to tell. Doctors and lawyers are ethically bound not to discuss anything related to their patients or clients," she countered.

"Perhaps if Lester had lived, that would be true. Now I don't know if those men will hold silent or not." Tears ran down her cheeks, but she did not wipe them away. "But it doesn't really matter. The undertaker will be coming soon. Mr. Larimore already arranged for him to come as soon as my brother died to prepare his body for burial. I simply can't do it. I don't even know how to do it. And then he'll know, too. And he'll talk. And I'll be forced to leave for the shame of it. And I have nowhere to go. And no one to take me in. And no one who cares."

She wept, her tears and grief finally ending her rambling.

Touched to the very essence of her spirit, Emma got up, knelt before the woman, and took both of her hands in her own. "Nothing like that is going to happen," she promised as she set aside whatever it was that this man had done to concentrate on helping the woman sitting before her.

"We simply won't let that happen. If it's the undertaker you're worried about, then we'll send him away. I'll help you with your brother.

I'll show you what to do. Whatever it is you're worried about, no one else need ever know."

Orralynne let go of Emma's hands to finally wipe away her tears. "Then you'll see for yourself and you'll know. Why would I expect you not to tell anyone what you see for yourself? Why should I believe you'd protect me from what my brother did?"

"It can't be as bad as all that," Emma argued. "What could your brother have done that was so awful—"

"Don't be kind. Please don't be kind to me," Orralynne snapped. "You won't want to be kind once you learn the truth, because the truth is that my brother deliberately set our cottage on fire. The roof didn't catch on fire because of the explosion or the other fires, like everyone thinks. Lester did it. Lester set the fire himself. And he did it on purpose so he could sue and get a huge settlement."

Emma gasped. Appalled, her heart began to pound. The very thought that Lester Burke would have turned the tragedy that had destroyed so many people's lives into a ploy to be used for his own gain made her mouth sour with bile. To act so belligerent and demanding afterward, when he knew the fire in the cottage was nothing but fraud, nearly left her breathless. "No. He didn't. He couldn't have done such a thing," she argued, simply because she could not believe anyone, even Lester Burke, could be that despicable.

"Well, he did. He crawled up into the attic with that bad foot of his and started that fire. I didn't know what he'd been doing up there, even after he came down and told me to get outside, but no one will ever believe me."

Orralynne dropped her gaze. "When he was up in the attic, he stepped on a number of nails. The puncture wounds got infected, but Lester was too afraid to send for the doctor because he knew his secret would be discovered. That's what killed him in the end. His secret. His terrible, terrible secret. And once everyone finds out what he did, they'll hate him for it. And they'll hate me, too, because they'll never believe that I had no part in my brother's scheme. None at all."

Emma sat back on her haunches. Orralynne was right. If anyone ever learned what Lester Burke had done, his name would forever be associated with the evil of his actions. Orralynne, unfortunately, would also be branded with the sin of her brother.

"So now you know the truth," Orralynne whispered. "Sooner or later, you'll talk to someone who will tell someone else, and eventually the truth won't be a secret any longer."

"I believe you. I do," Emma replied, "but we all have secrets we pray won't ever be known." Content to let the good Lord judge the man who had sought forgiveness in his very last moments on earth, she vowed to make sure that Lester Burke's secret would be buried with him so that Orralynne might find some semblance of hope in the very desperate future she faced.

33

ALTHOUGH MANY OF the curious had trudged up to Hill House to view the deceased on Friday, few offered more than a nod of condolence to Orralynne Burke, and none of them joined the small number of people gathered in the cemetery behind the church to lay Lester Burke to rest Saturday morning.

Snow flurries swirled in gentle gusts of wind and huddled on capes and coats and hats and bonnets as yet another storm threatened to bury Candlewood under more snow and bitterly cold weather.

Standing at the head of those gathered, Reverend Austin concluded the brief graveside prayers. Grief-stricken yet stoic, Orralynne stood with Mr. Lewis on one side and Mr. Massey on the other at the foot of her brother's grave. Mrs. Massey, obviously, could not attend. The Hill House family, including the travelers who had returned late yesterday afternoon, lined either side of the grave. On one side, Reverend Glenn, Aunt Frances, Liesel, and Ditty stood shoulder to shoulder. On the other, Zachary Breckenwith stood between Emma and Mother Garrett.

Out of respect for Orralynne's wishes, the mourners remained at the grave site until the very last shovelful of earth filled in the burial plot, which would remain unmarked until the tombstone could be prepared. Only Emma, however, knew that this gesture reassured Orralynne that her brother's secret had indeed been buried with him.

Saddened by the opportunities she had missed to be a better friend and neighbor to Lester Burke, she hoped to do better in the coming days and weeks as Orralynne confronted her very uncertain future.

After returning to Hill House and sharing a light meal together, one by one the mourners left the table. Reverend Glenn retired to his room with Butter. Liesel and Ditty left to go home to their families. Mother Garrett and Aunt Frances started cleaning up the kitchen, leaving Emma alone with the remaining guests.

She noted the sag to Orralynne's shoulders and the circles under her eyes. "Perhaps you should rest awhile upstairs," she suggested.

Orralynne moistened her lips, as if to say something, then turned to Mr. Massey instead and looked to him to answer for her.

"As it happens," he replied, "my wife and I invited Miss Burke to stay with us. Since Judith's mother isn't here, Miss Burke has kindly offered to help with the housekeeping and such. I promised Judith that I'd bring Miss Burke home with me as soon as she could pack her belongings."

"I packed my travel bag before we left for the cemetery," Orralynne offered. "It's upstairs in my room. I packed up my brother's things in the library, as well," she said, turning to Emma. "I was wondering if I might store them here for a spell until I know where I'm going to be living permanently."

"There's more than enough room in the garret," Emma assured her. She was surprised yet very happy that the Masseys had been so welcoming. "I'll see to his things for you, and please know that you are welcome to come back here to Hill House. Always."

Mr. Massey stood up. "I can move Mr. Burke's things to the garret. I have to go upstairs to get Miss Burke's travel bag anyway."

"Another pair of hands will make the task easier before I head back home," Zachary suggested, and they left together with Orralynne leading the way.

Emma shook her head and looked at Mr. Lewis. "It seems everyone has cleared out with plans of their own today."

Mr. Lewis cleared his throat and stood up.

"In truth, I'm going to take my leave, as well. I'd like to pack up my wagon and be on my way before the next storm hits, which appears to be soon. The Burkes' portraits are still in the library, and they need to dry more completely. I hope it's not an imposition to leave them here with you since Miss Burke is settling elsewhere."

"Not at all," Emma insisted as she got to her feet. "I was wondering if Mr. Burke ever finished the suit of clothes he was making for you."

"No," he said quietly. "As circumstances grew more serious, I rather thought he wouldn't have the strength."

"You're going to Pennsylvania, if my memory serves me right," she said, recalling their conversation in the library.

"Hopefully," he replied with a smile as he walked around the table toward her. He handed her a note, folded and sealed with wax. "I'm afraid I'm not very good with words, especially when I must say farewell. I wonder if you might forgive me if all I say is thank you for now. You can read this later, after I'm gone."

She tucked the note into her pocket alongside her keepsakes. "You've been a great help to all of us. Perhaps someday, if I get to keep Hill House, you might come back and do that stenciling in the hallway for me. Is there any way I could contact you?"

He shook his head. "I'm afraid I travel about, working wherever my whims at the moment take me. But one day, perhaps, I'll find myself back this way." He paused and swallowed hard. "God bless you, Widow Garrett," he whispered and left the room.

———

After the rush of packing up the carriage Mr. Massey had rented and Mr. Lewis's wagon and saying farewells, Emma joined the rest of her family in the west parlor. She would have collapsed and dropped straight down on the settee, except that Zachary was still there.

"It's been a long day for everyone," he commented. "I should leave, too, so you can all rest for the afternoon."

"Don't be so quick to run off," Mother Garrett said, waving him back into his seat. "You might enjoy hearing Emma tell the tale about sledding down the hill and skating down Main Street again. I know I would." A twinkle lit her eye as Emma took her seat with proper decorum.

Zachary grinned.

Emma groaned. "Maybe, just maybe, once this bruise is completely gone, I'll have one full day without being reminded that I might be too old to sled or skate."

Mother Garrett chuckled. "I wouldn't hold my breath waiting for that, so unless you have something more interesting to talk about, I'm afraid you'll have to tell the tale again."

Emma's eyes widened with sudden inspiration. "As a matter of fact, I do," she argued and slipped her hand into her pocket. "Mr. Lewis left me a thank-you note. I'll read it to you all." She nudged her keepsakes aside and pulled out the note.

"Read it to yourself, Emma dear," Aunt Frances suggested. "Maybe he wrote something he meant only for you."

"No more secrets, remember?" Emma teased.

"She's right. Read it to yourself first," Mother Garrett said quickly. "I doubt that man's note will be anywhere near as interesting as your tale is, which means you can't avoid sharing it with us again."

"Have it your way." Emma broke the seal and unfolded the note. Silently, she skimmed the words he had written to her. Shocked and well beyond disbelief, she read them again more slowly:

To the esteemed Widow Garrett:

In my room you will find a landscape I painted for you. Next to it, you will find a packet of papers granting you full and legal title to Hill House, in accordance with my wishes as the heir to my late uncle's estate.

May all those who dwell here, as resi-

*dents or guests, continue to find the peace
and hope and contentment you so lovingly
offered as His faithful servant.*

> *With gratitude,*
> *Malcolm Lewis*

Emma's heart pounded in her chest. Tears welled and threatened to spill down her cheeks. Her hands began to tremble. "I . . . I have to go upstairs. No, all of us. We have to go upstairs," she managed. "Come. Come and see. He left something in his room we need to see," she insisted, half afraid his words might be some form of cruel hoax, and too afraid to believe they were true.

"Upstairs? Now?" Mother Garrett grumbled.

"Now," Emma repeated as she got to her feet and shoved the note back into her pocket. "Everyone should come. Hurry, please," she begged, so excited she thought her heart might burst.

"You go ahead. Take Mr. Breckenwith with you," Reverend Glenn suggested. "He can carry down whatever it is so us old folks don't have to struggle all the way up those steps and back down again."

Mother Garrett sighed. "Go on. Even though I could keep up with you, I'll stay here to keep these two 'old folks' company."

"But I want you all to come," Emma countered.

Chuckling, Zachary got to his feet. "We could go upstairs and be back down again in a matter of minutes, or we could argue the issue indefinitely."

Emma sighed. Maybe it would be better if he looked at the papers Mr. Lewis had left for her first, just to make sure everything was legitimate. "Fine. We'll be right back. Are you ready, Mr. Breckenwith?"

He smiled. "As always," he replied, and he even kept pace with her as she rushed upstairs as quickly as decorum would permit.

When she opened the door to the guest room where Mr. Lewis had been staying, the moment she saw the painting, which was sitting on a small table near the window, her heart skipped a beat. She entered the room and approached the painting almost on tiptoe.

Out of the corner of her eye, she saw the packet of papers lying exactly where he said she would find them, but she kept her gaze focused on the amazing landscape he had painted for her.

Somehow, as if he had been sitting atop a cloud hanging low and just to the south, he had painted an aerial view of the property. Sitting high atop the hill, surrounded by a world dressed in glistening snow, Hill House sat beneath a winter gray sky. A single, gentle beacon of light, that shimmered as if it had come from heaven itself, broke through the clouds to shine directly on Hill House.

Trembling, with Zachary at her side, she stepped closer to the painting and pressed her hand to her heart. The detail in the landscape was utterly breathtaking, but specific details he had chosen touched the deepest recesses of her heart.

Light poured from every window of the house, with silhouettes of residents and guests inside. Two chairs sat side-by-side on the snow-covered patio, where a fire was burning in the outdoor fireplace, and she could just make out the corner of the pen she had had built to pro-tect the chickens in the back of the house. Be-yond the gazebo, the shadow of a panther crept through the woods. And in the distance, far be-yond the figure of a woman skating down Main Street, a lone wagon, much like the one Mr. Lewis owned, traveled south out of Candle-wood.

"The painting is exquisitely done," Zachary murmured. "The man has an amazing talent with the brush."

"He has an amazing heart, as well," Emma whispered, blinking back tears. She picked up the packet of papers and handed them to him. "I know you're not my lawyer at the moment, but would you mind if I asked you to look at these? Just to make sure they're valid?"

He lifted a brow.

"Please. Just this once."

He sighed, took the papers from her, and read through them. Twice. And then again. He shook his head, and his eyes mirrored the very same wonder she felt. "I'm not sure how or why or when—"

"But he was the heir? He was the legal owner of Hill House? And all along he was here?"

"That's what the documents prove. Mr. Larimore did quite a competent job," he admitted as he handed the papers back to her.

She clutched the papers tight in her hand. When Mr. Lewis had ridden back into town with Mr. Larimore, she had had no idea of the professional relationship that existed between the two men. Nor had she any suspicions at all during Mr. Lewis's stay that he might be more than he presented himself to be—a man who spent his life traveling and painting the lives of all he met with beauty.

Overwhelmed, she closed her eyes for a moment. Her spirit bowed to the awesome power and love of her Creator, who had answered each and every one of her prayers, as her heart showered the heavens with praise and thanksgiving.

When she opened her eyes, Zachary was gazing at her with such tenderness and affection, she knew with one gentle beat of her heart that the man who would love her and be her companion and helpmate was right here beside her.

He had been here all along, too.

IN EARLY MARCH, Reverend Glenn and Aunt Frances were married at Hill House.

Instead of flowers, which were still waiting for spring to warm them back to life, bouquets of multicolored cotton bows decorated the parlors, and a wreath of candlewood greens was on the front door and the porch railings. Even Butter wore a bow for the festive occasion.

In lieu of inviting a multitude of guests from the congregation, the couple chose to limit those in attendance to family and close friends. Still, between Reverend Austin and his wife, Aunt Frances's two sons and their families, Reverend Glenn's Hill House family, Zachary Breckenwith, the Masseys, and Orralynne Burke, who appeared to have settled permanently with the young couple, nearly twenty people witnessed the simple ceremony.

In keeping with tradition, after the new associate pastor and his bride accepted congratulations, they all filed into the dining room to share a meal together. Emma ushered the last of the guests from the parlors toward the dining room and walked behind them with Zachary as her escort.

He bent low to whisper in her ear. "Since everyone is here, shall we tell them today?"

She chuckled. "Not today. This is Reverend Glenn and Aunt Frances's special day. I don't think we should do anything to detract from that," she whispered back.

He frowned.

"Besides, I haven't agreed to marry you. I've only agreed to let you court me. And only after you've made this one last trip to New York City and return to Candlewood," she reminded him.

"Which won't be until next month," he countered, clearly anxious to share their news.

"April is such a lovely month," she offered. Indeed, this particular April was going to be very lovely. Spring would arrive, filling the world with color again. The canal would reopen, bringing a new season of travelers and guests on holiday. More important, her three sons, their wives, and Emma's grandchildren would all be together in Hill House to help celebrate her birthday—a perfect opportunity to introduce them all to Zachary Breckenwith.

"I rather like March," he grumbled.

"You also like surprises," she teased, reminding him of their conversation in the woods when she wanted to know where he had planned to take her on their first outing. "Since you never did take me riding again, I might reconsider your suggestion to tell everyone today if you can at least tell me where you were going to take me."

"I can't. It's a secret."

She tugged on his arm. "You told someone else, but you won't tell me?"

He grinned. "I promised Mother Garrett I wouldn't tell another soul."

She pouted, quite certain she and Mother Garrett were going to sit down later tonight to talk this out. "Then take me riding tomorrow."

"I can't. I'm leaving early tomorrow afternoon, remember?"

She tilted up her chin. "Speaking of which, I received some papers from Mr. Lewis's lawyer in Philadelphia. I thought we might meet for a short while in the morning to go over them. Just to get your advice," she added.

"You need a lawyer, remember? Hire one."

She grinned. "Perhaps I should just wait a bit longer before I do."

He cocked a brow. "How much longer?"

"Until I decide whether I should marry one instead."